DEAD
IN
THE
WATER

COPYRIGHT PAGE

DEAD IN THE WATER: A DEEP SEA MYSTERY WITH MERMAIDS

A Polyester Press Publication

e-Book ISBN: 9781939197054

Print ISBN: 9781954579347

DEAD IN THE WATER

DIANE VALLERE

Polyester Press

Part 1: Zoe

I was done following the rules. Sure, they may have been written to protect the inhabitants of Sirenia, the mermaid colony ruled by my mother, but those same rules only stifled my curiosity. Maybe it was unseemly for a mermaid to show interest in something from the human world, and maybe the human's curiosity about us was the reason the rules and regulations had been established in the first place, but just because I was a mermaid didn't mean I couldn't be curious about other things.

Exploration was thrilling, and there was *definitely* something thrilling about the old shipwreck that rested on the ocean floor below me. And now that I'd snuck away for the afternoon, I had a chance to find out what it was. I didn't care that I was in unchartered waters or that there might be a severe punishment if I were caught. I flipped a spray of water from the ocean with my pearlescent blue tail and dove deeper into the water.

Ever since I was young, I'd been the mermaid who got into trouble. "Zoe, leave that alone," they said when I showed interest in something unusual. Back then, it was simple things like waking sleepy barnacles or bringing home trash that someone tossed into the ocean. As I got older, I pestered mermen who patrolled the colony to tell me about the world outside our territory but even they tried to dissuade me. It wasn't that I looked for trouble, but I couldn't help myself. Mermaids existed to inspire humans to grand adventures and lofty thoughts. But honestly, I didn't understand how I could inspire adventures without experiencing some of my own..

I undulated about forty meters below the surface, through the deep blue-green water, passing two schools of fish and a crab. On another day, I might have dallied by the coral or even wrapped my tail in kelp to bring out the natural luster of my scales, but I was already taking a risk by being this far away from my sisters. Kyra would cover for me—she was the baby and always did what I asked—but I wasn't sure about Ava. She's my older sister, and the most dependable, which also made her the likeliest to rat me out. If Ava wanted, she could make my life miserable.

I was going to have to make sure Ava had no reason to make my life difficult.

As I approached the shipwreck, I twirled around in the water to slow my forward momentum and then hung back, behind a reef. Like yesterday, when I first snuck away to explore this area, I knew something had changed from the previous times I'd been here. The water was clear and I had no trouble seeing the details: rusted rivets, crumbling metal gashes, and tiny, shimmery, silver fish swimming in and out of the long out-of-use portholes.

But there was something else. Bubbles. Large, oblong bubbles that spilled out of the back of the shipwreck and floated to the surface.

Bubbles could be generated by pulling air from the surface to the water below like I'd done with the flip of my tail. But I was deep enough to know these bubbles didn't come from the surface. They originated from the far side of the ship. Just like yesterday. A shiver of anxiety climbed my spine like a family of overactive sand crabs. Bubbles meant one thing: I wasn't alone.

I floated behind some kelp and peeked between the blades. Slowly, I pulled myself along using the plant as leverage, until I was at the end of the shipwreck. The bubbles were meters away. They hadn't moved since I first noticed them. Whoever—or whatever—was there wasn't active, but I couldn't know who—or what—it was without getting closer. The rules of the sea were clear in cases like this. Turn back. Get help. Be safe.

I swam closer.

As I peeked over the side of the shipwreck, I spied a diver. A man! I couldn't see his features, but his close-fitting wetsuit indicated he was in good shape. His hair swayed in the ocean, fanning around his face, and his mouth was stuffed with a regulator connected to air tanks strapped onto his back. This stretch of the ocean was far beyond the waters that were safe for humans. Ever since the accident caused in the great shrimper/mermaid tragedy, there had been an understanding between humans and mermaids. A charter had been voted into law to keep them from risking their lives (and ours) by diving past the border—the same charter I ignored right now.

The diver was now beyond the border. Quite.

If he saw me, if he learned how close he was to Sirenia, he'd bring others. The merfolk freedom would be compromised. Greedy sailors would hunt us, catch us, and sell us to the highest bidders. At least those were the stories I'd heard at swim camp.

But I'd outgrown scary stories around the same age when I outgrew sleepy barnacles, and besides, I'd never seen an evil sailor up close. Despite the fear, the warnings, and the possibility of capture, I swam closer. Maybe, if I could learn something about the diver, I could report back to Sirenia and tell the others. They would listen to *my* stories and develop ways to defend themselves. I could be the one to save them!

Pride at the possibility surged through me, and the scales on my tail, which had dulled from the exertion of swimming this distance from home, now glowed a magnificent shade of coral. There would be no hiding amongst the kelp at this rate. I curled my tail to hide the bright color. The movement caught the attention of the diver, who looked directly at me.

I froze.

The diver watched me watching him. He didn't move. A thin stream of red floated in a cloud from somewhere below him. It was blood. I'd read about it in books from the Library Under the Sea. My pulse pounded through my arms and scales, and I hovered in place, waiting to see what he'd do now that he'd spotted me. He appeared to be considering his options as well because he did nothing.

I wriggled out from behind the kelp and closed the distance between us. When I rounded the corner, I learned why the diver hadn't approached me. His ankle was caught in a twist of sea kelp, keeping him tethered to the ocean floor. He kicked his foot, but the plant kept him bound. The cloud of blood, however, was unrelated to his current dilemma.

The blood came from the body lying on the ocean floor next to the diver's foot.

I had a choice. Save the trapped diver, or swim back home and return with the mermen patrol. (It wasn't that mermaids couldn't enforce the charter, but that with our talents, looks, and emotive abilities, we were the royalty of the sea. The brute force required to protect us fell to the mermen. It was a symbiotic relationship, but I sometimes wondered what would happen if we switched roles!) The mermen would take no pity on a diver who'd entered our restricted waters. Plus, if I told the mermen about the shipwreck and the dead body, they'd send me home, back with my sisters, to be a good mermaid while they managed the matter. I'd never know what had happened.

I wasn't going anywhere.

The diver bent toward his foot and yanked at the kelp twisted around his ankle. I already knew he wasn't going to be able to release himself. It takes more than human brute force to tear through thick, coarse kelp blades.

Were all humans like him? Did they think they could muscle their way through a crisis?

Air leaked from a tear in the hose that connected the diver's regulator to his air tanks. It was a thin trickle that was visible only by the tiny bubbles that slowly popped one by one from the hole, but I knew if he waited too long, if the ocean grew fierce, or if the hose tore further, the diver would die.

I swam toward him and pulled his hands away from the plant. I scanned the ocean floor for a helpful crab or jagged piece of broken shell. But the ocean floor was clear. The presence of the two men—the diver and the body—had scared away any of the sea life that called the shipwreck home.

The diver grabbed my arm. My whole body tensed, including my tail, which isn't the best thing for quick maneuvers and fighting back. This was it. Tricked by a human diver pretending to be tangled up in kelp on the ocean floor by a body. That probably wasn't even a real body. The stories from swim camp were right. Humans were sneaky!

His grip relaxed and he pointed to the body.

From the pictures I'd seen during human anatomy class, I'd say that was a real body.

Next to the body lay a silver tank like the one the diver wore. The regulator had slipped out of his mouth and rested in the sand by the man's head.

The diver pointed, this time more aggressively, and it seemed more accurate to say he wasn't pointing *at* the body, but at the underwater sea knife *in* the body. And then he put his hand around his throat and convulsed. He needed air.

The excitement made my tail glow even more than it had been. While my sisters were blessed with exotic looks: Ava with striking pink hair and Kyra with white hair and tail, I'd been born with a blue tail that blended in with the depths of the ocean. Changes in my mood brought out a warm coral hue that was impossible to ignore. With one powerful flap of my tail, I propelled myself to the body and yanked the knife out of the dead man's chest. I turned and swam back to the diver. His eyes were closing, and his body seemed limp. I sliced through the thick kelp and freed his ankle, then grasped his hand and pulled him up to the water's surface. He didn't have much time.

When we broke through the euphotic zone I felt the diver's grip on me tighten. He gasped for air. I guided him to a nearby boat that had the same yellow insignia as the one on the back of his wetsuit and gave him a boost with a kick of my tail. I dove down below the surface and watched his flippered feet disappear over the edge of the boat. I swam about fifty yards from where I'd been and resurfaced. The man sat in the boat, staring into the water.

I'd saved his life but risked my own. Would there be repercussions? I glanced to either side of me, my blue hair fanning out around my head. Nobody had followed me. Nobody knew where I was. If the diver left and never returned, my secret would be safe. No one would ever know I'd broken the rules.

It wasn't until that moment I realized I was still holding the knife I'd pulled from the dead man.

I'd heard rumors of the kinds of techniques humans used to catch their criminals. Chemicals that revealed fingerprints and blood and something called evidence. Their police had systems in place to figure out when one of them committed a crime. It wasn't like the sea at all.

But these were unchartered waters. I knew because of the paths I'd taken to reach the sunken ship. The diver and the dead man were beyond the territory protected by the treaty. Would the police risk relations between humans and the merfolk to get justice? Or was the ocean beyond their jurisdiction?

Was that why the man on the ocean floor had been killed this far out from where he belonged?

My tail was still bright coral. If anyone came around looking —for me, for the dead man, or for the trapped, now free diver—I couldn't hide. The safest thing to do was to go home and leave things as they were. I didn't know what to expect, but satisfying my curiosity wasn't worth risking Sirenia.

I released the diving knife and watched it land in the sand next to something that glistened silver. Ava collected sea treasures, and an unusual artifact discovered from the shipwreck might be just the thing to keep her from asking questions about my disappearance. I swam down to the ocean floor and buried the knife, and then raked my fingers through the sand to uncover a small, oblong item attached to a long silver chain. I hung the chain around my neck and swam home, leaving behind my biggest adventure yet.

On my way back to Sirenia, I stopped off at the Ebb Tide Emporium. My tail had dulled, but every time I thought about freeing the diver and finding the body, the coral glow returned. There was no way it would return to its natural shade by the time I got home, and the glow would raise questions about where I'd been. I had to cover it up and that meant a trip to see Mad Midge.

Mad Midge was an older mermaid who'd sustained injuries in the shrimper/mermaid tragedy. Her tail had been permanently damaged, her caudal adductor paralyzed on one side (which sometimes made her swim crooked), and she'd lost vision in one eye. She ran the most profitable booth at the weekly Ebb Tide Emporium and parlayed that success into eventually managing the whole shopping market. She was one of the few mermaids to have ongoing contact with humans after the treaty went into effect. Mad Midge argued that her livelihood depended on it, but I secretly believed too many merfolk depended on Mad Midge to procure the specialties they desired to reject her application. Her permit to travel was approved, and her business flourished.

In addition to running her booth, Mad Midge owned and bred electric eels. Eels were a known source of underwater electricity and illumination and were valuable commodities because of that, but their value was reduced by the fact that they couldn't be turned off. Their presence illuminated the water, which led sailors to occasionally see the underwater life that was supposed to be a secret. Because of this, eels had been banished.

Mad Midge had developed a paste made from pulverized abalone muck and algae that, when slathered on the eels, kept them near invisible. She sold the muck in jars, small and large. Between the sale of the muck and the rental of the eels, she was financially secure. Anything else she sold was extra, though that didn't stop her from stocking unusual items to attract people to her stand every week to see what was new.

There was probably a jar of eel muck at home, but I needed to apply it before getting there. When I arrived at Mad Midge's topical paste booth, she floated behind her stand, inventorying items in a large blue tub. As I neared, she closed the lid and straightened up.

"Hello dere, Zoe-girl," she said. She tacked the word "girl" on to the end of each of our names, just like she tacked "tuna" or "crab" after the names of the fish who frequented the emporium. "Din't expect customers today, no. The emporium doesn't open for two days. I'm just here waitin' for a delivery. Got special orders comin'." Her one good eye swept over me from head to tail, and she nodded at the coral glow of my tail. "I see you've got a bit of a problem, don'tcha now."

There was no point lying about what I wanted. "Do have any eel muck in stock?" I asked. To be on the safe side, I added, "the large size, please."

Mad Midge nodded in a knowing way. "Ya found yourself swimmin' around da dangerous parts of da ocean, didja now?" She kept nodding, this time as if agreeing with something she didn't say aloud. "I know what it's like, swimmin' out dere in da dark parts of da ocean. I know da secrets da ocean holds, yah."

Nobody knew how old Mad Midge was. She'd been around since before I was born, and aside from my limited contact with her at the market, I only knew of her from the tales other merfolk whispered behind her back.

"Ya gotta be careful now," she said. "Dere's dangers in dem waters. Dangers you mermaids have yet to encounter."

"Like the humans?" I asked cautiously.

"Nah, dem humans are okays," she said with a wave of her hand. "Dey bring me my supplies and buy da wares I find in da ocean, don't ya know. I wouldn't have a shop if not for da humans."

I couldn't understand how Mad Midge could be so forgiving to the very people who had been responsible for her disfigurement. "Why don't you hate them?" I asked, my earlier nerves now traded for curiosity.

The elderly mermaid tipped her head and considered me. The water massaged her choppy hair (she'd recently cut it short; "practical reasons," she'd explained to anyone who questioned her decision to go against expected mermaid ideals of beauty), causing it to fan out around her head like a sea shrub. She used colorful hair tonic on it to advertise the effects of the product, and the result left her rainbow-colored. "Zoe-girl," she said, "why should I hate da humans when they are da link between me and my income?"

"But they—the shrimpers—what happened—" I stammered. I didn't know anybody who asked Mad Midge about the shrimping accident directly. There must be a reason we only talked about her behind her back!

"There are always a few bad ones in every group," she said. "Ya can't expect da world to be a nice place an' you can't expect it to be a bad place. You hafta expect a little of both."

I was intrigued by her knowledge and forgot my fears. "But they left you blind in one eye and damaged your tail. They left you for dead. How can you trust them?"

"I said I didn't hate dem," she countered. "I never said I trusted dem." She reached below the booth and pulled out a large clear jar half full of a thick, greenish-gray substance. "Now let's get you settled. You wanted a jar of eel muck?"

"Yes, please." I looked away. "I don't have money with me. I can barter a song or bring money from my coin jar and pay you when we come to the market this week."

"How's about you use up the end of dis sample. I'll be needin' to break out a fresh sample when da market opens. You'd be doin' me a favor." She pushed the jar toward me.

I looked up at Mad Midge, surprised. I'd never heard of her giving away merchandise that she could sell and I'd never once heard of eel muck going bad.

"Go on, now," she prodded. "It's gettin' late and I'm leavin' after my special order comes in. Your mother will be worryin' about ya soon, and I don't need Mother Mermaid to be thinkin' I'm a bad influence on you girls." She reached forward and unscrewed the jar with her bony, spotted fingers. I slathered the gelatinous substance on my scales, coating the coral glow that had only gotten stronger since arriving at the booth, thanked Mad Midge, and swam towards home, stopping one more time to barter a batch of mussels from a shellfish vendor and have a plausible excuse for being away so long.

By the time I arrived home, forcing a leisurely pace that allowed my tail color to appear closer to normal, the food pantry was empty. I left the mussels in reserve and swam to my room. Kyra and Ava were out. Our coin jar, a receptacle where we collected human money that we found on the ocean floor, was empty, and my fishnet shopping bags were missing from the coral branch where I kept them. A lock of Ava's bright pink hair waved from the coral. If I hadn't already suspected, now I knew. Ava was the most comfortable borrowing my things without asking, a fact that never ceased to infuriate me.

It wasn't like we didn't share, but at least Kyra asked permission before helping herself. And here I'd brought Ava a gift! I balled my fist around the silver chain and turned away. Ava didn't deserve it. I slipped the chain into an empty clamshell, tied a piece of silvery phytoplankton around it, and nestled it under Kyra's pillow. At least one sister was nice.

When my sisters returned later that night, they were bursting with excitement. "You missed it!" Kyra said. She swam in a circle, her white hair flying behind her. "We were at the Library Under the Sea when a human swam up and asked for help!"

My tail began to glow. I tucked it underneath me and held an empty fishnet bag on my lap to cover it. "There aren't supposed to be humans in these waters," I said tentatively.

Ava snatched the second fishnet bag from Kyra and dumped a pile of books onto the counter. "I could tell something was wrong with him. He said he was a police officer, but he didn't have a badge or anything."

A badge. That's what the shiny thing was I'd found buried in the ocean floor. My stomach clenched, and I fought the urge to turn and look at the gift-wrapped mussel shell I'd left under Kyra's pillow.

"He had trouble breathing," Kyra said. "I was scared for him. Her eyes widened, like they had that day she discovered a tiny sea urchin had taken up residence in her bed. Being the youngest mermaid, she would always be wide-eyed and innocent, and she'd use that to her advantage long after losing the specter of youth. Ava exploited Kyra whenever she had a chance, though Kyra seemed not to mind in the least.

"Did he die?" I asked.

Ava studied me. "That's morbid. No, he didn't die. We sang him into a trance, and then two of the mermen accompanied him to shore, or at least as close as they were able to safely go. He'll either swim to the beach or wash up. Somebody will find him and take care of him." She shook her head. "If you ask me, the mermen took a significant risk by helping that diver. He could talk. If he crossed into unchartered waters once, he could do it again. The council should be warned."

"No," Kyra said. Her voice was quiet but had an unexpected strength to it. "He won't remember any of us. You know that's how humans are. He'll wash ashore and someone will find him. If he talks to the humans about us, they'll assume he had a hallucination when he ran out of air."

Kyra's defense probably had little to do with the diver and a lot to do with the mermen. Kyra never met a male she didn't like, and she didn't want to believe the same mermen she flirted with regularly would do something dangerous.

"Kyra's right," I said tentatively. "When the treaty was drawn, the police agreed to bury any reports of mermaid sightings. They have to blame it on a hallucination. If they listen to stories about us, they'll have to explore where he was, and that's beyond the barrier. They'd have to prosecute him for swimming that far and —" I stopped talking. I'd said too much.

Ava's stare was direct and intimidating. Her bright pink hair fanned out around her head, creating a halo effect. She crossed her arms. "Where did you go this afternoon?" she said, squinting at me. "You were supposed to be here when we went to the library. I covered for you, but mother has questions."

I'd anticipated this, which was why I'd stopped off after meeting with Mad Midge. I met Ava's accusatory tone with defiance. "I went to the mussel shoals. Mother said we were low, and I had free time to collect them."

Ava looked around the room as if taking an inventory. "I'm sure Mother will be thrilled. Where are they?"

"I left them in the food cubby. And you're right, Mother was pleased." I turned my back on Ava and shook my head so my hair fanned out around my head. It was less dramatic than Ava's pink hair, but it was still an effective way of letting Ava know the conversation was over.

Which was just as well, because when I turned my back on Ava, I saw Kyra at the exact moment when she discovered the gift-wrapped badge I'd left tucked under her pillow.

"What's this?" Kyra asked. Her voice raised and her hand closed around the clamshell. "A present? For me?"

"Yes," I said. There wasn't any other way around it. I snuck a look at Ava to assess her reaction. Ava was looking at her bed, probably for a gift of her own. It had been a lapse in judgment not to consider this scenario, but there was no correcting it. Now I just had to keep Kyra from opening the shell.

Mother's melodious voice sliced through the tension. It was her way of calling the merfolk and neighboring aquatic life to her table for dinner. Soon, our house would fill with mermaids and mermen and water sprites and selkies and manatees and dugong and possibly even some of the neighboring fish. It would be easy to disappear in the crowd, a fact I looked forward to for the first time in a long time.

Ava would remain by Mother's side. It was her role as oldest, to function as an extension of the matriarch, and she took her role seriously. She hesitated by the door, seemingly torn between her duties and her desire to see Kyra's gift.

Kyra dropped the mussel shell and twirled around twice, her white hair flying around her face. It was customary for mermaids to have long, colorful hair, and Mother had encouraged each of us to embrace our unique shades. Ava's hot pink tresses made her stand out wherever she went. She frequently braided her hair or wound it around her head like Mother. My blue locks blended in with the ocean. At first, I'd felt shortchanged, as if the other mermaids had something I didn't. When I realized my ability to blend meant I could come and go without being caught, I saw it as a blessing. Too many of the mermaids sat around preening and singing and not exploring. Curiosity wasn't a feminine trait, but I didn't care.

It was Kyra who acted like mermaids were expected to act. She used her wild, white mane to attract mermen. Tonight, her cheeks flushed and her tail sparkled. She would no doubt mingle with the party crowd where she'd easily be the center of attention. Although lately, she had engaged in a harmless flirtation with

Laker, a merman who had recently moved to our colony after migrating from a colder climate. Kyra gathered the front of her hair on top of her head and secured it with her favorite blue jewel of the sea, and then swam past Ava. She'd forget all about the shell before the evening was over.

But just in case, I waited until Ava left the room and then unwrapped the mussel shell and hid the badge and chain in the eel muck I'd bartered from Mad Midge.

There was too much to do during dinner to spend time thinking about the diver. Ava was in the kitchen with mother as usual, preparing salad and tiny delicacies that looked too pretty to eat. Kyra had volunteered for the job of hostess, which was fine with me. I secretly knew her motivation was to be the first mermaid our guests encountered when they arrived, which gave her a chance to flirt with each one individually and choose her suitor for the night.

Left with the task of setting the table, I unpacked cabinets of shells and set them out alongside eating utensils and serving spoons. As I caught sight of Kyra flitting between River, a green-eyed merman who had grown up in Sirenia and Laker, who stood out with his white-blond hair and bright blue eyes, I accepted that I'd likely be responsible for the cleaning duties as well. Another mermaid might have been resentful, but I applauded Kyra's outgoing nature and appreciated how she got me off the hook, so to speak, in situations like this. Between talking to mermen about their adventures or having my own, the choice was obvious!

River swam away from Kyra and joined me. "Hi," said River,

swimming into the dining area. "Shouldn't your sister be helping you?"

"Who, Kyra? She's the hostess."

"I know," River said. He looked longingly over his shoulder at Kyra, but she was too busy with Laker to notice. "She's too trusting. Look at her. She's paying too much attention to the new merman."

As I slowly swam around the table, I glanced up to watch Kyra and Laker. She swam in circles around him, her white hair flying behind her like a banner. Their coloring matched, making their playfulness seem choreographed like a dance routine.

Laker occasionally held out his arm to stop her and she changed direction quickly, never getting fazed. Kyra was a champion at anticipating moves such as these and had won blue ribbons in all of the school competitions. She was the fastest sprinter I knew but had no interest in using the skill for anything other than a flirtatious game of mermaid chase. River watched them dart back and forth but didn't join in.

I once heard Kyra tell Ava her biggest fear was that one day the merfolk and fish would stop paying attention to her. I wanted to tell my little sister that invisibility was the greatest quality of all. When nobody noticed you, you could go anywhere. But I couldn't say anything or she'd know I'd been listening in on their private conversation. (Even though that alone would prove my point!)

"Kyra knows what she's doing," I said to River. "She's the entertainment. Watch." I pointed to our view of her. In addition to Laker, she'd been joined by two manatee and a blowfish. A group of tiny crabs crawled sideways to them as well and snapped at the bottom of her tail. She giggled and swam in circles, then twirled. The more she performed, the bigger her audience got. It wasn't until Mother's melodious voice sang out that dinner was ready that the spectators looked away.

River put his hand on my arm. "There's trouble coming to Sirenia," he said. "Poseidon waived the curfew for the mermen so we can patrol the waters and be on hand should something happen. Laker showed up after the rules changed and was the first merman to take advantage of them. I don't think that's a coincidence."

"You don't like him because Kyra's paying him more attention than she does you." I smiled to let him know I didn't judge him for his jealousy, but he seemed angered by my response.

"Laker's up to something," River said. "I'm going to keep an eye on him." He swam off as the others entered the room and sat down for what turned out to be a spectacular meal.

* * *

The evening passed quickly. I was eager to finish my chores and go to bed, mostly so I could wake up and go out exploring. Twice I'd found people talking about the diver in low voices. Both times Ava had been close enough to observe the change in my tail color. And with the muck from Mad Midge now hiding the badge, I had more reason to keep the jar full than empty.

Living in Sirenia was a colorful experience, and we treasured our colony. After a representative from Poseidon's team negotiated the treaty, the finned females felt a level of safety we'd never thought possible. We accepted our newfound freedom tentatively at first, but slowly made Sirenia our home. Siren calls to other colonies brought visitors who moved in and the colony expanded.

Soon, it was bustling with mermaids and mermen and other fishy visitors. The coral, safe from threat of fishing lines, lobster cages, and crab nets, gradually spread around the region and created a natural border in shades of cerulean, magenta, and vermillion. Sirenia became a paradise under the sea, and Mother became the matriarch.

My two sisters and I accepted that our roles in life were different from the other mermaids, though no one knew the details about Mother's relationship with Poseidon. There had been nights when that question alone kept me awake long after my sisters had fallen asleep, but like the mysteries I pondered, I reached no conclusion.

Tonight, I laid in bed and thought about my day. I hadn't told a soul about my encounter with the diver, and if what Kyra said was right, then the police would ignore any mermaid tales the diver might live to tell.

None of that explained why he'd been there, who the dead man was, and what they'd been doing by the shipwreck.

My shipwreck.

Whatever it was, it couldn't be good for Sirenia.

I might not be able to tell anybody about where I'd been or what I'd done, but that didn't mean I wouldn't do it again. For the first time in my life, I felt truly alive. I could barely wait to return to the shipwreck to try to learn what had happened. First thing tomorrow. It was my duty.

* * *

Early the next morning, I removed the chain and badge from the eel muck, slathered my tail with the substance, and tucked the chain into my shell bra. I put a piece of shiny green sea glass into the original mussel shell and left it out for Kyra. I kissed Mother goodbye and was on my way to the shipwreck before the rest of Sirenia woke.

My mind was on the destination, not the journey, and I barely felt the water that rushed through my hair or past my scales. As Sirenia grew faint behind me, I pulled the badge and chain out and draped them around my neck. I arrived at the shipwreck in record time, but there was a problem.

The water surrounding the wreckage was cloudier than yesterday. It was cloudier than it had been since the treaty. I tipped my head back and looked up at the sky. Something was there, above my head. Something was blocking the ocean's surface.

It had to be a boat. And boats weren't allowed in unchartered waters. It was a direct violation of the treaty.

This time I knew I had to alert someone. Being inquisitive didn't negate the need for caution in a case like this. Before growing up and becoming a young lady mermaid (what Mother and the other lady mermaids called us, though I hated, hated, hated the term), I managed to avoid an audience with Poseidon. The thought of going to his office to report what I discovered— and the impulsive behavior that had brought me here in the first place—terrified me. I hovered behind the wall of kelp and waited for the water to clear so I could make a better assessment of what was going on, when a hand came around me from behind and clamped down over my mouth. A second arm snaked around my waist, pinning my arms against my torso, making it impossible to get free.

My instincts—and what I'd learned in the mermaid mandatory defensive maneuvers class—kicked in. I wriggled under the strong arms that held me, and with the benefit of the eel muck, spun free. I could tell my would-be captor didn't have experience holding a slippery mermaid, and I used that to my advantage. The hand shifted from my mouth and I prepared my throat to sound off a call for help when I recognized his face.

It was the diver.

He put his hand onto my mouth again, gently, but this time I wasn't scared. Mermaids were intuitive, and I instinctively knew he was more interested in my silence than in hurting me. I nodded and he let go. Tall leaves of kelp swayed toward and away from us, agitated by our movement. The diver's eyes moved to my throat and I remembered the silver chain with the badge. I reached my fingers up to the object and touched it self-consciously.

Kyra was the one who liked to decorate herself with sea jewelry, and Ava had that full head of long, pink hair. I blended in while my sisters didn't. I accepted my looks and rarely made the effort to alter or enhance my appearance. Wearing the silver medallion made me feel conspicuous.

The diver reached inside the collar of his black suit and pulled out a chain that held a badge like the one I wore. I hadn't recognized it initially, but now I did. It matched the image depicted on the treaty that protected Sirenia. The shield was a sign of peace. These were the humans we could trust.

The diver pointed up. I shook my head and pointed to the dark thing on the surface of the water. Swimming to the surface while a boat was nearby would mean almost guaranteed capture.

Yet there was no other way for us to communicate. That was the biggest problem with merfolk and humans. We spoke the same language, but humans lacked the biological makeup of the merfolk that let them speak underwater. Humans heard the bubbles and splashes around them. The delicate noises I'd grown up with and took for granted were loud, almost shocking to the human sense of hearing. For the two of us to converse, I'd have to default to his method.

The human world was very inconvenient.

I pointed to the bottom of the boat. The diver's expression softened, and he smiled. He took my hand and pulled me along with him. Occasionally he slowed and I glided to the side of him. He said something, but his voice distorted in the water, and I couldn't understand.

I grew impatient. I pivoted and kicked my caudal fin, which propelled me past the diver. He kicked his flippers and caught up. We broke the surface of the water side by side, yards from a long, flat pontoon boat. The diver swam past me and pulled himself onto the floating surface. The sunlight bounced off of his tanned skin and reflected back to me from eyes that matched the clear blue sky.

He thumped his chest. "I'm Seth. I'm a police diver. This is my boat. It's safe . There's no one else here."

"You shouldn't be out this far," I said. "It's dangerous for you in your little boat."

He turned and looked toward the shore, far enough away that his presence out here couldn't be explained as careless navigation. "My boat is safe. It's a triple-hull pontoon with a 150 horse-power engine."

"I don't know what that means," I said. Humans were always trying to show off with details that meant nothing to merfolk. "You're past the barrier, and you're not supposed to be here."

He looked down at his hands and rubbed his fingers. If he were contemplating an explanation, he seemed to decide against it.

I swam toward him but kept a safe distance. "What do you want?" I asked.

"To thank you, for starters. You saved my life yesterday. You didn't have to do that."

"It was nothing," I said, though I knew that not to be true.

"Where did you find my badge?" he asked.

I touched the silver medallion again. "This is yours?" He nodded. "I found it in the sand by the shipwreck." I pulled the chain from around my neck and held it out to him. He took it and gently rubbed his fingers back and forth over the textured surface, and then set it in the boat behind him.

"You shouldn't have been near the shipwreck," Diver Seth said. "It's dangerous."

"That's what everybody tells me." I tucked my chin and dolphin-dived deep below the pontoon, coming up on the other side of it. I loved creating bubbles and a froth of foam and rarely had the chance to frolic this close to the surface by myself.

I peeked to see if Diver Seth watched me. He was still facing the other side of the pontoon. "I'm over here," I called out. He turned around quickly and seemed surprised to find me floating on my back, flipping water into the air with my tail. I admit, I was showing off just a touch.

"What are you doing out here today?" he asked. "You're the last person I'd expect to see."

"I'm not a person," I said.

"I guess you're not."

"But I *am* curious." I rolled through the water, keeping my fins damp while the sun warmed my face. Should I trust Diver Seth? He had that shield. That meant something. I slowly positioned myself with my head and shoulders above the water and my tail below. "Did you kill the man in under the shipwreck?" I asked. There was no fear in my voice, just interest.

He seemed taken aback at the question. "No. He was dead when I got here." He seemed concerned. "This whole time, you thought I killed him?"

"I don't know. Humans do silly things."

"Do you think killing someone is silly?"

I considered his question. "No," I finally said. "I suspect if you killed him you had a reason. A motive," I added. "Are reasons and motives the same thing?"

"To some people, they are."

I laid back on the surface of the water and flipped the water higher into the air. The spray fell onto my face and arms. I tipped my head backward and used my hands to scull the water past me, letting the sun glide over my limbs and scales as I made a giant circle through the ocean. When I came back up, I slowly straightened until I was upright.

"Why were you here yesterday?" I asked Diver Seth. "And today? The shipwreck is—"

"It's past the border," he said, cutting me off before I could finish.

I learned this about humans a long time ago, from watching Mother converse with a boat of sailors who'd gotten lost. They were eager, impatient, even, to show off what they knew. The mermaids found this a funny trait, that humans who lived on land believed they knew more about the ocean than the merfolk. It would be like me pretending to understand those colorful boxes with wheels they used to get from one place to another.

"What does a police diver do?" I asked.

"The same things a policeman does, but sometimes under water."

"But there aren't people under water," I said.

"There was yesterday," Diver Seth said. His eyebrows dropped low over his eyes and he grew serious. "There's no legitimate reason for a human to be out here," Diver Seth admitted. "Not him, anyway. My job is to find out *why* he was here. What he was doing. And collect evidence."

"Evidence of what?"

"I think that man's body was dumped out here."

"You think someone killed him and put his body out here so it would never be found?"

"Yes, but I can't prove it."

This information was troubling. Murder was a concept that was known from lesson plans only. It was part of our education, to be aware that threats like these existed when we were away from the safety of a mermaid colony.

Sirenia was one of several mermaid colonies. The colonies spanned the ocean, run by strong female Mer-Mothers who raised daughters and welcomed visiting mermen and other sea life. Mermaids were expected to have a stationary home from which to be educated and learn mermaid skills. We wanted for nothing thanks to our birthright, and those things that weren't free were easily bartered for with a song.

But the one thing a life in Sirenia hadn't provided was adventure.

The ocean was ripe with life, and, in addition to plants, fish, selkies, water nymphs, and shellfish, colonies of merfolk were numerous. It wasn't unusual for strangers to arrive as guests in one colony and remain indefinitely, and then move on or return home.

Once upon a time, the merfolk world was a secret. Our lives revolved around fear of discovery. It was inevitable that, as humans ventured deeper and deeper into our waters, they'd discover signs that we existed.

Mother was instrumental in opening up our way of life. She'd suggested changes. Poseidon had implemented them. We'd allowed in visiting professors who could broaden our minds with knowledge about life on land. During my formal education, I'd learned that the mermaid way of life was more like a series of neighborhoods on land than neighboring cities or states. I didn't understand why humans would want to live this way. Wasn't it better to have one inclusive community that sprawled across the ocean floor, where everybody lived by the same rules and accepted each other without question? It was the guiding principle that let the vastness of the ocean feel like home.

Mermaids were the royalty of the ocean. Peaceful, beautiful, elegant, and intuitive. Water sprites often lived within our communities, as did water nymphs and naiads. Generations of underwater life had blurred the lines between us, and our peaceful coexistence populated the waters to numbers the humans would find unbelievable. It was handy, knowing others underestimated how many of us there were. If the humans knew just how much elegant sea life existed beyond the barrier in the unchartered waters, they probably wouldn't place such a high value on a mermaid sighting!

When I graduated from Coelacanth University (the premier school of higher learning for mermaids, also called "Sea U"), I vowed to explore every inch of the ocean. Soon after, I learned some humans had a violent side. Several mermaids had been caught in a net and died in their struggle to get free. Sirenia had been particularly quiet for days after as we absorbed the true differences between ourselves and the humans, and not just because we could breathe under water.

"Is that why you were here yesterday? To find out what happened to the body on the ocean floor?" I asked Diver Seth.

Seth nodded and shielded his eyes. "I've been investigating that man for some time. He's a known criminal, and he has lots of enemies. He recently served time for counterfeiting currency."

"Counterfeiting currency?" I asked. I was an avid reader—Mother had insisted that all of us learn words outside of our daily needs—but this word was unfamiliar. I thought it had to do with the currents of the ocean but couldn't figure out how or why someone would fake them.

"Currency is money," Seth said. I was still confused and Seth continued. "When you want something, how do you pay?"

"I barter with a song," I said.

He shook his head. "Things are a lot simpler under water," he said to himself. To me, he continued. "On land, we have something called money. We give it to people, and they give us what we want. This man made fake money. Sometimes he made fake objects that he sold for real money."

"What do people do with fake money?"

"They use it to get things for free."

"That's not nice," I said. "Somebody should make him stop."

Seth looked down into the water. "I think somebody did."

knew how the other mermaids would react to news of the dead man's murder. Fear would send them back to the safety of their small, isolated lives. But I couldn't swim away. Mother had said that for as long as she could remember, she knew I would never let fear run my life. Being the middle mermaid had often left me feeling forgotten in the mix. Not the oldest like Ava who had additional responsibilities, and not like Kyra, the baby (who was well into adulthood and encouraged adult thought from the mermen who constantly surrounded her!), forever being treated as if she were somehow more fragile than her sisters. I learned quickly that I could get away with more simply because no one was watching me.

It was what had brought me to the wreckage yesterday, what allowed me to notice that something was different than the other times I'd visited, and why I'd come back today even after I knew it may not be safe. It was why I wasn't afraid of Seth and why I wanted to help him find the answers he sought.

"You asked me why I was here yesterday," I said. I dove back under the water and swam below the pontoon. When I surfaced, I was startled by Diver Seth's feet dangling in the water. He kicked a splash toward me and I flipped water back at him with my tail. "There's something wrong with the shipwreck," I said.

"That's why it sank."

"No!" I giggled. "It sank because of a storm. I remember that. I've been coming to visit it whenever I can. I know which parts dangerous, and which parts are safe. I know how it landed on the ocean floor and which fish I'll find when I visit it."

Diver Seth leaned forward. I could tell he hadn't considered that I might be a witness or offer him valuable information, and my tail glowed coral. Enough of the eel muck had rubbed off when I slithered away from him that there was no hiding it even if I wanted to.

"You said something was different yesterday," Diver Seth prompted.

"That's right. Normally the shipwreck is lousy with fish swimming in and out of it. It's like a playground for them. The crabs, too. Once they get inside, they climb around it. One time I saw a crab swinging from the ceiling!" I laughed, but then quickly sobered. "But the day before yesterday, there weren't any fish."

Diver Seth rubbed his eyes. "If someone came out here to dump the counterfeiter's body, then the fish would have been startled. They'd swim away, right? That would explain it."

"No," I said. "There weren't any fish here, and there wasn't a body. That's why I came back. Something scared the fish before your currency counterfeiter was left here."

I impressed myself with how easily I discussed Seth's case. Mermaids overly emotive, and as such we didn't focus on facts and logic, but on feelings. My powers of empathy weren't traits that would normally allow me to help a detective, and the idea that I was different than the others made me preen.

An idea came to me, and I blurted it out without thinking. "I can help you," I said. "I can see underwater, talk to the fish, and look for your evidence. I can help you find out what happened to the man down there."

Seth shook his head. "That's not how it works. You shouldn't even be here. You're corrupting the crime scene."

"You're corrupting my ocean."

"That doesn't make sense."

"*You* don't belong here. *I* do. And as for your crime scene, there have been fish swimming around it for days."

"According to you, there *haven't* been fish swimming around it for days."

"That's right," I said. "*According to me.* You wouldn't even know that if I hadn't told you. What else don't you know?"

Diver Seth did not seem pleased by my version of logic, but he did appear to accept it. Again, he rubbed his eyes. What was it with humans and their eyes? If they were so dry, why did they wear those funny masks when they dove into the water?

I grew bored by his lack of response and occupied myself by twirling in the water. I dunked my head down and came back up, flipping water into the air. I couldn't imagine what it would be like not to live surrounded by the waves and the brightly colored plants, the soft sand on the ocean floor, and the constant company of the fish, sea horses, crabs, and eels. The only ones I wouldn't miss were the sharks, who flexed their muscle when they wanted to scare the other sea creatures and make everyone believe they were in charge.

After a series of twirls, somersaults, and a stretch of floating on my back and warming my face with the sun, I flipped and dove deep. If this whole investigation meant I couldn't return to the sunken shipwreck anymore, then today was my last day for fun. Using my hands as paddles, I propelled my body through the water, deeper, deeper, deeper, until I was inches from the wreckage.

If Diver Seth were unconvinced that I could bring him

information he couldn't gather for himself, there was one sure-fire way to prove to him that I could. I pulled myself along the sea-worn exterior bow of the shipwreck until I reached the side where the body had been and searched for a clue.

It wasn't what I saw that struck me as odd. It was what I didn't see. The body. The currency counterfeiter who'd been lying on the ocean floor yesterday wasn't there.

I swiftly circled the shipwreck and darted in and out of portholes looking for him, but he was gone. I rested against the outside of the shipwreck to consider what this meant. Someone else had been here since I had. Someone had a reason to remove the body.

That's when I noticed something that on any other day would have seemed quite normal. Long, pink gossamer threads caught in the branches of coral that sat by the sea kelp where Diver Seth's foot had been caught. Except I knew, without getting any closer, that the threads weren't threads. They were strands of mermaid hair.

My sister Ava's hair. She was the only mermaid in Sirenia who had hair the color of pink fire. I was as sure of it as anything.

Ava had been to the shipwreck. Recently. She'd violated the rules of Sirenia and hadn't said a word. It was more unlike her than anything I'd ever known and I couldn't fathom what had lured her to misbehave so egregiously. What I could understand was that Ava may be in trouble.

This was exactly the kind of clue Diver Seth would want to know about, and I had to find a way to hide it from him—until I found out how it had gotten there in the first place.

I could have stayed under the water indefinitely. I could have balled the long pink strands of Ava's hair into my fist or hidden them under the scales of my tail. I could have left the shipwreck and swam back to Sirenia and tucked the strands under my pillow until I had a chance to confront Ava. But I knew Diver Seth was on top of the water waiting for me. The dark shadow from the underside of his pontoon hadn't moved, and if I disappeared now, I'd constantly worry about what else he might find and when he'd come knocking on our door. (Knocking being a metaphor, of course, since mermaid colonies do not have walls. Duh!)

I'd have to play along. At least until I knew more. But first, I freed the strands of Ava's hair and braided them in with my own.

The human world saw mermaids as exotic creatures with hypnotic voices and mesmerizing beauty. Before the treaty, brave, daring, drunk (or all three) sailors would venture into our waters seeking mermaid sightings for luck or capture. The threat led to mermaid seclusion, racing to hide inside our protective coral fortresses until the sailors were out of range.

I flashed back to the story of the shrimper tragedy. Five shrimpers had ventured out further than usual under a full moon that bathed the surface of the water in glowing, sparkling, near-intoxicating light. They cast their net not for shrimp like their license had approved, but for mermaids. And mermaids, they caught. Five of the loveliest creatures to live under the sea tangled in the thick rope net. The mermaids were unprepared to fight for their freedom, and their struggle was ineffective. Four mermaids died. The injuries sustained by the fifth destroyed the beauty the humans had come to expect in a mermaid.

That fifth mermaid was Mad Midge.

When the greedy shrimpers discovered their bounty was worthless, they dumped the mermaid bodies and returned to land. That first night they'd set out, fueled by folk tales rum. But now they knew: one mermaid may be a hallucination, but five were real. Five mermaids, caught in a net, struggling for freedom, indicated there were far more mermaids than anyone had thought.

The shrimpers returned. The boat capsized. The men drowned.

An investigation was requested. Granted. Representatives from both sides pieced together what had happened and told the story. The humans declared the fate of the shrimpers the result of inexperienced sailors in choppy waters. Though no mermaid believed that to be true, the findings went unchallenged.

There were rumors that the mermaid elders knew what the shrimpers had in mind on their return trip. And that it was they who caused the mass wave that capsized the boat. Though the rumors circulated for a long time in underwater gossip, they were never confirmed.

The risk of exposing ourselves became less important than the need to establish boundaries to establish a peaceful coexistence. Humans and merfolk arranged a summit to discuss the tragedy. Soon after, the charter was drafted, defining the barrier that separated the mermaid territory from the public areas of the ocean. Mother, acting on behalf of Sirenia, signed the charter, as did the chief of police. That was also the day I understood the power Mother held over Sirenia, over Poseidon, and over the humans. That power would one day transfer to Ava, though not for hundreds of years.

Despite the charter, the mermaids relied heavily on protection from porpoises and whales, both of which were smart enough to recognize the potential danger to all of us. It was then the mermaids learned the value of our voices. One song could attract attention—sometimes the wrong kind.

But sometimes, the attention was worth it. Conjuring visitors to Sirenia allowed the mermaids to show off our multi-variegated tails and hypnotic movements. The charter allowed a peaceful coexistence between the humans and mermaids. Ships filled with men exhausted from too many days at sea would throw down an anchor and hope for a sighting to renew their spirits. It was a perpetuated myth that a mermaid sighting could help a tired sailor find peaceful sleep and wake refreshed, renewed, and reinvigorated for his mission.

Because of this, or perhaps in spite of it, mermaids learned to enhance our appearances. Even with shimmery scales and hair that cascaded down to our waists, we found ways to accessorize. Underwater industries that catered to mermaid beauty popped up. Jewelry made from perfect pearls offered up by oysters, coral branches from the sea life outside our colony, and stems of plants could be used as clothing, hair embellishment, earrings, necklaces, and pendants.

The art of self-decoration was as much a part of our education as the history lessons and the understanding of murder. But like murder, it was a lesson plan I never expected to use.

The information helped me now. I trusted that Diver Seth would either not notice the strands of pink braided into my blue hair, or that he would see it as part of the mythology of the mermaid. My tail had changed colors, so why not my hair?

Besides, I didn't have any other ideas.

When I surfaced, I found Seth on his hands and knees with his face peering closely into the surface of the water. He wore his black wetsuit and flippers. His air tank and regulator sat on the pontoon next to him.

"I thought you left me," he said. "I was about to dive in and make sure you were okay."

I giggled. "Why wouldn't I be okay? I live here. You're the one who wasn't okay."

Diver Seth did not appreciate my version of events. "If anybody else comes out here, you're not going to tell them that, are you?"

His question held more information than he may have wanted to share. It told me that just because he was alone now did not mean he wouldn't come back with others. And that more humans would come looking for him if he didn't return. It hinted that he expected me to be here. It assumed I would be as trusting to another human as I was to him.

Until I knew more about what had happened by the shipwreck, I wasn't making any promises.

I lay on my back and wiggled my tail to put distance between myself and the pontoon. When I felt safe, I let my tail sink and sculled the water with my hands to keep my head above. "Your secret is safe with me," I said. I tipped my head backward and used my arms to complete a backward flip in the water before unwinding and laying in the water again. All of this was for misdirection, of course. I wanted Diver Seth to be distracted by the sum of my magical mermaidness and not the individual parts like the strands of pink hair I'd acquired while under the sea or the nervous tremble that controlled my arms.

He watched me, at first amused, but then impatient. He

checked the device on his wrist and pulled his feet out of the water and stood. "I'm going to pass on your offer," he said. "I'm already looking at a ticking clock on this case and if you're going to play around in the water, I'm never going to catch who did this."

I got serious. "You'll have to violate the charter to conduct your investigation," I said. "Won't that be a problem when it comes time to present your case? How are you going to enforce the barrier if you tell people you went past it?"

It was a bold, risky move on my part. I remained almost still, with the sun beating down on my face, neck, and shoulders, and waited for his response. He didn't look away from me this time and I sensed it would mean something if I were the one to break eye contact.

I stared back. After enough time for a school of fish to rush past me, he spoke. "This is off the books. And confidential. And you are to check in with me before you explore and report to me what you find. Okay? I don't want anybody coming and going until I've collected every bit of evidence I can."

"We can," I corrected. Diver Seth glared at me. I smiled, aware that I'd won a small battle. A small buzz radiated within me, and I fought to remain calm. The water all around me turned orange as it reflected off my tail.

Diver Seth's face glazed over and he looked confused. He stared at a spot above my head. "What's that?" he asked.

My hand flew to my head and I felt my cheeks flush. "It's nothing," I said.

But he didn't seem to hear me. It was then that I realized he'd been placed in a trance. And there was only one thing that would put him in a trance—a siren song. I'd been so distracted by the need to protect my sister Ava that I hadn't realized she was right there, sending me a warning—from somewhere down below.

Diver Seth would remain in a trance for as long as Ava kept up her song, but since the song was aimed at me, I knew Ava would come looking for me if I didn't respond. And until I knew what was up, I didn't want Seth to know Ava existed.

I ducked under the water and answered Ava's call with a warning song of my own. I waited a few seconds to make sure Ava got the message, and then resurfaced and splashed water on the pontoon. Diver Seth snapped out of his trance. He looked confused, and then closed his eyes and shook his head quickly and opened his eyes back up.

"What did you say?" I asked.

"I said something?"

"Yes. You said you had to leave but we would meet here tomorrow and you would send me down to the shipwreck to find your evidence."

Diver Seth looked at the thing on his wrist again. "It's not late," he said. "We can keep going."

"You said you had to go back to shore." This was a bald-faced lie. But I feared he would find something else that related to Ava, or worse, evidence that Ava had killed the dead man. I shouldn't feel bad about that, because I knew the dead man was a bad man who made fake money, but something about the story didn't make sense.

"I said that?" Diver Seth asked. This time he looked amused.

"Look, mister," I said. I put my hands on my hips right by where the skin transitioned to scales and fluttered my tail to keep my head and shoulders above water. "Even if you do wear that gold shield around your neck, you aren't supposed to be here. And if the whales find out you are, they're going to banish you and you won't learn anything. Whoever killed that man did a bad thing, but that means two people were out here where they don't belong. You need to go back to land and let me find out what the merfolk know before you get into trouble with the council."

He nodded. He shielded his eyes from the sun and pulled up the anchor that kept his pontoon in place. "Same time tomorrow?" he asked.

I wasn't 100 percent sure what he meant by time, but I knew I'd be back at the shipwreck before he was. "Yes," I said. I'd figure out the details later. Before he had a chance to say anything else, I turned and dove far below the surface and undulated my way back to Sirenia.

* * *

During my swim, I considered how I was going to bring the subject up to Ava. But before I worked out an answer, a large bluefin tuna blocked my path.

"What were you doing with that human?" he asked.

(This was not an unusual occurrence. Centuries of coexistence between merfolk and fish had taught us to communicate as a way of warning each other against possible threats to ocean life. Conversing with a fish was as easy as conversing with a human. Easier, perhaps, since the fish understood words under water.)

I shivered. The bluefin hadn't asked if I'd seen a human, or why a human was beyond the barrier. His question indicated he already knew the answers to those questions.

"Who wants to know?" I asked with more confidence than I felt. Tuna and mermaids didn't spend a lot of time together, and this tuna was unfamiliar to me.

"Charlie," he said.

"Where is he?"

The tuna laughed. "I'm he. And I'm asking the questions." The tuna swam in circles around me, quick and close. Tuna were among the fastest fish in the ocean, and Charlie was no exception. He kept one eye on me while he circled, and even though I tried to turn away, his laps around me made it impossible to ignore his stare. "You know the human was in violation of the charter," he said.

"Is that what's bothering you?" I asked. "He's part of a dive team to collect evidence about a body that someone dumped by the old shipwreck. He has a shield. He's safe."

"He'd like you to think that," Charlie said. He slowed his pace and glided in front of me. "But did he tell you how he found the body? Why he was at the shipwreck? What he was looking for?"

He hadn't. I had trusted him as soon as I saw his shield, but Charlie was right. What did I really know about Diver Seth—other than the fact that he'd been trapped in the water not far from where a body rested? How did I know he wasn't responsible?

Maybe he'd lied about being the killer!

There was no faking the glow of my tail to Charlie. The tuna —really, all underwater life—would know what that meant. The color-shifting glow was a genetic anomaly found in only a few mermaids, but what it meant was no secret. Just because Mad Midge could sell me an eel salve to downplay the intensified glow didn't mean I could get away with faking it indefinitely. And now that Charlie knew, he could tell the others.

I was lucky to have an excuse to leave. "Get out of my way, Tuna," I said in my most commanding voice. "Mother expects me home and if I'm not there, she'll send out the mermen."

Charlie's scales turned a dull gray. He circled me twice, and then swam a few feet away. "You're in dangerous waters, mermaid. Watch yourself or somebody might clip your tail."

He turned and swam away, leaving me scared and exhilarated at the very same time.

I was no closer to knowing how to approach Ava about the shipwreck when I arrived back home, but it turned out not to matter. Ava had gone shopping with Mother, leaving Kyra alone. Kyra had taken advantage of the moment to be with Laker, the cute merman she'd been trying to attract. When I arrived, Laker was chasing Kyra in and around the tall reef and branches of coral that ran around our family house. Mermen, I thought. What good are they? Always chasing you around. I didn't see the point.

What I did see was an opportunity to snoop around Ava's room. The three of us shared a space, but each had claimed a corner. Ava made a show of storing her personal items in a giant clamshell. She'd spotted it a few meters away from the colony and convinced the mermen to retrieve it for her. The shell was lined in bright, cobalt blue, and when the shell was closed, it looked like it was wearing blue lipstick! Ava had made it clear that Kyra and I were not to borrow her items without asking, but tonight, I ignored that rule.

I convinced myself I was doing it to save my sister, not to steal from her. I hoped Ava would see things the same way if she found out.

I swam up to the clam and forced the shell open. Inside were Ava's mother of pearl comb and mirror, her set of waterproof cosmetics she'd bartered from Mad Midge, and a bottle of something I'd never seen before. I unscrewed the lid and found bright pink hair tonic inside.

Ava didn't need pink hair tonic. She had bright pink hair all on her own.

But if someone else got ahold of this, they could make their hair look like Ava's. They could go places they weren't supposed to go and if they left evidence behind, everyone would suspect Ava. It was the kind of surprising find that I knew could explain the long strands of pink hair I'd found by the crime scene, but what possible explanation could there be for Ava having it?

It was only one of two questions that troubled me. The second was worse. If Ava could get a jar of the pink hair tonic, then could someone else as well? Ava's role as Mother's assistant left her with few friends and fewer allies. Did someone dislike her enough to use the pink hair tonic to frame her?

That night, the three of us set the table while Mother prepared a feast of scallops and linguini. Mad Midge had started stocking fresh pastas. The source was a secret, and no matter how many songs the mermaids promised, Mad Midge and her eels wouldn't talk. It was just as well—being able to buy fresh pasta was more fun than having to go out and catch dinner—a task that often fell to me while Kyra practiced her music lessons and Ava acted as intermediary to the council.

Another reason being the middle mermaid sucked.

After dinner and clean up, Ava and I went to our room while Kyra remained behind to flirt with the mermen. I climbed onto my bed with a book but was too distracted by thoughts of the dead body and Ava's secret hair tonic to read. It wasn't until the school of glowing fish that provided our evening light finally left and cast Sirenia in darkness that I set down my book and confronted Ava.

"I have to ask you something," I said. "It's important."

I suspected Ava knew there was something on my mind. I hadn't flipped a page in almost an hour and I was known as the bookworm amongst the mermaids. I watched Ava's face, trying to gauge whether she was going to cooperate or tell me to mind my own business.

"Are you in trouble?" Ava asked.

"No, but I think someone else is. Someone in Sirenia." Ava watched me closely, and it was wrong to beat around the bush. "You," I added. "I think you're in trouble, and I want to help."

Ava's expression froze, and her bright pink hair flared out around her. "How much do you know?" Ava demanded.

This wasn't the question I anticipated. It was practically a confession. Now it was up to me to determine which direction to go: trust Ava and protect her no matter what she'd done or tell Diver Seth what I knew and make him uphold the treaty that said he couldn't prosecute mermaids beyond the barrier. Both options put me in an uncomfortable position, but I knew where my loyalties lie.

Mermaids were devoutly loyal to their kind. It was part of being a member of a genus that was part fish and part human. We could make friends with fish and people, but ultimately, there was no one else like us and it behooved us to only trust other merfolk. I wished things were different, but Poseidon had mandated the mermaid code of loyalty above all. It was the single most important law in Sirenia and without it, chaos would ensue.

I considered the various ways I could ask Ava about the pink hair tonic I'd found. Admitting to snooping would put Ava on the defensive. Could I pretend Ava left it sitting out? No, Ava would never do that. There was only one way, and it was the truth.

I leaned forward and looked out of our room to make sure Kyra was still preoccupied. (She was showing off the tricks she'd taught her pet seahorse while the remaining merfolk watched.) "Yesterday I found a dead body by the old shipwreck," I said. "And a diver trapped in the kelp, too. I cut the diver free and he swam away, but when I went today, he was back. He has a gold shield like on the treaty, so I knew I could trust him."

"He's a member of the police?" Ava asked.

"He's on a dive team sent to collect evidence."

"Did he find any?" Ava asked. "Evidence?" Her expression was—hopeful.

I expected anger, accusations, or maybe even distrust. I hadn't expected hope.

"Ava, did you have something to do with the dead body I found?" I asked directly.

"Yes," Ava answered, "but not how you think."

I sat upright and tucked my tail underneath me. I hadn't expected a confession so quickly, but even with Ava's admission, I knew there was more to the story than a simple explanation.

"The council suspects humans of violating the treaty," Ava said. "Of crossing the perimeter to use the unchartered waters for nefarious business. But there's been no proof. Poseidon's cabinet recruited volunteers to patrol the perimeter and report anything unusual."

"You're one of the volunteers," I correctly guessed.

"Yes." Ava sighed. "Sometimes accompanying Mother to the council meetings can be boring. I'm not important enough to have my own opinion, and people think of me as little more than an attaché. Mother can speak for herself. She prefers not to engage with many of the others, and that makes me look standoffish."

I hadn't realized Ava knew how she looked to the others. Behind Ava's back, the merfolk mocked her, saying she was as close as she'd get to being a mother mermaid herself since she showed no signs of interest in dating or settling down. She took charge of the household while Mother was away, and even Kyra was resentful of Ava's bossiness. Who knew Ava was resentful of it as well?

"Did you kill the dead man?" I asked.

"It's not that cut and dried," Ava said, using an expression she'd picked up from some sailors. (I'd tried to talk like the sailors too, but when Mother heard, she made me sit in hot water. My tail hadn't glowed for a week after that!) "I've been circling the perimeter regularly. A few days ago, I saw men hiding trunks inside the shipwreck. I waited until the men left to look inside the trunks. They were filled with money. Human money."

"The diver told me the dead man made fake money and used it to cheat people out of what they were selling," I said.

Ava shook her head. "I don't think that's true. I took a handful of coins back to the council and they said they were real. They coordinated an effort to retrieve the trunks so the men would have no reason to come back."

That plan showed some of the simplistic thinking I often found amongst those in charge of Sirenia. That the most important goal was to keep humans from swimming in our waters. Not to capture those who did or find out why they violated the treaty.

The humans had their police force, a group in charge of capturing people who broke their laws and making them serve time without freedom as a punishment. They learned from the people they caught and were more prepared the next time someone broke their laws. Their crime rate was on the decline. Meanwhile, the mermaids put our trust in a treaty that had been broken as recently as a few hours ago.

In the sea, capture meant death. It was the singular threat of humans in our stretch of ocean. The treaty allowed for sailors to apply for safe travel through Sirenia, and sailors were often rewarded with mermaid sightings to inspire them while on their journey. But when sailors arrived unannounced, there was no way to tell from our view below if they were peaceful or predatory. Mermaids had learned to remain far below the surface when we saw ships invade our waters unannounced, but that didn't keep shrimpers from dangling nets with which to capture us.

But despite the mermaids' firsthand knowledge of the ways of humans that threatened our lives, the laws of the sea were to deter crimes, not to punish them when committed. If someone was found in the act of breaking a law, the governing body instituted a catch and release policy.

To my thinking, if someone crossed into unchartered waters to hide trunks filled with valuable money, they wouldn't simply go away when the money went missing. They would return. They would become desperate and bold. They would take risks they otherwise might not, and those risks would involve hurting anyone who got in their way.

When I had first seen the strands of Ava's long pink hair caught in the shipwreck, I'd suspected Ava might be in trouble. But this was a different kind of trouble than we'd known.

I reached up to my hair and undid the braid that contained the pink strands. "Ava, your hair caught on the branches of coral by the shipwreck. I didn't know I was going to find something that would link back to the mermaids, especially you. I thought it might be fun to help Diver Seth with his crime scene."

Ava said, "You violated orders to stay close and not wander off by yourself."

"Didn't you do the same thing? Just because the council sanctioned it doesn't make it any less dangerous." Both of us put ourselves in danger because we wanted more than what life in Sirenia offered us.

We *were* sisters, after all.

Ava and I sat in silence for a few minutes. It had been good to clear the air, but now we had a secret to keep from Kyra. And it wasn't just because Kyra was more interested in boys than adventure. It was to keep her safe.

"Like I said," Ava started, "I took a handful of coins to the council and they tested them and told me not to worry. They assumed that would be the end of it. I was assigned to a different area for patrol, but I managed to swim past the shipwreck twice a day to keep an eye on things. That's when the humans came back."

"Humans? More than one?" I asked.

Ava nodded. "Two of them."

It sounded like Ava would be able to fill in the gaps of what had happened. She might even be able to make a positive identification. This was excellent news! I could go back to Diver Seth and tell him the story and he could search for the second man on land and the shipwreck would go back to being my favorite spot to explore. Maybe a few of the coins had fallen out of the trunks when the mermen collected them . . .

"You can't go back," Ava said, interrupting my thoughts. "No matter what. The council has put the shipwreck under watch and siege, and if they catch you that far out, you'll be captured. It's not worth it."

"But I have to go back," I said. "Diver Seth expects me to help him. He doesn't know I found your hair, and if I don't go back, he'll dive down and find more evidence that links back to you. And you said yourself, there were two men with the trunks, not one. The other one might have seen you, and he's already crossed into unchartered waters once. He won't be kept out by the treaty."

"What do you suggest we do?" Ava asked.

This was the first time Ava had treated me like an equal, and I wanted to prove that I'd earned her confidence. I had an idea, a vague one, but I believed it would work. "We'll go back together,"

I said. "We can search for clues before anybody else does and clear any evidence that points to you."

"It's risky," Ava said. She considered things for a moment and then shook her head. "No. It's my job to keep you safe. I can't let you do this." She floated up and pointed a finger at me. "I know you mean well, but if anybody catches you near the shipwreck, it'll come back to me, and we'll *both* get thrown into containment. The only one of us who has a reason to be there is me. I'll take care of this." Ava turned and swam away.

Now *that* was the behavior I knew far too well. But one thing she'd said was true. Ava was the only one who had a reason to be there.

Which meant if I was going back, I was going have to look like Ava in order to protect us all.

When I was sure Ava wasn't going to return, I pried the giant clamshell open and grabbed the pink hair tonic. I poured the liquid onto my hands and quickly rubbed it into my long, blue locks, and then replaced the bottle where it had been.

The mirror gave me a shock. I wasn't used to being noticed, but there would be no hiding with this hair.

"Kyra?" called a merman's voice from the other side of the coral. Was that Laker? Did Kyra expect him? Was he comfortable enough around Sirenia to come in without knowing if she were here?

This was no good! If anyone who knew Ava saw me now, they'd tell Ava and she'd know what I was planning to do. I swam into Mother's room, borrowed a swim cap, and tucked my now-neon hair underneath. (Mother wasn't willing to cut off her hair like Mad Midge, but she did recognize that sometimes having her hair secured under a cap was the more convenient way to travel.) I snapped the strap under my chin and swam away, into the dark, nighttime waters, to take care of the evidence myself.

* * *

I left Sirenia and swam to Mad Midge, who assigned two electric eels to accompany me. The eels provided enough light to illuminate my path. I could trust these fish to keep my secret since eels weren't able to talk. Everybody knew that.

As unfamiliar as the feeling of a swim cap was, I left it on until I reached the shipwreck. Bright pink hair flowed out in all directions. It caught on the rusted edge by the porthole and yanked me backward. I plunged my fingers into the tangle and worked the hair loose and then twisted it together and held it in one hand. Several strands broke off and waved at me like Ava's hair had earlier, and I realized how ill-conceived my plan was. In my desire to clear evidence that pointed to Ava, I was creating more!

I pulled the cap back on and jammed my long hair underneath. I spent a minute removing the pink strands and hiding them in a satchel that I'd brought along for my mission and then set to work searching the bottom of the ship for something more. The eels circled about, in and out and around the wreckage, making it appear ghostly and radiant. I searched the ocean floor for footprints or errant coins, anything, really, that would indicate what had happened. But as is the case with an ocean floor, days of currents and the action of sea critters had leveled the sand, possibly burying but more likely simply erasing tracks that had been made in the scuffle.

It was later than I usually went out by myself. Satisfied that there was nothing to incriminate Ava in the investigation of the dead man's murder, I wriggled out of an opening and found myself face to face with Ava.

But instead of reprimanding me for disobeying her, Ava pointed up. I looked. I hadn't noticed how dark the water was thanks to the electric eels, but now I saw the surface of the water was blocked by a large, flat object. I recognized it from swimming back and forth under it all morning. It was Diver Seth's pontoon.

I pulled Ava into the shipwreck. "It's okay," I said. "That pontoon belongs to the Diver Seth, the police officer investigating the crime. He told me he thought the body was dumped late at night. He must be out here watching and waiting to see if the killer is going to come back."

"No," Ava said. She pulled me into the deepest corner of the shipwreck and twice glanced over her shoulder to make sure we were alone. "He's not here to watch out for the killer," she said. "He *is* the killer. That's the pontoon the two men used the day I saw them dump the trunks filled with coins. You have to trust me, Zoe. That's the man who committed the murder."

I wanted to argue the point, to tell my sister she was wrong. Diver Seth had a shield. He was police. He was part of the solution, not part of the problem.

I'd agreed to help him.

But before I could form a response, I saw a shadow approach the shipwreck. The shadow of a man in a wetsuit. The glow of the eel reflected off his face and I recognized Diver Seth and amidst everything I now doubted, I knew with certainty that Ava and I were in danger.

Diver Seth swam past the shipwreck. Ava and I stayed still. We pressed against the deepest recesses of the boat's interior, and there was no place to hide. Thanks to the swim cap, I was able to blend in with the background. The same could not be said for Ava.

I knew what I had to do. I handed the swim cap to Ava, and then pointed to herself and the front of the wreck. Ava shook her head emphatically. I pushed the cap at Ava and swam past her.

I counted on two things. One, that Diver Seth would be too preoccupied with covering his own tracks to think much about my presence, and two, that I could distract him long enough for Ava to get away. I swam out of the wreck and let my newly colored hair flare out around my head. Within moments, Seth's underwater dive light shone in my direction. I twirled a few times like I had earlier that day and then slowed and stared at the light and the man holding it.

Recognition flashed across his face, and he smiled. I had his attention. *Now,* I mentally cried out to Ava. *Go now!* I didn't dare turn to see if Ava had read my mind. I left the safety of the shipwreck and swam, past Diver Seth, up toward the surface of the ocean. A layer of foam, frothy from the bubbles caused by the tumultuous waves against the anchored pontoon, covered the water like a thin veil. The foam clung to my tinted hair and flushed skin. The moonlight reflected off the surface of the water.

"You look more magical than you did earlier today," Diver Seth said. He trod water about five feet away from me.

I was on the verge of denying the observation or blaming it on my newly colored hair. Neither of which would help Ava. I simply allowed myself to drop down, below the surface, slowly, and then resurface with my hair slicked back, off my face, in a column behind me. My heart pounded from the danger I knew I was in, but it made me feel important in a way I hadn't known.

"What are you doing here tonight?" I asked.

"I could ask you the same question," he said.

"But you won't, because you know only one of us is supposed to be here."

Diver Seth's smile wavered. "Isn't there a mermaid curfew?" he asked. "I was under the impression that no one was supposed to be in the unchartered waters at night."

It was true, and I should have expected him to know that. It was in the treaty. There was absolutely no reason for it to have included in the text, but one of the mermen had let it slip during negotiations and the humans thought it worth mentioning. Their explanation was that while the waters were off-limits, there was less reason to patrol and enforce the treaty during the curfew.

Anyone who knew that small fact would have known the middle of the night was the best time to cross the barrier and dump a body.

Diver Seth's having mentioned the fact so soon after discovering me did nothing to remove the cloud of suspicion that hung over his head.

"I guess we're both overachievers," I said. "I'm a middle child. What's your excuse?"

I hoped to establish a playful tone with him, but he remained serious. "There's little chance of solving this case. And every minute that passes, that chance gets even smaller. I lied to you earlier when I said I was part of a dive team sent out here to find evidence. There's no team. There's just me. I rented the equipment and the pontoon."

"And the funny black outfit?"

"The wetsuit is mine. I like to surf on my days off."

I moved my hands back and forth in the water, cupping it and then turning my hands outward and pushing it back. Over and over. The motion allowed me to stay put, in one spot, swaying ever so slightly without having to move my tail. Only my head and shoulders were above the surface, and the water distorted the view of my arms, torso, and tail below. If the eel were in the area, they were far below and no longer visible, making the ocean seem very scary indeed.

"I don't think you're going to find any evidence," I said quietly. "I think you should leave and never come back."

"If I leave tonight, I'll never find answers," he said, his face drawn and pale.

I wondered how long he could keep himself afloat. Twice his mouth had dipped below the surface and he kicked his flippered feet and rose back up. But I could tell he was tiring. I could see it in his eyes.

I'd surprised him by being here. He hadn't counted on that. But he also hadn't tried to hurt me or scare me off. He'd shown no violent tendencies. I closed my eyes and tuned in to my emotive sense to read him. And what I got was . . . sadness?

A mermaid almost can't bear to be around a sad person. It is the hardest emotion to absorb, and at the core of the mermaid is the desire to inspire joy and happiness. I felt an immediate need to do something, and before I put any thought into what that something would be, my mouth opened and I began to sing.

The sound of a mermaid singing can't be described in everyday words or explained to those who have never experienced it. We manipulate our vocal cords in a way that creates a frequency that makes no audible noise. It tickles spines and melts hearts and lulls senses and excites spirits and sets forth a trance that temporarily erases all conscious thoughts. Our mermaid songs have been responsible for conceding armies, calming pirates, and pacifying drunken sailors. We've inspired simple minds with magnificent thoughts that turned ordinary men into philosophers and great thinkers.

Tonight, my song erased the sadness in Diver Seth's face. I watched him relax in the water and prepared to swim forward and carry him from the choppy waters to his pontoon where he'd be safe for the night. I intended to remain close until morning when he woke and returned to shore forever.

None of what I planned would come to fruition though, because as I completed my song and opened my eyes, I sensed we weren't alone. I ducked under Seth's pontoon to hide just in time to see a harpoon pierce the water and strike Seth from behind.

Diver Seth's body slowly sank below the surface. A thin trail of red blood flowed out of a hole in his wetsuit where the weapon had struck his shoulder. He hadn't woken from his trance, and if I did nothing, Diver Seth would have less to fear from the harpoon than the water that would soon fill his lungs.

If I did nothing, he would drown.

I reached my hand out and grabbed Diver Seth's wrist. I pulled him under the pontoon with me and swiftly pulled the harpoon from his wound. Soon the scent of the blood would alert the sharks who would care not a whit about the mermaid treaty. They were the thugs of the ocean, they would take what they wanted with no concern for territories, laws, or respect, and if they found a half dead diver, they'd finish him off for sport.

Something about that thought bothered me, but I had no time to follow it through. I unzipped Diver Seth's black rubber suit. I removed my satchel and pressed it against his shoulder and pulled the zipper back up to the top. The satchel stanched the flow of blood, but now he needed air.

Mermaid physiology allowed me to breathe water. I could extract the oxygen I needed to survive and not drown the way a human would. But taking an underwater breath and then breathing it into Seth's lungs would mean sure death to him. It was the number one reason humans and merfolk were ill-fated matches. Short-lived summer romances had been known to spring up from time to time, but only between well-informed, consenting adults who recognized that such a dalliance had no future.

There was one way to save him. Get him above the water's surface. But whoever had shot him was still here. Who? It couldn't be coincidence that the incident took place directly above the shipwreck where I'd first found Diver Seth trapped by the kelp.

There was a second way to save him.

I remembered the oxygen tank tangled in the kelp, how I'd cut Seth free with the knife that had been in the dead man and how the tank had remained behind when the two of us had swum to the surface. I hadn't seen the tank earlier, but Ava had startled me. That meant it was probably outside the shipwreck, partially buried in the ocean floor.

I had to leave Seth in order to retrieve it and I didn't think that was a good idea.

I swam to the edge of the pontoon and peered around the surface. I popped to the surface long enough to fill my lungs with a rather large gulp of nighttime air and, unnoticed, returned under the pontoon and breathed the air directly into Diver Seth's mouth.

He convulsed with the much-needed air. His eyes opened. He sputtered out a water-filled exhale. When he gained control of his lung spasms, I pointed up. He seemed to understand where we were. I pressed my hands together in a silent plea and pointed down to the shipwreck. He nodded.

Quick as could be, I dove down, down, down to the ocean floor and buried my fingers in the sand by the kelp. I dug around, waking hermit crabs and other critters who had expected to be in for the night. A lobster pinched my hand, and I cried out. He let go and crawled away, and my hand closed upon the object that I'd sought, the one thing that didn't belong on the ocean floor. The air tank that had slipped off the dead man.

I pulled the silver tank out of the sand and snapped my tail to propel me back to the pontoon. I practically jammed the device into his mouth in my haste to help him breathe. He seemed not to care about my unexpected forcefulness. For several long seconds he inhaled and exhaled, his chest expanding and contracting, his mouthpiece giving way to thousands of glistening bubbles that caught on the underside of his pontoon and slowly crawled to the edges and disappeared into the waves alongside of them.

I could have left. Perhaps I *should* have left. But I felt responsible for Diver Seth. Twice he'd found himself in mortal danger in mermaid territory, and I now believed Ava had been wrong. Whoever had been responsible for dumping the body by the shipwreck, it wasn't him.

But if I couldn't get him onto his pontoon, he might share the same fate.

The night held one challenge after another. I couldn't think about the punishment that awaited me when I returned to Sirenia and Mother learned where I'd been and what I'd done. I questioned why Ava hadn't sent help and worried that she had encountered trouble of her own. Neither concern could be addressed until I felt comfortable leaving the shipwreck.

When Seth indicated he was okay to surface, I clenched his hand and pulled him out from under the pontoon. Our heads popped out above the water next to one another. Seth tipped his back and breathed the crisp night air. I took the tank from him and set it onto the pontoon. I pulled him to the side and got behind him, putting my hands on his and raising each one to the edge of the pontoon.

Once his fingers had curled around it, I ducked below the water, under his feet. I felt his flippered feet tentatively press down on my tail, and then harder as he leveraged himself. With a forceful kick, I sent him out of the water and onto the pontoon. When I was satisfied that he'd landed, I flipped in the water and then rose and surveyed the damage.

Seth had successfully made it onto the pontoon, where he sat amidst a large pool of water that had splashed onto the pontoon with him. As water dripped off his head and face onto the deck around him, I stifled a laugh, though there was nothing funny about his predicament.

"You can't stay here," I said. "You need to see a doctor about the wound on your shoulder."

"No," he said. "The ocean is dangerous for you tonight. It's late and you're alone. There's blood in the water and you're well past your curfew. There's nothing to protect you on your way back to your colony."

He was right. The waters were dangerous for numerous reasons. But he needed to get treatment before morning. The heavy salt content in the waters would help sanitize the harpoon wound, but now that he was out of the water, he had to worry about infection. It seemed the only true option was for us to go our separate ways and hope for the best.

As if to underscore the caution Seth had expressed, something very much alive and unexpected brushed past my tail right below the surface.

I curled my tail instinctively to pull away from whatever was in the water with me. Remaining in place was not an option. If it were a shark, I'd have to swim for my life and even then my chances were less than favorable.

Without a word, I plunged my head under the water and snapped my tail to propel me down below. I dove deep, seeing nothing but darkness, a greenish black that muted the colors I knew made up my underwater world. A branch of coral scraped my arm and I overcorrected my path, swimming headfirst into an underwater plant covered in sea urchins. The small, sleepy critters scattered, waking tiny crabs and minnows in the process, and generating a cloud of sand from the ocean floor.

I hadn't realized I was that deep. I put my hand out in front of me and touched the bottom. My fingertips sank into the basin. A body in motion appeared in front of me and I twisted to change direction. I felt a hand glide over the scales on my hip and I flipped onto my back.

It was Laker.

River had mentioned something about mermen being exempt

from curfew in times of distress. I hated that they had autonomy while mermaids were not, but that was a battle for another day. Tonight, I knew Laker could help me get Seth's pontoon to shore and then chaperone me back home safely.

Laker's white-blond hair fanned out around his face. If his eyes had been any color other than their bright blue, I might not have been able to see it, but the unusual light color was impossible to hide. He had a canister strapped to his back, a quiver, I was certain, filled with sharp harpoons to use in the event he needed to defend himself.

Laker held out his hand. "Come with me. I'll accompany you home," he said.

"Not yet. There's a pontoon above us. With a human who is injured. He needs help getting to shore."

"The safety of humans is not my concern," Laker said.

"It's our duty as denizens of the deep to allow no harm to come to those who find themselves in our waters," I protested.

Laker seemed torn between helping me, a task that would benefit him doubly when word of his heroics reached Kyra and helping a strange human who had no business being where he was.

I pulled away from Laker. "Leave, then," I said. "I'll get him to shore."

I turned and swam back toward the pontoon. I hadn't explained my disappearance to Diver Seth and wondered if he even knew I was gone. A quick look above the surface told me he hadn't. He lay on his side, eyes closed, one arm wrapped around his torso.

I also knew something nefarious was taking place by the old shipwreck, and Diver Seth was a part of it. If he died, there would be no one with answers, and I would live in fear. That wasn't an option if I wanted to go on living the only life I knew. And if it meant giving up my adventures away from Sirenia, I would. But I had to know one way or the other.

It took two flips and a twist for me to position myself under the pontoon. I wriggled my tail and snapped it upward to give the pontoon momentum and direction on the water. Laker appeared beside me and shook his head. I turned away and made a series of shallow dolphin dives through the water.

The pontoon swayed, dangerously at first, and then caught the rhythm of my undulations. Laker pulled to the front and mirrored my movements. Soon the pontoon was moving along the water thanks to the current we generated. Before long, we were in shallow waters where the pontoon glided onto the beach and came to rest in a sand dune.

"Come on," Laker urged. "We have to get out of here before anybody sees us."

"Wait," I said. I swam as close to the pontoon as I could, with my head and shoulders and upper torso out of the water, propped on the edge and my tail barely submerged in the shallow waves that washed up on the beach.

I closed my eyes and sang a quiet song, one that would cause humans to wake but not know why. Diver Seth stirred on the pontoon and I reached out and touched his gold shield. I had no words to offer to him and didn't know if he could hear them if I did. I rolled down the beach, back into the water, and took Laker's outstretched hand. Together we swam back to Sirenia. The fate of the Diver Seth was out of our hands.

The next morning, I woke slowly. The memory of the previous evening clouded my mind like the waters that surrounded the shipwreck. Had I really spent most of the night in the dark ocean, unchaperoned, while undeniable danger lurked nearby?

Something tugged on my head, and I rolled over. Ava sat next to my bed, slathering my hair in a gelatinous substance that stank like rotting anchovies. In a bucket below, blobs of pink goo dripped.

Even if everything else turned out to be a dream, I now knew the hair tonic was real.

"Ow!" I cried.

Ava clamped her hand on my mouth. "You need to sit still and let me get this tonic out of your hair before Mother sees it. I covered for you last night, but you're not out of trouble yet."

I was quiet while Ava worked the goo through my hair and wrung out the last remnants of the tonic. She dragged the bucket to the portal that carried waste out of Sirenia to the processing plants that recycled it into new products. Aquatic life had learned how destructive garbage could be from the humans who saw the ocean as a giant trash receptacle. Now all underwater creatures worked together to reduce, reuse, and recycle. For a moment, I forgot about the dangerous situations I'd been in while I contemplated what form the stinky pink goo would return as. Maybe a set of jewelry or hair ornaments that Kyra would barter from Mad Midge? I giggled and then tried, unsuccessfully, to hide my laughter. It was too late.

"You have nothing to laugh about," Ava said. "You were told not to swim to the shipwreck, and you did. You made friends with a killer, and the investigation is going to implicate a mermaid."

I rolled over. "I don't care," I said. Ava knew more than she'd admitted, but I didn't yet know if it was worth calling her out on her secrets. I might learn more by playing it cool.

I also might learn that my sister was a killer.

* * *

It was hard to act like things were normal around Sirenia that day. With everything that had been going on by the old shipwreck, I had lost track of the days and was unprepared for the chaos that happened when the Ebb Tide Emporium received their new merchandise. Mother planned to shop, and the rest of the mermaids knew that "shopping" for Mother meant "carrying" for us. Each of us was responsible for filling a net and swimming it back to Sirenia. I was eager to talk to Laker and be sure he would keep our midnight swim to himself. I was sure he would be there because the mermen always helped the merchants unload the wares they intended to sell.

As I approached the emporium, I watched crowds of fish and sea creatures mill about, bartering for objects to take back to their homes. History lessons had taught me that once upon a time, there had been no marketplace to procure unusual items. Merfolk and ocean life had made do with what existed in the sea. Can you imagine?

Fortunately for us, we had more than enough to choose from. Booths made from reinforced braids of kelp lined row upon row of merchandise. To my left was the booth that housed electric eels, and past them were tanks of fresh food from the human world. The emporium didn't just stock utilitarian items. There were brushes and combs to use on mermaid hair, jewelry made from mother of pearl, colorful garments to wear for dress up, and an entire booth of beauty products meant to improve and enhance the appearance of mermaid scales.

Kyra had a whole trunk of makeup. She once spent an hour detailing the outline of the scales on her tail in phosphorescent paint that made her glow in the dark like the eels! When Mother found out, she used up four jars of eel muck to remove the paint. The topical temporary color had left Kyra's tail sensitive for the following month and she'd had to withstand a series of tail-conditioning sessions to bring her scales back to their regular state, but as soon as she recovered, she was quick to sample Mad Midge's next batch of makeup in secret. Some mermaids will never learn.

On this trip, Mother visited the necessary booths and placed orders, and it was up to my sisters and me to courier the filled orders back to Sirenia. Both Ava and Kyra had made two trips already. I stayed behind and killed time in the bookstore while Mother shopped and read three chapters of an adventure novel before a familiar voice distracted me.

"Did it come in yet?" asked Charlie the Tuna. "It was delivered two days ago." I peeked around the book to see Charlie's audience.

"If you tell me what it is you're waiting for, I can go look for it," said a chubby manatee.

"Trunks," Charlie said. "Two of them. And don't get any ideas about opening them. I paid good money for privacy."

Charlie the Tuna was waiting for a special order from Mad Midge? Trunks? And he paid extra for privacy?

Mad Midge had said something about waiting for a special order to come in. She'd said it the day I swam back from saving Diver Seth (and seeing the dead body).

What if there was a connection? The dead body and the trunks Ava had seen and Mad Midge's special order and Charlie the Tuna? Could it be?

Did that mean the currency counterfeiter was working with Mad Midge?

Or Charlie?

Did they know the other diver was dead?

Had one of them killed him?

Questions came into my mind with such rapidity that I couldn't keep up with them. I vibrated with energy and my tail got so bright I reached out and squeezed a sample squid pen so I could hide behind the resulting cloud of ink.

I floated forward so I could hear better. Charlie seemed to become aware of my presence and looked right at me. I pretended to read, but the cloud of ink slowly cleared, revealing me. Charlie was not pleased.

"Come back tonight," said the manatee. "Mad Midge said the trunks got mixed up when we unpacked them, and nobody is allowed to open them but her."

Charlie grumbled something I couldn't understand.

A moment later, he spoke to the manatee. "You make sure Mad Midge knows I want my trunks before the emporium closes."

"Yes, Charlie," the manatee said. Manatees were mammals of

very little brains and I suspected he'd forget Charlie's demand long before he encountered Mad Midge.

But *I* wouldn't. Because Ava had said she'd seen trunks by the shipwreck. Trunks filled with coins. And what better reason to pay for privacy than knowing your special order was something a human had been killed for?

It was hours before I finished with my tasks. Ava kept a watchful eye on me, swimming alongside me both times I left with a net filled with purchases. It wasn't like I was planning to get away—I knew I'd been lucky not to have been caught on my other solo trips and had decided to play it safe today—but still, I bristled at Ava's overbearing proximity. Everybody knew Kyra was the one who tried to get out of working! When Mother finally called on Ava for her opinion on new books for the Library Under the Sea, I circled the aquatic marketplace in search of the mermen.

I found my younger sister instead.

Kyra rested on a giant clam with her face in her hands. Her lustrous white hair billowed around her shaking shoulders. I dropped my own agenda to make sure she was okay. "What's wrong?" I asked.

"Laker," Kyra said. "He said he would meet me behind Mad Midge's booth today, but he didn't show. I asked around and one of the other mermen told me he saw Laker swimming with another mermaid last night after curfew." Kyra blinked her wide eyes, and her thick, curled lashes created ripples in the ocean. If Laker had moved on from Kyra to another mermaid, he was a fool.

Except I knew *I* was the other mermaid. One of the other mermen had seen us. And worse, my hair had been pink. Whoever saw us would have thought I was Ava. If Kyra heard that her older sister had stolen her latest beau, she'd be crushed, and the bond between us would be shattered forever.

I was torn. If I told Kyra I'd been the one with Laker, all sorts of questions would come up. Kyra was sweet and innocent. She didn't understand things like murder, evidence, sneaking around late at night, and ignoring orders. She could just as easily tell on me for my late-night excursion as she could plant a handful of sand crabs in Ava's bed to punish her.

But as much as I hated to see her hurt, I knew the truth was too risky. Laker staying away from her would be a good thing for me.

"Kyra, everywhere you go, you're surrounded by mermen. What's so special about Laker?"

"He's new," she said. "I didn't grow up with him like the other mermen."

"Why does that matter?"

She looked up. "I would think you'd understand that better than anybody."

I lowered myself onto the clamshell next to her. It was slightly smaller than the one she was on, and even though Kyra was on the petite side, I had to look up to address her. "Why would you think that?"

"Because you're all about finding what's new. You go exploring because you've seen everything in Sirenia. I saw how excited you got when Ava and I told you about the human at the library. The second you heard something exciting happened that you weren't a part of, you started asking questions. Ava told me not to tell you anything else about him because you'd end up wandering off to see if you could find him."

She did, did she?

"What else is there to tell?"

"See? You're doing it just like she said!" She pointed at me as if she'd caught me in the act of, well, fulfilling Ava's prediction.

"You made it seem like big news, but when I told Laker, he just shrugged it off."

I felt a vibration of nerves through me. If Kyra brought up the human to Laker, he might have told her about my involvement. "When did you tell him?"

"At dinner," she said. "He said it was no big deal. Everybody knew about the diver by the shipwreck."

I was stunned. I'd spent so much time trying to keep secrets from my sisters, and here it turned out they both already knew what I knew.

It seemed there was no point hanging around looking for Laker now. My so-called secret was common knowledge. "Laker's probably just busy with his project for Poseidon," I said. I put my arm around Kyra's shoulders. "Let's swim back to Sirenia and help mother unpack what she bought."

I floated up from the clamshell and held out my hand. Kyra grasped it. We swam to the Ebb Tide Emporium exit and checked in with one of Mad Midge's employees, who pointed us toward a rather large pile of bulging nets. We each grabbed one and swam it home, the first of many trips that kept me occupied for hours.

Despite the distractions of the day, there was no escaping my thoughts. The more time I spent hauling nets of merchandise back to the colony, the antsier I got about the idea that danger existed in the near vicinity. Everywhere I turned, I found more questions about who was lying—and why. After lugging the last of the cargo nets back to the colony, I swam away from the others and rested for a moment.

That's when I saw the trunk.

It was a nondescript worn leather box, deep brown with rope tied around it to keep it closed. The rope wasn't a natural resource, and while it wasn't impossible for one of the merchants to repurpose a piece of trash that had floated their way, it was odd that no one had carted the box away with the other items. In fact, the trunk was positioned almost as if someone wanted it to go unnoticed.

Which made me all the more interested in its contents.

There wasn't much time.

The size of the trunk was about the size that Ava had indicated when talking about the trunks she'd seen by the shipwreck. And if there was money inside—well, first things first. I needed to know what was inside before I determined what it meant.

I worked half the knot loose when I heard voices. Quickly I flipped over and sat on top of the trunk. I put my hands behind me and turned my face up, as if stretching my back and neck and shoulders from too much physical strain that day.

Two male mermen swam around the side and seemed surprised to find me there. It was River and his younger brother, Creen. I smiled. "Hi, Zoe," River said. "Is Kyra with you?" he looked around.

"No. After our last trip, she stayed back at Sirenia. I came back to make sure we got everything."

Creen swam in circles around River and me, slowing to pick up a stick from the ocean floor and jab a sleeping crab. The crab scurried sideways to get away, which interested Creen even more. River and I watched him, as if having a mutual focal point gave us a reprieve from having to converse. I had a personal stake in outlasting River. I was sitting on it!

"So, I heard one of the mermaids was out with Laker last night," River said. "Kind of unusual behavior, don't you think? Swimming around in the dark, unchaperoned."

I fought not to react. "I don't know," I said. "Ever since the treaty was enacted, the unchartered waters have been safe. Aside from the water being dark, there really aren't any dangers around here, are there?"

River chuckled. "That's the thing about dark waters," he said.

"You can't tell what's lurking in them. I bet Mother Mermaid would lay down the law if she suspected one of you of trying to get away with something like that." River grinned again, but this time his smile seemed less friendly and more sinister. "She might even banish Laker from coming to Sirenia and spending time with her daughters."

If I hadn't been sitting on a partially opened trunk possibly filled with enough money to make someone commit murder, I would have gotten up and swum away with no further word. River implied that he thought Kyra was the one who'd broken the rules, and he was willing to tell on her to keep them apart. He was willing to turn Mother against Kyra for his own purpose. Mother had been strict with us when we were in school, but for good reason. Hearing someone else mock her protectiveness raised my ire. "You should really be controlling your brother's behavior more closely," I said. "A boy with a stick is no match for an antagonized crab with sharp pinchers."

I said this while staring at Creen, who apparently heard me as well. He looked away from the crab, and the crab seized the opportunity to do exactly what I suggested. He clamped his sharp claw onto to the boy's bare hand. The stick dropped to the ocean floor, and Creen cried out. River went to him.

"Come on," he said to Creen. "We're going home." He cast a quick look at me, hesitating for just long enough to make me wonder what he was thinking. Whatever it was, he seemed to make up his mind. He and his brother swam away without saying goodbye.

I wasn't willing to take a chance on someone else finding the trunk. I rose and hauled it out of the sand and swam it back to Sirenia. After making sure my sisters were busy unloading new purchases with mother, I raised the lid and looked inside.

I'd been right that this was one of the trunks Ava had seen by the shipwreck. It was full of enough gold to be suspicious. But what was worse was that the gold wasn't in the form of counterfeit currency or sunken treasure. No, the weird gold coins Ava had seen weren't coins at all. They were small gold shields like the one Diver Seth wore around his neck. The police badge I relied on to believe in his innocence.

Gold police badges like the one I found buried in the sand by the shipwreck overflowed from the trunk. These were most likely the reason one man was dead and another was wounded. This trunk was what a desperate person was trying to get, and now it was in my possession. In Sirenia.

I dug my hand into the trunk and scooped up several of the badges. When I had seen the one hanging from the chain around Diver Seth's neck, I trusted him. But the number of shields in this trunk made them look as unimportant as a basket of sea glass. If the badges were this easy to come by, it would be impossible for us to know who we could trust.

Another thought struck me. This was the identification the police wore on land. I was afraid for the mermaids and mermen and underwater life, but what about the humans? Would people use these badges to pretend they were in charge so they could commit crimes and get away with them?

Were humans that devious?

I was torn. I knew the mere presence of the badges in our

room was not only suspicious, but dangerous. Whoever was responsible would come looking for them.

They already had.

I suddenly remembered hovering inside the old shipwreck with Ava while Diver Seth approached. Ava had been afraid of him and had cautioned me that he was bad. I hadn't wanted to believe her—all because of that stupid shield. It was frightening how much power one small symbol held.

But I remembered Diver Seth's face as he swam toward us in the shipwreck. Ava's warning had provided enough doubt that I questioned my own judgment. And what had changed? The harpoon that struck him in the back. The victim couldn't be the criminal. He needed help, and the attack triggered my emotive side. I'd given up my hiding spot to swim out and help save him while giving Ava an opportunity to swim to safety.

With the relative silence of the mermaid house, I was able to think clearly for the first time all day. Ava had seemed genuinely scared of Diver Seth, but why hadn't she sent help? And I remembered what it was that had bothered me after Seth had been struck by the harpoon. The blood in the water, just like the blood that streamed from the body that had been lying on the ocean floor the day Seth's foot had been caught in the kelp.

There should have been sharks. Both times, there should have been sharks.

There weren't.

Why?

And what had happened to that body?

Other questions filled my mind, like bubbles that escape from the mouth of a sleeping tuna. Why was Ava hiding a bottle of pink hair tonic when she had naturally pink hair? How did Laker know to come find me last night after curfew? What had tipped off the council to form a volunteer patrol? Who confided in Charlie the Tuna? Was it a coincidence that Mad Midge was ready with a supply of paste to help me hide my glowing tail? How did River know Laker had been out with another mermaid? Where was the second trunk?

Was there a second trunk?

Until I had answers, I didn't know who I could trust. Even Ava's story of patrolling the edges of our territory felt off. I had heard nothing about such a mission, and that was unusual. Rumors spread quickly through the ocean because it was impossible to get away from sea life. Barnacles, abalone, and crabs were all where you'd least expect them. Sometimes what appeared to be a random shell could house a curious clam who would pass information along to other sea life. Other times, a shell was just a shell.

If I could talk to someone about everything, it would help. And there was one place I knew I could go, one confidante I could turn to, one who would advise me. The conversation would not be easy and it may result in a punishment far worse than anything I'd ever experienced, but I knew. I had to talk to Mother.

I hid the trunk of badges under my bed and swam off in search of the matriarch of Sirenia. If we were all in danger, we would need more than just me to survive.

When I entered the grand corridor of the housing structure, Mother was sitting on an ottoman made from woven seaweed. Unlike Ava, Kyra, and me, Mother's appearance reflected the signs of maturity and power. Her eyes were the palest blue, and the color had left her hair, leaving translucent locks that she braided in a thick plait and wrapped around her head. Atop her braid was a small crown from the ceremony when she assumed power over Sirenia. Once she'd received it, she'd never taken it off.

Her physical appearance projected strength and power, though I had never been able to identify what it was that communicated it just so. She had a presence to her that I'd never seen in any other merfolk, and she instantly commanded respect wherever she went.

She had a book on her lap and a tall glass on the mother-of-pearl-topped table next to her. (Humans did not understand that our possessions did not float away under the ocean.)

"Mother?" I said gently. "I would like to talk about a threat to Sirenia." The words, spoken aloud, sounded too heavily weighted, but anything less would have downplayed what I feared. Mother appreciated honesty and directness, both of which she believed eliminated confusion in our communications. It helped that we could easily read each other's emotions. Mother would know without hesitation that I wasn't merely being overly dramatic (something Kyra was constantly accused of—rightfully so!).

Mother Mermaid closed her book and set it on the table next to her chalice. She crossed her hands over her lap and nodded to me. "Speak, daughter," she said.

I wrung my hands together and then, realizing how unbecoming the gesture was, released my hands and forced them to my sides. "I've been exploring by the old shipwreck," I admitted. "Even after you told me not to go back, I did. For this, I am sorry."

"Are you?" Mother asked gently. I wasn't sure why Mother had asked. I apologized because I knew I disobeyed orders and thought it was the right thing to say. At my hesitation, Mother continued speaking. "You went to the shipwreck despite being cautioned not to. That demonstrates a great interest in the exploration of your surroundings. That is not something to apologize for."

"I was apologizing for disobeying," I said.

"It is important to know when to obey and when to disobey. And there are times when we need to accept our actions and stand behind them, whether they were condoned or not. Are you sorry that you explored the shipwreck? Consider your answer before speaking."

I pressed my lips together and thought about Mother's question. No, I thought to myself. I was not sorry I'd gone exploring. My older sister had more responsibility than I did, and my younger sister was coddled. The rules that applied to me had little do with my skills, desires, and talents, all of which leaned toward curiosity.

"No," I said. "I am not sorry that I went exploring. I enjoy exploration and I'm good at it. I've explored all of the areas of Sirenia that I'm allowed to explore, and I ventured out in search of a great adventure."

"Did you find one?" Mother asked.

It wasn't the question I expected. "I don't know," I answered.

"What did you find?"

"I found trouble," I said. "I've been raised in a protected environment, and I'm unfamiliar with how to handle it."

I floated in the water, barely moving, waiting for Mother's inevitable question and lecture. There would be no way to confess the full extent of what I'd found without implicating Ava, and while I felt that coming to Mother for counsel was the right thing, I didn't relish the idea of getting my sister in trouble too. It was one thing to be responsible. It was another to be a tattletale.

A long silence stretched between us. The whole time, Mother's eyes studied my face, and then ran down my torso and tail. It was as if Mother were taking stock of me for the first time. I adjusted the set of my shoulders a little straighter and lifted my head. I wanted to pass this inspection even though I didn't know what passing it meant.

"Zoe," Mother said, "You showed great bravery by going off to explore the shipwreck by yourself. I did not know you were so inclined. But adventure without the goal of seeking knowledge is folly. You have gained knowledge from your adventure, and it is up to you to decide what to do with it."

"But I've come to you for counsel," I said.

"And my counsel is this. Follow this adventure. Find the answers you seek. You must see this through for yourself or you will never understand the satisfaction that comes from discovering the solution to a problem."

"What if this problem means danger? Great danger? Not just to me, but to others?"

Mother folded her hands in her lap. Her lips turned up ever so slightly, a hint of a smile that indicted both understanding and restraint.

"It is your choice, Zoe. You can be adventurous, or you find a place like your sisters, but you cannot do both. Were anyone to tell you what to do, you would never know if you followed your true path. Only you can decide."

"But Ava and Kyra know what their paths are. I thought—"

"You thought you were overlooked? Or that I never considered your skills?"

Well, yes. But it was one thing to think those things to myself. It was quite another to admit them to Mother without sounding petty and filled with self-pity.

"I've been patient," I said cautiously, "waiting to see what was in store for me."

"You have tried to be patient, but the very act of exploring past the barrier indicates you were not confident that the decisions you awaited would fulfill you. As the oldest, Ava was born into her position. She didn't have a choice. And Kyra enjoys the life she has here in Sirenia. This may be your destiny, Zoe. This is your chance to experience the adventure you desire."

I thanked Mother and swam through the coral branches that marked the house entrance and back to my room. This was entirely new to me. Up to now, everything I'd done had been because what was expected of me. It was the way of the mermaids. I'd been bored by the routine and had sought out excitement for myself. I imagined a lecture, maybe a punishment. I thought I'd unburden myself and either Mother would tell me what to do or the problems I'd uncovered would be assigned to the mermen or taken to Poseidon. I never anticipated being given a choice in the matter.

And without overthinking things, (which I tended to do), I knew what I would do. I'd set out for the shipwreck because I wanted—needed—more than what life in Sirenia offered me. I'd taken that chance because the unknown attracted me. I wanted to see this through until it was finished, no matter the cost.

But just to be safe, I went in search of my sisters to say a proper goodbye.

Ava was sitting outside the wall of red coral reading a fashion magazine. Her hair billowed out around her head, framing her face in a cloud of fuchsia. Puffs of air shot upward from sand crabs who'd burrowed into the ocean floor and buzzed Ava's scaly mermaid tail. My presence startled her and she jumped, quickly going from surprised to annoyed.

"I saw you talking to Mother," Ava said. "I suppose it's just a matter of time until she grounds me."

"I did talk to Mother, but I didn't mention you," I said. Ava's reaction was both self-centered and hostile, and I enjoyed being able to take the high road. "Our conversation was about me and my future."

"What future? You're a mermaid."

"So are you," I pointed out. "And you have a future. You have an important volunteer role as well. That's all I want, Ava. I want my own role."

Ava ran her tongue over her teeth inside her mouth, causing her lips to pucker up like a guppy. She tipped her head down and looked at me from under her eyelashes. She could never compete with little sister Kyra in a competition of eyelash batting, but Ava had learned her best angles and used them well.

I looked away. I didn't want to be caught in Ava's spell, or worse, compelled to tell Ava the details of my conversation with Mother.

"Ava, why do you have a jar of pink hair tonic?" I asked. "You were born with pink hair. It doesn't make sense."

She looked down at her hands. "Mad Midge told me one day the color would leave my hair like it has with Mother. She gave me the tonic as a precautionary measure. She said all the human women use it."

Mad Midge's business thrived on her ability to find and sell unique items. She'd found a way to make Ava want the one thing Ava would never need. But—gave it? Mad Midge didn't give away anything.

She gave me a sample of eel muck.

Was there something behind Mad Midge's new, rarely seen generosity? Or was she hiding something and buying our silence?

"I'm going out," I said abruptly. "Back to the market," I added. "I brought something home that doesn't belong to us and I think it's best to return it before anyone notices."

"How do you know no one's noticed?" Ava asked.

"I don't. I'm taking a chance."

Ava turned her attention back to the magazine and flipped the page. "You better get going," she said without looking up. "The longer you hold on to something that doesn't belong to you, the more people will think you took it in the first place."

It wasn't the first time Ava had attitude over something I did, but it was the first time I chose not to let it get to me. Ava was right. The sooner I returned the trunk to where I found it, the sooner I could sit back and watch who retrieved it. I would set my own trap.

But before I set my trap, I removed a handful of gold shields from the trunk and buried them in the ocean floor under my bed. If things went wrong, I wanted there to be something left behind to prove what I'd known.

I slipped the trunk into a cargo net and swam away from home. I didn't have much of a plan, but I felt certain the simple act of returning to the shipwreck would draw out whoever was behind this. I didn't know if Diver Seth had gotten medical help after Laker and I swam him to shore, or if he'd died on the beach where we had left him last night. There were many things I didn't yet know: who the dead man was, where his body had gone, who had thrown the harpoon that injured Diver Seth, what someone planned to do with a trunk filled with badges, and why Diver Seth cared so much about it all that he'd broken mermaid law to research it himself.

It was this last question that bothered me the most, and I suspected the answer was the key to everything.

By the time I reached the Ebb Tide Emporium, I was
exhausted. The trunk containing the faked badges was
heavy even with the weightlessness of water. The cargo
net created drag, and I felt like I'd worked twice as hard to reach
my destination. I glided toward the open clamshells that Mad
Midge had positioned by the entrance and sat for a moment to
rest. The cargo net holding the trunk remained by my tail. It was
careless not to hide it first, but the market had closed for the day
and everybody knew if you stuck around too long, Mad Midge
would put you to work. For that reason, the emporium was as
popular after hours as the old shipwreck.

Once again, my mind returned to the sunken ship. Before I
happened upon the mystery surrounding the ship, it had been my
secret hiding place. My place to go to get away from my sisters and
the expectations of being a mermaid. Sometimes I took a book,
relaxed inside the ship, and read. Sometimes I swam in circles
around the wreckage. Once I used a broken shell to dig a hole in
the ocean floor, though the currents made my efforts futile.

Shifting sand and silt leveled the hole as quickly as I dug it out and I abandoned the project shortly after beginning.

Maybe that's why the trunks were abandoned inside the shipwreck. The dead man thought he could bury it but discovered the idea of buried treasure in an ocean was only possible when the ocean itself did the burying?

But something else bothered me. Ava said she had taken a handful of coins to the council when she'd discovered the trunks, and they'd verified them and coordinated efforts to retrieve the trunks. If that were the case, then was this trunk one of them? Where had it come from? Was it possible that someone had intercepted the trunks before the council was able to take possession of them?

Now that I'd started asking questions, they wouldn't stop!

I briefly wondered if this was why mermaids weren't supposed to go nosing around for adventure. But to me, the questions were thrilling. I wanted to know what had happened and eliminate the threat to Sirenia, but a part of me knew this was the most exciting thing that had happened in my life. Once it was over, I'd go back to being plain old Zoe, middle sister, practicing for voice lessons and pretending to care about how to be a muse.

Boring, boring, boring.

But that was the life of a mermaid, and it was the life I knew to protect. It was the reason I'd brought the trunk back here, away from home. Whoever was skulking about stealing badges and killing divers wasn't someone I wanted around my family. It was more important for me to protect my sisters than to go out on my own.

And then it hit me: what if danger came to Sirenia because I'd gone out exploring on my own? What if *I* was the one who had brought danger to our colony?

I floated up from the shell and gathered the cargo net in my arms. The short respite had been welcome but I couldn't relax, not just yet. I carried the net to where I'd found the trunk in the first place and turned the net upside down so the trunk tumbled out. It landed upside down, the knot of the rope on the underside. I cast the cargo net to the side and tried to right it when I heard voices.

"Ya shoulda thought a dat before ya ordered dem," said a voice that could only be Mad Midge. "Da humans don't mind me usin' a line of credit for unusual items, ya know, but when it's somethin' like dis, dey expect to get paid right away."

"I told you, I have the money," said Charlie the Tuna. "Just have to move a few investments. You're in business. You understand."

"I understand how our relationship works better dan you, ya know," she said. "You give me da money, I give you da trunk. Do ya see me givin' away the rest of my wares on credit?"

"But you got them, right? All of them? Like I asked?" Even without seeing Charlie's face, I could hear the greediness in his voice.

"I got dem," Mad Midge said. "But I'll just be sittin' on dem until you give me my clams. I took a lot of risks for dis order, and I've got my own plans. We had an agreement, Tuna."

"Give me one more day," Charlie said. "I'll have your money by this time tomorrow."

"This is it, Tuna. The last special order for you. I can't be goin' out on a limb for you if dis is how it's gonna be."

I should have been prepared for the abrupt end of the conversation, but I wasn't. There was no way for me to get out of there without being seen. I ducked inside the clamshell benches and pulled the top half of the shell down on top of me. Even with my tail bent, I barely fit. Worse, the upside-down trunk that I'd brought back to the emporium was on the ground not far from me, and the cargo net was who knows where. Evidence of my presence was all over the place. I closed one eye and spied out the small gap between the clamshell to see what Charlie would do when he discovered the trunk, unattended, right there in front of him.

But Charlie didn't notice the trunk. He swam right past it and took off in the direction of the shipwreck.

I knew I should get out of the clamshell and swim after him. After everything that happened, I knew I shouldn't let him out of my sight. But to tell you the truth, the clamshell was comfortable and maybe tracking an angry tuna wasn't the most important thing for me to do. I rested my head against the bottom of the shell and closed my eyes. Just for a moment.

Just.

A.

Moment.

More.

I fell asleep. I must have. Because when I opened my eyes, I was completely confused about where I was. It took me a second to identify the smooth pearly interior of the clamshell, and it took a second more to remember why I'd climbed in at all.

I'd been so tired I could have slept there all night. Something had woken me. What?

I peered out into the water. Mad Midge's electric eels had been corralled for the night and no longer lit up the entrance. I pushed the top half of the clamshell up and sat up. My joints were stiff from sleeping in the shell and I needed a rigorous swim to loosen myself up. I floated out of the shell and swam a few yards away, and then turned to look for the trunk.

It was gone.

Just as I was about to leave, I realized why the water seemed so dark. On the surface of the ocean, in the euphotic zone, was a large rectangle. It was Diver Seth's pontoon. He was here. At the Ebb Tide Emporium.

I couldn't imagine a single honest reason for him to be right here, right now.

I'd saved him. I'd helped him. I'd trusted him.

And here he was, at Mad Midge's market. Mad Midge, who was the only mermaid allowed to do business with humans. What had she told me? She didn't hate humans, but she didn't trust them.

"Zoe," said a voice. I spun quickly and my blue hair fanned out around my head. It was Laker.

"Shhh," I said. I held my finger up to my lips and pointed to the pontoon. Laker immediately recognized it. "You were right," I said quietly. "He's trouble."

"We need to get you out of here," Laker said. "Give me a minute to make sure Mad Midge isn't in danger and I'll chaperone you back to Sirenia."

I nodded. Laker swam off, into the deepest part of the emporium and I waited. As time passed and he didn't return, I panicked. After what had happened to Mad Midge, I didn't believe for a moment that she would turn her back on us for profit, but I did wonder if she was capable of exacting revenge for her injuries.

I'd brought much of this trouble on the mermaid community. I couldn't trade others for my safety. I shifted direction and swam into the darkness. Seconds later, my arms and tail were twisted in a tangle of rope, cotton, and mesh.

I'd been caught like a fish in a net.

I'm ashamed to admit that the first thing I did was struggle. It wasn't smart, and it wasn't going to get me free. And if I'd been more prepared for a trap, I mightn't have wasted precious time and energy with the effort. Whoever had cast the net into the water knew exactly what he expected to retrieve, and a mermaid with a bright coral tail was probably at the top of the list.

Especially if the net caster knew I was down here.

I'd told Diver Seth the story of the captured mermaids. I'd told him because I trusted him. His betrayal stung like an attack by a thousand angry jellyfish. I resolved to never save a human again. Not that I expected the opportunity to go saving humans to continue to pop up willy nilly, but still, the resolve had been made and there was no going back.

As I gave up the struggle against the net, I considered my options. First: warn the others. If a human dredged for mermaids, he may not be content with the capture of one. I opened my mouth and sang out a warning song, casting vocal vibrations through the water that would be heard all the way to Sirenia. Soon, a response reached me. *Help is on the way.*

No, I sang back. It's too dangerous. It's a trap.

This time I was met with silence. The merfolk knew I was right. I was on my own for one last adventure.

The boat on the surface of the water started to move and the net dragged along the bottom. Had I spent my first moments thinking instead of thrashing about, I might have thought to free the electric eels from the tank to give me light, but as the humans say, that ship had sailed. Oh, the irony.

As the ship pulled me along, I scanned the passing sea plants and bittersweet relief flooded me. We were headed away from Sirenia, not toward it. My sisters would be safe.

Another thing struck me. The path we traveled was familiar. We weren't going to shore; we were going toward the shipwreck. We were headed to where I first met Diver Seth.

Which meant we were headed to where I'd buried the diving knife.

I pushed my hand through an opening in the coarse weave of the rope and trailed my fingers through the ocean floor. Occasionally I woke a crab, who quickly burrowed a new hole into the sand. Come on, I thought to myself, where did I leave it?

I remembered. I'd buried it somewhere between the shipwreck and Charlie the Tuna's hangout. We were nearing it; we had to be. We had to be. I trailed my fingers in the sand and tuned into the frequency that allowed me to sense my surroundings. I felt the vibrations of the ocean and the presence of sand crabs and the movement of the aquatic plants and the familiarity of the journey. At the precise moment where the vibrations were at their peak, I dug my fingers into the sand, pulled out the knife, and sliced through the rope to free myself.

And I considered swimming back to Sirenia, yes, I considered it very much, but I knew, deep down, that the danger was still there. With one hand gripping the knife, I used the strength of my tail kick to propel myself through the water, to the shipwreck, ahead of the boat. I was surprised by how slowly the boat moved through the water, but I used it to my advantage.

I reached the shipwreck and saw the shadow of a man inside. The ocean water was dark and cloudy, like it had been the day that I'd discovered Diver Seth and the dead body, but a light on the figure's head provided a halo and I recognized him. Diver Seth. In the shipwreck.

Diver Seth? In the shipwreck?

If Diver Seth was in the water, then who was on the pontoon?

A terrible thought occurred to me. A terrible, terrible thought that was only half-formed, like the piece of sand that is destined to become a pearl but never gets the chance because the shell is opened too soon. It was a thought that explained so, so many of the questions I'd had from the very first day that I'd discovered the body, the diver, the trunk, and the knife. It explained how close I'd come—we'd all come—to trouble.

Hesitantly, I stopped short of letting Diver Seth know I was there. I sang another siren song, this one to Kyra. *Has Laker returned to Sirenia?*

The answer was no. The sadness was evident in the lilting quality of her song. I heard her sobs, like ripples along the bottom of the ocean. Mermaid tears had the power to change the tides, and Kyra's broken heart would cause all sorts of problems to sailors who'd hoped to safely navigate our waters tonight.

But that didn't matter, not tonight, not to me.

Laker. Who'd come to Sirenia from another, warmer climate. Laker, who'd heard of my adventure by the shipwreck. Laker, who'd appeared out of nowhere the night I was with Seth, who'd advised me to let him die, who'd been at the Ebb Tide Emporium, who'd pretended to go for help before I'd been caught. Laker, who helped me propel the floaty pontoon from underneath.

Laker, who could have tossed out the net to catch me, feeding into the biggest fear of every mermaid in Sirenia.

Laker, who swam with a quiver, which held harpoons like the one that had injured Diver Seth. I was certain that the merman was behind our troubles, but I didn't yet understand his motivation. Violence wasn't common among merfolk, and even under Poseidon's direction, Laker would have had options other than murder.

I swam toward the shipwreck and entered through a porthole. Even through the cloudy water, my excellent mermaid vision allowed me to recognize Diver Seth, who looked surprised to find me there. He pointed up to the surface and I understood. I swam to the surface quickly, forgetting he needed to make a slower ascent to keep from cramping. (Humans had all sorts of issues.)

He finally surfaced a few feet away from me and pulled the regulator out of his mouth. "Zoe," he said. "It's past curfew. You shouldn't be out here unchaperoned."

"You have to leave," I said urgently. "The waters are dangerous tonight."

"No," he said. "I haven't been completely honest with you, but you have to trust me. I came back to stop what my brother started out here."

"Your brother?" I asked. I spun in a circle, looking for someone else in the water. By the time I finished a full rotation (less than a second), I was sure we were alone. "Your brother?" I asked again.

"My brother was the body you found the day you saved me. I caught him counterfeiting police badges. He was using the shipwreck to hide his inventory. I followed him out here to make him stop. He was breaking the law—human law—but by coming out here, he was breaking the mermaid law, too. I wanted to save him from doing something he couldn't undo."

"You were too late," I said quietly. And the missing pieces

unfolded. Diver Seth's brother hid the trunks. Laker found him. Shot him. Killed him. Left him.

Laker had no interest in the counterfeit badges. Nobody did. They were evidence of a human crime, not one that mattered in the merfolk world. Those badges were nothing but junk to us. Kyra might find a way to string them together, into a necklace of sorts, but other than that, they were useless.

But when word got out that a merman had killed a human, there would be questions. And Laker was new to our community. He'd be banished for committing an act that would cast aspersions on the integrity of Poseidon and his promise of peaceful waters.

I'd resolved never to trust a human again, but that was exactly what I had to do.

"Your brother was in unchartered waters. If he were approached by a merman and acted hostile, he would have been shot."

"My brother was working with bad people," Diver Seth said. "He was desperate. If caught by anyone other than me, he would not have been peaceful. Even I expected a fight."

"So," I said.

"So," Diver Seth said.

An uncomfortable moment passed while I tried to figure out where we went from here. It was Diver Seth who volunteered the solution. "I'll mourn my brother, but his fate came about the day he chose his path. I am a police officer. I will not seek out the responsible party. The crime committed was not of mermaid concern. All I want is the evidence. It needs to be destroyed."

"That's what you were looking for the other day," I said. "Why?"

"Because I prefer to protect my mother from the truth. Without evidence, my brother's memory can be protected. It is less painful this way."

It was then that a third head—with white-blond hair—broke the surface of the water. Diver Seth tensed. My tail lit up, and the resulting glow discolored the water surrounding me. I feared for Laker and Diver Seth and a little bit myself but the emotion in Laker's crystal blue eyes wasn't anger or fear. It was hope. "Do you mean what you just said?" Laker asked.

Diver Seth looked into the water. "You could hear us?"

Laker nodded.

"I give you my word," Diver Seth said.

Laker looked at me and I smiled. "This is a human world problem," I said. "It is not our role to get involved."

"But we are involved," Laker said. "How do we know this diver will do what he says? How do we know he won't come back and capture us?"

"We don't," I said. "But it is not the merfolk way to live in fear or to let corruption change us. We are simple of joy and pure of spirit and strong of will." I turned back to Diver Seth. "The trunk that you seek is hidden inside the Ebb Tide Emporium. Mad Midge is the only mermaid who does business with the humans. If anybody finds the trunk, they'll assume it's part of her inventory."

And that is how it came to be that an unlikely mermaid helped a police officer shut down a counterfeit identification scheme, solve a murder, and restore peace to Sirenia while protecting the memory of a brother who had given in to the dark side of human nature.

Zoe never did find out what was in the trunks that Charlie the Tuna awaited from Mad Midge. Satisfied it had nothing to do with the business by the shipwreck, she resolved not to bring it up (but she did put him on her new surveillance route.)

The mermaid world returned to normal, with one noticeable change. Every day, after voice lessons and before dinner, Mother sent Zoe away from Sirenia to explore. It was, as Mother put it, Zoe's destiny.

As for Mad Midge? Shortly thereafter, she closed the Ebb Tide Emporium for a week. It seemed she'd recently come into a sizeable amount of cash from a transaction with a human police officer and said it was time she treated herself to an adventure.

Zoe couldn't have agreed more.

Part Two: Kyra

"Like I said, I'm not jealous of Zoe," I said to my music teacher. "She's my sister, and I love her. And she did help the human police solve a case they'd been working on, and the ocean is safer because of her, and now she has a job working as liaison to the divers."

I know how it sounded, but I meant it. I wasn't jealous of Zoe. But this new development, the job that had been created for her after Mother met with Poseidon, had changed things around Sirenia. My sisters and I had been schooled in mermaid ways (literally, as that was the curriculum at Coelacanth University—otherwise known as Sea U). Plus there were chores and lessons. We each excelled at different things, and our assignments were aligned to our talents. Now, with Ava serving as Mother's assistant on the mermaid council and Zoe spending time swimming by the unchartered waters to look for clues to help the human dive teams, I was often left alone.

Maybe that's what bothered me. Zoe was the one who wanted adventure, and because she swam out and found it (or it found her, the counter point she used in the argument she had with Ava a few nights ago), she now gets to have adventures every day, which means I'm left behind by myself. Yesterday, I even put on a new luxury eye shadow that I bought from Mad Midge at the Ebb Tide Emporium's monthly luxury sale and nobody was around to notice!

Today will be different, though. I have singing lessons with Diatomic Jones. He's the most musical of the mermen and lives on the outskirts of Sirenia by the algae garden. He's an unconventional choice for a music teacher, (the other mermaids get their lessons at Coelacanth University—Sea U—where vocal lessons are part of the mermaid coming-of-age curriculum), but the scholars told Mother to provide me with additional learning opportunities. Of all the teachers I've had since then, Diatomic Jones is my favorite.

Diatomic Jones was what other merfolk called a hippie. His pad is filled with instruments made from shells and plants and even some he bought from the emporium, but he's most known for playing the upright sea bass. The first lesson I had, he was inside, playing bongo music on a sea urchin. I never heard drumming like that, and the rhythm inspired me to dance. Diatomic didn't miss a beat (quite literally) and we didn't speak for the first fifteen minutes of the lesson. After that, we both relaxed a bit. Turns out he was as reticent about schooling me as I was of being schooled by him. I guess some mermaids don't appreciate music the way I do.

Mother said Diatomic chose to live an unconventional lifestyle independent of the mermaid colony. At first, I was nervous about going to his place for lessons. I'm not naturally brave like Zoe. But Mother said if I wanted to pursue the underwater musical arts, then I had to be sure to round out my education, and I'm glad she did.

He calls his place a crash pad because it's known throughout the ocean that other musicians are always welcome. Because of that, you never know who you might find or what you might end up singing. Diatomic had arranged for a group of the top jazz musicians in the ocean to assemble for our lesson today. And the idea of singing and dancing along with their jam session was so exciting that, of course, I had to dress up.

Where my sister, Zoe, was born with a blue tail that glowed coral when she was antagonized or nervous, mine was white like my long hair. Before performances, I coated it with a glitter-infused silicone gel. The substance smoothed my scales and eliminated their protective functionality, so I saved it only for those occasions where appearance was more important than comfort or self-preservation.

I secured my hair to the top of my head and let long tendrils hang down on either side, and then decorated it with blue gemstones. My sisters thought it was stupid to spend my allowance on makeup and jewelry at the market, but pretty things made me happy. Mother encouraged me, too. She said being the center of attention was part of being a performer. I bet if Zoe had been born with a melodious voice, Mother would have had a challenge!

Today, Sirenia, the mermaid colony where the merfolk live, was quiet. Mother and Ava were at a Mermaid Tribunal to discuss the possible tour of a sculpture that had been gifted to Mother when she first inherited Sirenia, and Zoe was probably doing laps around some old, rusty shipwreck. The mermen were busy weaving palm fronds into a divider outside the wall of coral. A new family was moving into the village, and new families meant new living quarters. Once they moved in, there would be a party and a welcome ceremony, and I'd be asked to perform. And since I heard Ava tell Zoe there was a merman my age in the family, I had every reason to make sure my voice was in top form.

That's the other part about being a performer. It's not all about appearances. You have to have talent to back things up or else you're just a flash in the pan (a human expression that was particularly creepy to any of us who lived in the sea!).

I swam away from Sirenia to Diatomic Jones's pad and was so lost in my thoughts about my lesson that I almost didn't realize I'd reached the Nautilus Vault. It was a massive underwater structure that housed a vast collection of rare and valuable mermaid treasures that had accumulated in different colonies for generations. Whenever a new item was to be added to the vault, rumors about what it could be spread through the ocean. Because of Mother's rank in Poseidon's cabinet, we were among the first to know about new acquisitions, and sometimes we even got an opportunity to view the latest artifact in a private setting before the vault was resealed.

The Nautilus Vault was under protection by a legion of specially trained mermen. Zoe says the reason I like going to Diatomic Jones's place for lessons is because I get to flirt with the mermen guards who protect the vault, which may or may not be true.

There's nothing wrong with that, is there? I mean, it *is* the shortest distance between two points, and we learned at Sea U that just because the shortest distance between two points is a straight line, the best way to get someplace depended on the varying currents within the water column. There was no one way to get to Diatomic's pad, which meant a certain flexibility existed in my path.

I relaxed my tail and glided through the water, looking for mermen. The water was cloudier than usual. Too late, I realized exactly what had caused the inky darkness and what it meant. I turned, prepared to put a safe distance between myself and the Nautilus Vault, and got hit in the face with a stream of blue squid ink.

23

The dark ink blossomed into a cloud that enveloped my head and torso. I shook my head and my hair came loose. Long, white tendrils moved around my face. As my hair absorbed the color, the water in front of me cleared.

I brushed my hands against my exposed skin and scales, but the ink didn't budge. I couldn't show up at my lesson looking like this. I dove to the ocean floor and grabbed a fist full of sand and rubbed it against my discolored skin. The granules were rougher than the exfoliant I kept at home, but it worked. The inky coloration faded.

When provoked, cephalopods squirt ink to confuse their attackers. Octopuses gave off black ink, and cuttlefish gave off brown. Blue was from squid. The cloudiness I'd noticed in the waters indicated the ink had been produced before I got here.

The rules of the ocean were drilled into all of us at an early age. When schools of fish suddenly started zig zagging, it indicated a low oxygen content. When large objects blocked the rays of the sun from reaching the depths of the ocean, it indicated boats filled with humans on the surface of the water. And when bursts of ink were present, it indicated a threat to the cephalopods.

I hadn't done anything to provoke the squid, which was well and good for them but not so much for a mermaid with white hair and new glittery makeup. The efforts I'd taken to dress up for my lesson had been undone with one quick squirt.

I was less concerned about my appearance than the squid. My heart went out to all the creatures of the sea, and the presence of the ink told me something had aggravated the squid. Some*one*. The murkiness that surrounded me was a warning sign. If there were a threat outside the Nautilus Vault, then the mermen should have spotted it. Where were they?

I veered away from my path and approached the outside of the vault. Enough ink colored the water to make it difficult to see the structure. I swam closer and caught my reflection in the shiny exterior walls of the building. I was blue. Head to toe. Hair to fin. Scales, skin, and all. I blended in so well with the cloudy water that I felt invisible.

I wanted to cry.

But before I gave in to self-pity (which would have gotten me into major trouble at home), I noticed movement by the corner of the building. I kicked my tail and glided close. Horrified, I saw a trio of squid bound together by rope and tethered to the outside of the vault. They were clearly agitated, releasing bursts of blue ink at erratic but frequent intervals.

Squid weren't supposed to be tied up. No wonder they were squirting ink!

I snapped my tail into a powerful kick that propelled me straight up to the vault and used my long, nimble fingers to untie the kelp that bound the creatures. Two additional bursts of ink colored the water, making my rescue attempts more difficult. When the squid were free, they sped away like wild branzino. I didn't blame them. If someone tied me to the side of a building and I had a chance to escape, I'd act like a wild branzino too!

"Kyra?" asked a deep voice. I spun around. Diatomic Jones floated in the ocean about ten feet in front of me. "Is that you?"

The aging merman's hair was long and gray, not lustrous and brilliant like mine, but translucent, like it had lost its color. It was tied into a braid behind his head. He had a mustache and goatee, both of which had not yet gone translucent and thus were darker than his hair, and his face, chest, and arms were a dark, leathery-tanned shade that came from spending too much time by the surface of the water. He kept his torso covered in garments made from woven algae, but I'd once caught him without his shirt on and saw a series of scars across his back. Rumors about him said they were injuries made by a trident. The scars were in lines of three, as if made by the weapon carried by Triton, Poseidon's outcast son. Nobody talked about Triton or if there were other reasons Diatomic Jones lived outside of Sirenia besides personal choice.

"You're late," he said. "I came looking for you to make sure you were okay."

"I was on my way," I said quickly. I fought the urge to see if the squid had gotten away. I was unnerved by their presence, and the sudden appearance of Diatomic out of context was curious. He'd never once met me on my way to his pad, and for a reason I couldn't explain, I sensed his proximity to the vault today had less to do with me than he wanted me to believe.

Diatomic kept his eyes on me and held out his hand. "Let's go," he said. "I can't let people think you didn't get your full lesson." He tried to make it sound like a joke, but I knew him well enough by now to detect a different note in his voice. Diatomic wasn't just trying to get me to my lesson. He wanted to get me away from the vault. He was troubled by something.

I swam toward him, at first tentative and then faster. I took his hand and we glided side by side to his pad, leaving the curious scene behind.

Propelled by two tails, we made the rest of the trip quickly. I excused myself the moment we arrived and tried to scrub the blue squid ink off in his bathroom. It didn't work. There would be no avoiding questions when I returned home later today.

When I re-entered the rec room, Diatomic was floating by the drum set, idly staring at an oblong instrument in his hand. It was his new guiro, a hollowed-out gourd that one of his musician friends had given him in exchange for a temporary place to stay. Music lessons at Sea U focused on lyrical notes, occasionally incorporating words, but sometimes just vocal triangulations that spoke to all sea life through delicate manipulations of the underwater sound waves. Siren songs were a part of every mermaid's education, and for fun, Ava, Zoe, and I sometimes sang harmonic folk songs that had been passed down through generations of underwater life.

But today, Diatomic had promised something different. Bossa nova, he called it. A jazzy fusion sound that he learned from humans. He had shown me how, with his guiro and a filed-down seashell, he could create a unique rhythm. I wasn't surprised to find the instruments set up, but I was surprised to find them vacant.

"Where is everybody?" I asked.

"It's just us today," he said.

"But you said—"

He cut me off. "I was wrong." He set the guiro down and turned his back on me. "Take a seat and let me hear your scales and arpeggios."

"Scales? You mean to warm up before we get started?"

"No. We're working on scales today."

"But you said you would teach me jazz," I said, finishing my thought this time. The disappointment in my voice made me sound like a child who'd been promised a high-calorie seasoned seaweed snack.

Diatomic turned around, and his eyes—one green and one brown—flashed anger at me. "You need to practice the fundamentals more. Your mother isn't paying me to broaden your repertoire. Let's go." He set the instrument down and tapped a steady beat on the sea urchin drum. Several moments passed with only the sound of his tapping. I expected him to stop when I didn't start singing, but he didn't. He kept tap, tap, tapping. After it became clear we weren't going to discuss anything else, I opened my mouth and sang, but my heart wasn't in it. I was sure Diatomic knew it, too, but he never once stopped me or asked if I wanted to talk.

Do you want to know what's hard? Singing scales and arpeggios when you're busy thinking about tied-up squid. But that's exactly what I had to do. Because the more I thought about what I'd seen at the Nautilus Vault before my lesson, the more I knew something bad had been taking place. And I couldn't help thinking about why Diatomic showed up when he did and why he wouldn't talk about it now. If he cared so much about my lessons, then he would have pointed out how off-key I was, but he didn't do that either.

"Let's take five," I said. "I need to clear my head."

"Sure," he said, though he seemed not to like the idea.

"Can you get me something to eat?"

He glared at me, and I batted my eyelashes. I had enough experience around mermen to know how to distract them. I'd never flirted with Diatomic before, though, and felt a little foolish. He seemed not to notice. He nodded and turned away, swimming into his small kitchen.

As soon as he left, I swam to the music stand. As originally planned, the agenda spelled out several jazzy tunes that Diatomic had mentioned at our last session. For some reason, he'd changed the lesson plan. I picked up the top page of music, and the pages behind it fluttered off the stand and floated to the ocean floor.

The music was written on a series of kelp blades, just like the pages of the books in the Library Under the Sea. There was no fear of water damage, though occasionally, when the grocery shopping hadn't been done, we needed to use spare kelp as a garnish. I admit, I'd gotten very confused the first time I heard a human say, "eat your words," since that was occasionally what we did out of necessity!

When I stooped to pick up the fallen pages, I saw that they weren't sheets of music at all. They were rudimentary renderings of the layout and floorplan of the Nautilus Vault, with special attention paid to the quadrant that held the most precious of pieces in the collection. It was also right behind the doorway where I'd freed the bound squid.

24

Whatever was happening at the Nautilus Vault, Diatomic Jones knew. Him not talking told me he was thinking about it too. I set the floor plan renderings back on the music stand and covered them with the sheet music.

"What are you doing?" he asked, surprising me with his quiet return. He'd gone to get me something to eat, but there was no food in sight.

"I was looking at the new sheet music," I said. I held up the top page. "Can we go into this next?"

"We're done for the day." He swam toward me and took the music from my hands. In a quick move, he swept the other pages off the stand and rolled them together in his hands. The whole time, he kept his heterochromic eyes on me. I felt uncomfortable under the intensity of his stare. "You're too boy crazy, Kyra. Forget about chasing mermen around the Nautilus Vault. You need to learn to shut out distractions and work on your focus."

"You think I was chasing mermen?" I asked. The concept was ridiculous. "I've never chased a merman in my life. If anything—"

I stopped before finishing my thought. Did Diatomic really believe that's what was on my mind? Or was this his way of warning me to stay away from the vault?

"If anything, what?"

"Nothing. You're right. I need to practice focus." I swam to the doorway.

"Where are you going?"

I turned back. "Home. Sirenia. You said we were done."

"We are, but I'm coming with you."

"Why?"

He stared at me again, this time the silence between us stretching even longer. "I owe it to your mother to make sure you get back safely."

Even though I was considered the baby (and sometimes accepted it too easily when people treated me so), I had an immediate response to Diatomic's suggestion that I needed to be protected. "Your assumption that I need an escort to swim through the ocean where I've lived my whole life demonstrates a lack of confidence in my education. You owe it to my mother to have faith in my upbringing and my ability to take care of myself."

I was surprised by the intensity with which I spoke. I'd never been one to assert myself in regular mermaid circles, though music and dance gave me a confidence that made me feel invincible.

I pulled myself up straight, flicking only the very tip of my tail to keep myself upright. Zoe might be the adventurous one, and Ava might be the one who attended mermaid council meetings, but I didn't just sit around waiting for mermen to protect me. None of us did. We protected ourselves.

Mermaids were strong, able, and smart. Daughters of matriarchs like Mother were expected to one day start colonies of our own, and we were trained for that from early on. Everybody in the ocean knew it. There was a code among the mermen that the mermaids were to be escorted, but Diatomic was acting like I couldn't take care of myself. It was so outdated of a concept it might as well have come from the human world.

There was another possibility, one I hadn't wanted to consider. Diatomic had another reason for volunteering to chaperone me back to Sirenia. He wanted to keep me under his watchful eye. It was very nearly possible that Diatomic wasn't as concerned about my safety as he was about his. I swam away, on my own, not giving him the chance to stop me.

* * *

On the way home, I encountered Fen, a merman about my age who had recently relocated to Sirenia. He had short dark hair that fanned out around his head and blue eyes that were the same color as the water. Unlike Diatomic, Fen was bare chested. Unlike me, his exposed torso was the color of merman flesh.

"Kyra," he said, eyeing me. "You're blue. Is that the latest fashion?"

"New beauty product," I said playfully. "Mad Midge gives me samples that she gets from her suppliers." Fen circled around me and I twirled a couple of times. His scales brushed against mine and a smudge of squid ink transferred onto him. "You better get that off before you get back to Sirenia," I cautioned. "Otherwise you'll get questions . . ."

He rubbed his thumb against the smudge. "I'm not heading back to Sirenia just yet."

"Why not?"

He dove deep into the water and rolled over, folded his hands behind his head and floated up to me. "I've got some business out this way."

"Anything I can help with?" I asked. I smiled and twirled a few more times. On any other day, my long white hair would have billowed out around my face and created a mesmerizing display of luminescence, but the squid ink had left my appearance dingy. Mother had cautioned us against situations like this. Showing any doubt about my self-worth based on my appearance was a direct violation of the mermaid code and, if reported, would lead to an enforced curfew. Even if I couldn't wait to get the blue ink off myself, I had to act like it was the most natural thing in the world.

Fen seemed to have forgotten all about my physical appearance. "I wish," he said. He looked over his shoulder toward the vault. I followed his stare. There appeared to be no other fish or merfolk in the vicinity. "I can't," Fen said. "Tomorrow, maybe?" he asked hopefully.

"Maybe," I said noncommittally. "Or maybe not. We'll see." I flashed another smile at him and swam home. I'd traveled this distance by myself thousands of times, but today, I couldn't shake the feeling that I wasn't alone.

* * *

By the time I reached the mermaid village, I was sure about only one thing: I'd done the right thing by freeing the squid. I'd always made friends with the other sea life: keeping sea horses as pets, hiding a family of crabs in my room, and even taming an electric eel so I read under the covers late at night. I didn't care if the squid were responsible for discoloring my hair, skin, and scales. That wasn't permanent. But keeping them tied up was a form of torture, and I knew that was wrong.

Mother and Ava had left for the Mermaid Tribunal earlier that morning, so I half expected to return home to an empty village. Sirenia was frequently filled with all sorts of visitors and merriment, but that was thanks to Mother's role as matriarch of the community. She hosted a formal weekly dinner, but there was a steady stream of visitors most nights, simply because our doors were always open.

Well, not doors per se, since the colony was made of coral branches, but you know what I mean.

But with Mother and Ava away, Sirenia was empty. I felt relieved that I'd have a chance to de-blue myself and went into my room to find a suitable cleanser from my stash of beauty products. I swam straight into Zoe, my middle sister, who was supposed to be spending her day by some old shipwreck.

"Hi," I said, pulling up short. "I didn't think you'd be home."

Zoe eyed me suspiciously. "Mother asked me to keep my hours short while she and Ava are gone." Even though Zoe's eyes never left my face, I knew she couldn't help but see my top-to-tail temporary discoloration. Whether or not she'd comment on it remained to be seen.

"Why are you blue?" Zoe asked.

"Squid," I said carefully.

Zoe's eyes narrowed. "Squid," she repeated. "Where?"

"On the way to my music lesson," I said quickly. I wasn't as accustomed to thinking on my tail like the other mermaids were, and for that reason I followed the rules and rarely, if ever, lied. I felt the scales on my tail stand out, a sign that I was nervous. It wasn't as obvious of a tell as Zoe's tail changing color, but it was something.

One of the reasons mermaids were believed to be exotic muses of the sea was because our physical appearances had the power to transform and mesmerize. It happened not consciously, and sometimes the shifts were quite inconvenient. Take Zoe, for instance. She had a perfectly lovely blue tail that blended in with the water, but when she was excited, nervous, or agitated, her tail glowed coral from within, alerting anyone around her to her presence.

Ava was blessed with a mane of long, bright pink hair that

billowed out around her. When she wore it loose, she was easily the most striking of the three of us. Her dark violet eyes added to the exotic image, and when she swam by the surface of the water and allowed sailors to see her, she was a vision so intoxicating she could stun them without trying. But Ava didn't care about things like that. Sure, on the nights of the full moon when we were expected to appear to the humans, she did what was required of her, but Ava was far more comfortable by Mother's side, learning to run Sirenia and waiting for her turn at the throne.

Then there was me. I lived for the attention of others. Something happened when I performed. I felt alive and my whole body hummed. I'd learned how to use everyday situations to get a taste of the sensation, flirting with mermen, befriending fish, and practicing my feminine wiles. I may not have been born with Ava's exotic appearance or Zoe's natural curiosity, but I knew how to become what others wanted me to be.

The encounters of the day left me flushed. My tail fluffed out and gleamed, the ink-stained shade taking on an almost reflective quality that mirrored every gorgeous shade in the ocean. For the first time since being squirted with ink, I saw an upside to being blue.

"The water outside the Nautilus Vault was cloudy," I continued, sensing Zoe was waiting for more of an explanation. I relied on the facts to establish my story. I'd never had much of a reason to lie about where I'd been or what I'd done in the past, but I was afraid of admitting I'd been close to danger and being told not to return to my lessons.

Zoe swam around me. "That's not a shot of squid ink. That's a *lot* of squid ink. What did you do to provoke them?"

"I wouldn't provoke the squid," I said. "They're my friends. They trust me."

"And?"

"And what?"

"Kyra, I've been hit by enough squid ink to know what happens when they get you. I can tell from your scales that you're not lying about the water being cloudy, but your face and shoulders are covered in it. This isn't some new beauty product from Mad Midge, is it?"

I was silent for a moment. That was the lie I'd told Fen, and if Zoe jumped to that conclusion on her own, then it was as plausible as the truth. I wasn't like Zoe, who had to figure things out. Maybe whatever was happening at the Nautilus Vault wasn't my business. But Zoe was in charge of investigating reports of trouble. She might know something. Was it smart to tell anybody that I had been there and freed the squid? Diatomic knew where I'd been. That couldn't be helped, but I hadn't told him about what I'd found when I was there.

"Zoe, have you heard anything about Mother's sculpture going on display from the Nautilus Vault?" I asked.

Zoe circled me. Her eyes only left mine when I purposely twirled the opposite direction and looked away. "Why?"

"I've heard things. Mother and Ava are at a council meeting to discuss it, and today, when I swam past the vault, something didn't seem right."

Zoe laughed. "'Something didn't seem right.' That line never worked for me, so why you thought it would work for you is crazy. Kyra, I love you, but if you want a cover story to tell Mother, you're going to have to produce something better than that."

"But it's the truth," I said. "Have you heard anything about the vault?"

Zoe reclined in the water and floated on her back. "From what I heard, the Siren Sculpture is going on display to celebrate the expansion of Sirenia. Ava can probably tell you more. Whatever you saw, it probably has to do with that. I wouldn't lose sleep over it. If there's a ceremony, they're going to expect you to perform. That's where your focus should be."

Zoe was right. We each had a job to do, and entertainment was mine. It was entirely possible that the whole thing *was* a misunderstanding. Maybe the secret legion of mermen was arranging security for the sculpture. Maybe the request for the statue to tour was approved. Maybe a new artifact was being added to the collection, or there was scheduled maintenance, or, well, something. That was probably it.

Zoe was also right about asking Ava. If there were important business being conducted at the vault, it would have been approved by Poseidon himself. They'd discuss it at the tribunal. For all I knew, Ava had talked about it before she and Mother left. I never paid attention to politics or law enforcement. Those were subjects for my sisters.

Still, I couldn't help but be troubled by the squid that had been tied to the balustrade. Tomorrow, I'd leave extra time and make sure they were okay. But before I had that chance, I had to find a way to keep Zoe from digging into the truth. Because freeing some squid was one thing but being caught in a lie and having to tell Mother meant a punishment I had spent my life trying to avoid.

I'd hoped Zoe would lose interest in grilling me, but she didn't. "What's the real story, Kyra? You know I'm going to find out whether or not you tell me."

"I smiled at her. "You know Mad Midge and her potions," I said carefully.

Zoe shook her head at my apparent naiveite. "One of these days, she's going to give you a sample of something that makes your scales fall off." She reached under her bed and pulled out a jar of eel muck. I knew Zoe bought the stuff in bulk because of her glowing tail situation, and now that she had the job working with the divers, she glowed practically all the time. "This will get it off," Zoe said. "You better use it before anybody sees you."

I took the jar and slathered it over my torso and tail. The thick black substance, developed to apply to electric eels to hide their natural illumination, broke down the squid ink and returned me to my original shade. Was lying to Zoe the right thing to do? I didn't know. She didn't seem to believe what little I'd said so far. If I told her, my concerns might stop weighing on me, but if Zoe brushed it off or told me I'd imagined it, then I'd be out of luck.

***

The next day, I woke early and prepped for the day. I twirled my hair and pinned it up with coral combs and accessorized with matching earrings and rings. Vanity was as innate of a behavior to me as Ava's bossiness or Zoe's curiosity. It wasn't that I did it out of obligation but that I recognized that being a mermaid muse was my gift. It was the one thing that left me feeling in control and not babied in the way others tended to treat me. It was where I found my confidence.

I knew it drew the attention of the mermen, and I played that to its full advantage at social occasions, but what the others didn't know was I was scared that this life was all I would ever have. Ava's future was secure. As the first born, she would inherit Mother's throne and carry on as the leader of Sirenia. And Zoe's turn helping a human diver solve a murder had given her a role investigating underwater crimes. But someday I would lose my looks, and then where would I be?

I never told my sisters this, but this was the reason I spent so much time with Mad Midge. The one-time booth owner turned proprietor of the Ebb Tide Emporium had been injured in the now-historic Shrimper/Mermaid tragedy. A group of drunken sailors had set out to capture mermaids for profit. As the events unfolded, an unexpected horror forever changed the relationship between humans and merfolk in the sea.

Lives had been lost on both sides: human and mermaid. Mad Midge had been one of the loveliest mermaids in the ocean, but thanks to that attack, she'd been scarred permanently. She was older now and had developed a gruff personality to match her appearance, and that's how the merfolk treated her. But I had learned that underneath it all, Mad Midge was just like me. She had seen things and lived through things that other mermaids had not. She'd once relied upon her appearance and when she lost it, instead of being bitter or hiding from the other creatures in the ocean, she found a way to take care of herself and become invaluable to the village. She'd come away from it all with a strong business sense and a determination to make the best of her life.

I respected that. I even thought that one day I'd like to have a booth at the emporium like Mad Midge. This was a secret I didn't tell the other mermaids because I knew that wasn't the life I was being trained for. A mermaid like me, daughter of the matriarch, working at a booth! They would laugh, and some might even wonder what was wrong with me that I would waste my pretty face and take a job. It was ludicrous.

To me, it wasn't ludicrous. To me, the idea felt exciting and important, like I would be doing something with my life aside from batting my eyelashes and flirting with mermen.

When I was fully accessorized, I flitted through the house and found Zoe practicing defensive maneuvers. (Basic maneuvers were part of the curriculum at Sea U, but Zoe was an overachiever.) Zoe's biggest problem wasn't her ability to defend herself, it was her tail. Like I said, she had a genetic anomaly found in a rare percentage of the merfolk population, and it was the one thing that would hinder her new role as underwater investigative liaison to the humans. I had watched Zoe double down on her exercises and then meditate after her tail glowed to try to control the color change. So far, she'd been unsuccessful, but I didn't doubt she would eventually triumph. Zoe was like that.

"I'm going to my voice lessons," I said.

Zoe ceased her activities. "You had voice lessons yesterday," she said. She narrowed her eyes. "How come you're going back so soon?"

"The ceremony," I said quickly. Even though I'd pretended not to know about the ceremony, it now seemed to be the most plausible explanation. "Diatomic said he was working on a special gig, and I think it might be the ceremony you mentioned. Are you sure you don't know anything else about it?"

Zoe shook her head. "No, but I've been out of the loop.

Talk to Ava. She's had a lot of council meetings lately. If she doesn't know about this, she can find out."

* * *

Shortly thereafter, I was undulating through the waters on the way to see Diatomic Jones. I hadn't been lying about the lesson, just exaggerating. I *was* on my way to lessons, and Diatomic *had* said something about performing. Therefore, it was the truth.

It was no lie to say I enjoyed my lessons, but today was different. A hum vibrated through my body while I swam. It was a new sensation. I knew the thrill of performing and the flush of flirtation, but this was different. It was curiosity.

I recognized the cloudiness of the water as I approached the Nautilus Vault and veered from my path toward the building. A squad of squid, bound to the doors, struggled to get free, releasing inky blue liquid into the waters. I nimbly untied their bindings. They swam in circles around me, their way of recognizing my effort, and then disappeared, trailing tendrils of ink along with them.

I twirled in a counter direction as the squid left the area. I imagined them getting as far away as possible. When I could no longer see them, I squinted through the murkiness to determine where I was and which way I should go. I was facing the vault doors. They were open.

Again, there was no guard.

I swam inside. Something was wrong. This structure housed the most important merfolk artifacts that had been acquired in centuries. Pieces of art that had been displayed on earth and bartered in exchange for peaceful co-existence were kept here, in a climate controlled environment. Rare plants that were used to create restorative elixirs were nurtured in the botany wing, and the occasional item from the human world that had been dropped into the ocean, or gifted by someone of power, had been placed under cases carved from sea glass.

But today, the contents of the vault were disrupted. Items that should have been secure lay about willy nilly. A branch of a formerly pure white sea lily floated past, now tinted blueish as the roots absorbed the squid ink of the recently discolored water. As it glided by, I noticed something—or rather, didn't. The pedestal that used to hold the bronze siren statue that had been gifted to Mother when she assumed control of Sirenia, was empty.

I tentatively approached the empty pedestal and peered through the water. Had it been knocked over? Or simply shifted with a passing current? Even though I knew neither of these options made sense, I couldn't help but hope for the best possible scenario. It turned out not to be so.

The sculpture was gone.

Of all the items that could be missing, that one was the most personal to me. I swam in circles around the pedestal, wondering what it meant and who I should tell.

Every time Sea U took a trip to the vault, I signed up to join the group. I made excuses to stay behind and study the object and read about it at the Library Under the Sea.

In classes at Sea U, the merfolk learned about the relationship between human and merfolk as illustrated through art. The lessons were an interesting way to view how the two groups saw each other. Crude drawings and roughly shaped sculptures demonstrated the unsuccessful attempts sailors had made to capture the essence of merfolk, but it was impossible to fully grasp the beauty of aquatic life in two-dimensional renderings, because what made a mermaid attractive wasn't purely rooted in physical beauty. We learned early on that our appearance was what would gain us attention, but it was our emotive side, our intuition and overwhelming empathy, our soothing voices, and most of all our overflowing gift of love that cocooned all who encountered us and left them mesmerized. You couldn't see those other things, and sometimes it seemed like humans were so silly they didn't believe in things they couldn't see.

But I had always loved the crude siren sculpture. It could be described as incomplete. The simplicity of it, a siren holding two tails—one in each hand—while floating upright, displaying little more than the crown that adorned her head, spoke of poise, serenity, and power. It represented the simplest elements of life in Sirenia and how confidence that came from within was more important than any jewelry, makeup, or clam-shell bra. It was one of the most important artifacts in the vault, considered to be among the most accurately representative depictions of a mermaid done by a human, and rumors persisted about the artist and how he was able to capture a mermaid's essence so lovingly without fully knowing her. But where was it now? Had it been removed for display at the ceremony that Zoe had mentioned? If so, why did the interior of the vault look so chaotic?

Zoe was the one who mentioned the ceremony, and if there was a ceremony, then I'd be expected to perform. There had to be someone around who knew more than I did.

Diatomic Jones. He'd be my accompaniment. Perhaps that was the reason he was pushing me to rehearse all the time. Yes, I would go to his pad and ask.

I peered closely at the ocean floor, hoping to see something unusual (When Zoe regaled me with tales of helping a human solve a murder investigation, she said some of the clues she found had come from the ocean floor. I had always been more distracted by fellow fish with whom I could play and spent little time staring at the ocean floor. Sure, I could spot a sand crab once in a while but trying to play with them invariably led them to burrow into the sand, thus ending the game!)

If the sand crabs had been aware of activity by the pedestal, they'd burrow deeper so as not to be noticed. As time passed (after their initial fear), they'd return closer to the surface, and their positions would be marked with tiny little holes and divots from air pockets. If that were the case, I may be able to coax one out and watch how quickly he burrowed himself bac into the sand—an indication of how traumatic the morning's event had been to him in the first place.

What I found when I got close to the sand wasn't a series of tracks from a sand crab or an uninterrupted smooth surface that indicated the crabs were still scared. It was a pattern of three marks that scored the base of the pedestal and left tracks in the sand that hadn't yet been erased by the current of the water. The familiarity of the marks was not lost on me. They made the same pattern as the marks that Diatomic Jones kept hidden under his seaweed shirt—the pattern of three that I'd heard had been inflicted by Triton, Poseidon's outcast son.

A sound outside the vault sent me deeper into the recesses of the structure to hide, never once considering how I was going to get back out. As I cowered behind the case of human artifacts, I couldn't help but feel exposed. If whoever it was gave anything more than a cursory glance toward the interior of the vault, I would be seen. There was no way out other than the main entrance.

I was slight, as was characteristic of the youngest mermaid in a family. I had grown up coddled and treated as if I were breakable, and the focus had been on my voice and rhythm talents and not those of a physical nature. I'd managed to get through the classes on defensive maneuvers at Sea U but only barely. Right now, I wished I'd paid better attention like Zoe.

What I did have going for me was my coloring (on days when I hadn't just swum through squid ink): white, almost translucent hair and tail. I might have blended in if not for my inclination to wear makeup and jewelry, both of which were natural for someone in the entertainment field.

I unclipped the gems that adorned me and scrubbed my face clean of ink and makeup. Void of decoration, I blended in. If I remained very still, I convinced myself no one would notice me. The problem was that as I kept myself curled into a ball, unmoving, and concentrating on not drawing attention to myself, I sacrificed being able to see who had entered.

It was very nearly possible that I was witness to a crime in progress, if only I had a point of view!

But I was too scared to take that chance. I remained where I was and squeezed my eyes closed, not because of fear, but because it allowed me to tune into my other heightened senses. I concentrated on recognizing the presence inside the vault. And I did, very much feel that I knew whoever it was that was there. So much so that I shivered with the idea that danger was closer to home than anybody would have believed.

When the waters stilled and I felt confident I was again alone, I came out from behind the case of human debris and darted out of the vault. It was only then that I discovered the reason someone had been able to gain access into the vault and ransack the place without being caught by a Nautilus guard.

The Nautilus Guard lay on the ocean floor, limp and unmoving and very possibly dead.

I immediately knew I was not equipped to handle the situation by myself. A squad of squid hovered by the perimeter of the building. They seemed to recognize my fear. They came closer and hovered over the body. As if performing a routine for an audience, they released a burst of ink that clouded the water and made him seem to vanish. They were protecting the body so I could get help. Whatever it was that had happened there, the squid were witness to it. They may not communicate like other fish in the sea, but they were as threatened by the danger as I was. I was so absorbed with the question of what to do next that I didn't realize I was no longer alone.

"Who are you?" asked a lean and sinewy merman. While I had never seen him before, I knew him by the three-pronged weapon he held. It was Triton.

I immediately felt a buzz in the water, the way it felt when I swam close to the electric eels. Triton was unlike any of the mermen I'd met before. My already heightened emotions skyrocketed, but Triton seemed not to have any more reaction to me other than curiosity. His long black hair was pulled back away from his face and secured behind his head, though some of it had come loose and waved by his forehead and cheekbones. His eyes, the shade of green that I had only formerly seen on the underbelly of a giant sea turtle, pinned me in the exact spot where I floated.

"I'm Kyra," I said. "I'm the youngest daughter of Mother Mermaid who presides over Sirenia."

Triton swam around me "What are you doing here?"

"The guard—he may be dead. If not, he most certainly needs help." I turned toward the body and flapped my tail at the water. As the ink dissipated, the body became visible. Triton left my side and pressed his fingers into the flesh of the guard, and then pulled away. "He is dead," he announced. "There will be no helping him. Let's leave."

"But we can't just leave him," I said. "He was killed. The council must be notified, and his death must be investigated."

Triton swam in a wide circle. He kept his trident in his grip, the pointed tips of the large golden fork glowing as he swam. "What do you suggest, youngest mermaid daughter?"

"We need to notify the authorities," I said.

"I suppose . . ." Triton glided to the outside of the vault and leaned back against it. He tipped his chin down and watched me as though waiting for me to do something less boring.

On any other day, I would have been instantly intrigued by this dark, bad boy of the ocean. Triton's misbehavior was legendary, and I had outgrown the attention of the mermen who I'd grown up with. But today, I was angered by his flip reaction to the tragedy of the dead guard. I drew myself up like I'd seen Mother do, threw back my shoulders, and looked directly into his mesmerizing green eyes. "We are close enough to Sirenia that I will treat this guard as though he's part of my village. Whether you help is your choice, but I will make sure Mother knows of the behavior of Poseidon's son when it becomes time to inform her of the events of my day."

It was obvious to me that Triton did not know I had identified him, and the threat of his behavior getting back to Poseidon seemed to be enough to snap him out of his cool-guy mode. He propelled himself through the water to the body and circled it again. "Go for help," he said. "I'll move him into the vault."

"No," I said. I surprised both of us with my objection. "I'll help you move him to a safer location and we'll both go for help. I have a friend not far. We can go to him." Remembering the scars on Diatomic's back, I purposely kept his name out of my response. Something told me I'd rather see the two mermen interact with my own eyes.

It took little time for me and Triton to move the body of the dead guard out of the exposed ocean current and into the Nautilus Vault. The ocean could be harsh, and a deceased merman or mermaid was an easy target. There were ghost stories about critters who gnawed on merfolk scales, leaving behind little more than an exposed skeleton. I did not think that was a particularly lovely legacy, and I knew there was only so much the squid could do to protect the guard's body before the bottom feeders moved in.

After the body was laid to rest alongside the empty pedestal, Triton grasped my hand and pulled me outside. "Lead the way, youngest mermaid daughter," he said.

I snapped my tail and felt his arm jerk as I headed away from the vault and toward Diatomic's place. A tiny part of me reveled in the notion that he hadn't expected me to move so fast. I may have been the youngest mermaid daughter, but I was, perhaps, not as innocent as he thought.

Triton caught up to me and took my hand. We swam side by

side. As Diatomic's place came into view, I felt Triton slow. I pulled my hand out of his and looked at him questioningly.

"Diatomic Jones lives there," Triton said.

"Yes. He's my friend," I said. "He can help us."

Triton resisted. "He can help *you*. Diatomic Jones has a problem with me, and I don't see this working in my favor."

And before I could say a word, the bad boy of the ocean did a one hundred and eighty degree spin and swam off.

There was no time to deal with the brooding merman. I turned my back on him and burst through the entrance and called out for my music teacher. "Diatomic! Diatomic!"

His house was empty. I swam deep inside, through the living room, into the kitchen. I left the kitchen and swam into the communal area, down the hallway, past rooms filled with instruments, to his sleeping quarters. I hadn't meant to enter or linger by his bed, but that's where I was when I heard his voice.

"Kyra."

I whipped my head around so fast my hair tangled in a piece of rope art that hung on the wall. "Diatomic," I said. I swatted my hand by my hair to free it. Diatomic swam closer and gently untangled it. Before he could question me about violating his privacy by entering without being invited, my words tumbled out. "Something happened by the Nautilus Vault today. A guard is dead and the interior was ransacked. The—" I was about to tell him that the siren sculpture was missing, but I remembered the floor plans I'd seen hidden on the music stand.

"The squid seemed nervous," I finished somewhat lamely. I looked away from his face to his chest, and then, distracted, to his lower half. Embarrassed still, I stared at a spot on the floor and then looked up and batted my eyelashes in the hopes of distracting him.

He didn't seem to notice.

Diatomic grabbed a shirt that had been left draped on the top of his drum set. He pulled it on and then crossed his arms. "Slow down. What's going on? What happened at the Nautilus Vault?" He seemed to see me for the first time since I'd entered.

I didn't have time to consider the rudeness of barging in. I swam forward and grabbed Diatomic's forearm. "A guard was killed. The vault was robbed. I need your help."

Diatomic's eyes flashed with anger. "I told you not to hang around there," he said.

I let go of his arm and backed up. "Someone left the guard exposed. The squid were watching over his body when I—" I stopped myself from admitting that I'd been inside the vault. I still didn't know what it was I'd discovered or how it connected to the guard's body outside. I thought of Diatomic as my friend, but what if he wasn't? I'd seen the sketches of the interior of the vault right here in his living room, and he'd been acting suspicious. Maybe coming here had been a mistake.

I flipped my tail forward, putting more space between us. Too focused on him, I lost track of where I was in relation to the instruments and backed into them. The bow fiddle tipped, hit Sea Bass Stan, the ill-tempered sea bass who had recently joined our trio, and woke him up. He opened his mouth and let out a rather loud bass clef note, accompanied with a bubble of air. His glossy eyes surveilled me for a moment, and then he swam away, past me, past Diatomic, and into the kitchen.

I collected myself. I couldn't waste time convincing Diatomic to help me. I quickly spun and swam out of his front door, back to the vault. There was no one else to ask for help, but as scared as I was, I had to find the courage to handle this on my own.

It wasn't long before I was back at the vault, aware that my suspicions had been wrong. A crew of aquatic life tended to the body of the guard. Triton and I had moved the guard inside the vault, and I didn't know who had moved him back outside.

Among them were two octopi who engaged all eight of their tentacles to lift the body, shoo away spectators, clear the evidence, and transport him to an extra-large clam shell to transport his lifeless body. Their movements were graceful, but with so many tentacles flying about in every direction, the waves they generated kept the rest of the sea life out of their way.

A hand grabbed my upper arm. I turned and stared into Diatomic Jones's eyes. He'd caught up with me. His grip wasn't painful but was firmer than I would have expected.

"I told you to stay away from this," he said.

"I told you I couldn't. The guard was murdered. His body was left exposed in the silt outside the entrance. He needed help. That's all I wanted when I came to find you."

"What are you going to tell your mother and your sisters when you get home?" he asked.

I couldn't help but be unnerved by the question. What would I tell them? I'd already lied about having lessons, and if anyone checked my story with Diatomic, he'd deny it.

Unless he needed—what did Zoe call it when she discussed that case she helped solve—an alibi?

"I told Zoe I had lessons today," I said. "We didn't have a chance to practice our arrangement yesterday and I came to you hoping we could jam."

I studied his face closely, hoping for a hint to let me know if I could trust him. He turned and looked over his shoulder, as if checking to see who else might be listening. When no one presented themselves, he turned back to me. "Kyra, what's going on at the Nautilus Vault is dangerous. It's not the kind of business a petulant mermaid like yourself should allow herself to get involved in."

I had an immediate, visceral reaction to the comment. "Maybe I'm not as petulant as the merfolk think," I said. I yanked my arm out of his grip and spun away, leaving a cloud of kicked up silt in the water between us.

First Triton had treated me like a child, and now Diatomic called me petulant. So what if I was the youngest? I was still born into the family of the Sirenia matriarch, and that came with a certain level of understanding about the aquatic world. And if I lacked experience with the dangers of the sea like my sisters? That was because I'd lived a sheltered life.

What I lacked in dangerous experience, I more than made up for in feminine wiles and coquettish behavior. And as I learned at Sea U, lady spies who had played a role in history had been more naturally aligned with my talents than those of Zoe or Ava. I would just have to find a way to use what I'd been given.

They could all think I was too innocent and inexperienced to figure things out on my own, but they weren't right. I knew it. I'd let them keep on believing in the Kyra they knew, but on the side, I'd take on a different role. One that would allow me to find out things nobody else could.

I was filled with an enthusiasm I'd not yet known. The desire to be something unexpected, to prove to others and to myself that I was more than a pretty face, gave me a purpose. By the time I reached Sirenia, I recognized the fringes of a plan to find out what had happened at the vault and what it meant to my community—and how I could fix things so it would never happen again.

Sirenia was buzzing with activity. Mad Midge's delivery manatees unloaded crates by the back entrance, and a swarm of eel circled the exterior walls, casting their glow across branches of coral and the occasional anemone. Ava rested on a giant clam shell watching the activity and instructing the manatees to carry things inside.

"What's going on?" I asked.

"We're throwing a party," she said. "It was a last-minute thing. Mother and I were at the council today, and she learned of a visitor to our waters. She extended an invitation quite spontaneously, and after it was accepted we left and started planning the event."

"A visitor?" I asked. "Who?"

"Nobody you'd be interested in," Ava said. "Some visiting dignitary. He's an expert in Sirenian culture and has authenticated several of the artifacts in the Nautilus Vault. He approached Poseidon about a project involving a few of our pieces, and Poseidon told him to coordinate with us."

I couldn't help wondering how this fit in with what had

happened earlier. "Did he say anything else? About which pieces he wanted to see or why? Maybe he went on his own?"

Ava eyed me suspiciously. "What's with the questions? First Zoe, then you. It's like the Spanish Inquisition around here."

"The what?"

Ava rolled her eyes. "Didn't you pay attention in Human History? It's this thing that happened on land. I know you're not really interested in anything going on around here. I just don't know why you're pretending to be."

I didn't like what Ava's statement said about me, but I couldn't disagree. I'd barely made it through Sea U, and it had been my high grades in music theory and dance that offset the low scores I'd earned in history, language, and math. I'd never before been bothered by my poor performance as a student, but right now it seemed my lack of interest had painted a picture of me that kept Ava from taking me seriously.

That was just great.

It was at that moment, filled with the self-awareness that my own lack of interest in the world around me had led Ava to treat me just so, that I decided to change. It was more conscious than any decision I'd made before, even the time I committed to learning Calypso. And that had been hard!

Before long, our home was filled with guests. A few manatees who usually worked for Mad Midge hovered by the buffet, and a group of mermen knocked a small hollowed-out sea urchin shell back and forth with their tails. Laker, a merman who had recently moved to Sirenia and made some questionable decisions in the hopes of gaining popularity, hung back, watching the group. He waved to me. I smiled but quickly looked away. I wasn't in the mood to flirt tonight.

I went in search of Zoe. It was one thing for Ava to dismiss me. Ava spent more time in mother's world than in that of the other mermaids. Zoe at least had grown up anxious and in search of something herself. She'd been a tomboy, always getting into scrapes by leaving the safe areas and investigating shipwrecks and trouble. I knew if anyone were going to be able to help me find out what had happened at the Nautilus Vault, it would be Zoe.

But I didn't make it to Zoe. When I turned the corner by the large branches of coral, I came face to face with the last familiar face I was prepared to see. Fen, the merman I'd encountered yesterday by the vault when I was blue from the original blast of squid ink.

I hadn't given much thought to Fen's presence at the vault yesterday. At the time, I had been more concerned about being caught and being blue. But there had been a nervous element to his behavior. I remembered how nervous I'd been, and how I'd lied about the blue coloring. I remembered flirting like I always had, and how he'd seemed too preoccupied to pay me the attention I was used to receiving. That alone had confused me, since the one course I excelled in (outside of music theory and practice) had been Becoming the Muse. But it occurred to me now, after everything I'd seen and discovered, that Fen may have had his own reasons for not paying attention to me—ones that indicated he may have something to hide.

"Fen," I said quickly. I batted my eyelashes at him, but my heart wasn't in it. "I didn't expect to see you here."

"Kyra," he said back. Today, he seemed less nervous, more self-assured. "I had to come. This party is for my dad."

"I thought the party was for a visiting dignitary?"

Fen seemed bored. "That's him. He's an expert in mermaid culture and somebody contacted him about a statue."

"The siren," I said.

Fen looked surprised. "You know the piece? I didn't get the feeling you were into intellectual stuff like art."

I forced a smile even though his words stung like an insult. "I love the piece. It was gifted to Mother when she assumed control of Sirenia. I try to visit it at the Nautilus Vault whenever I can. Have you seen it yet?"

He shrugged. "Unless my dad says it's worth something, I'm not interested. I don't know why any merfolk care about something the humans made." Fen turned his head and looked at the impromptu stage where Diatomic and Stan were setting up. A third musician, Scat Catfish, had joined them. It looked like the beginning of the jam session I'd been hoping for at Diatomic Jones's place yesterday.

It was easy to be distracted by the activity on the stage, but Fen seemed to have something other than anticipation over the set list in mind. "If I were you, Kyra, I'd spend less time worrying about what's going on inside the Nautilus Vault and more on what's happening under your roof. I wanted to warn you to keep an eye on Diatomic. He says he's here to perform but I have it on good authority that he was told to stay away."

At that moment, Diatomic turned and looked directly at us. Fen quickly averted his gaze, making it even more obvious that he'd been staring at the music teacher. I stared back, gauging the emotional connection between Diatomic and me to see if he was hiding something. The only thing I read from his current expression was annoyance that I hadn't yet joined them on stage.

"Thank you for the warning, Fen," I said, "but Diatomic is my music teacher. If he learned there was to be a performance at Sirenia, he would have taken the initiative to pull together a band to back me. He has every reason to be here."

I started to swim away, and Fen reached out and put his hand on my arm. "Be careful, Kyra. You trust everybody, but someone out there might take advantage of your innocent nature."

There it was again. I was too innocent, too inexperienced, too trusting. Did nobody believe I could handle myself?

I swam away from Fen without replying and joined the band. In addition to lessons and flirting with the mermen, I was going to have to start watching Zoe and Ava and see how they communicated to the world that they didn't need anybody's help. It seemed a worthwhile lesson to learn.

***

The night wore on with a mix of music and merfolk mingling. I spent much of the evening center stage, a position that had the great side benefit of allowing me to keep an eye on everybody there. The only attendees who remained where they should have been were the other musicians on the stage. When the last song had been sung, a particularly peppy number that engaged Scat Catfish in a jazzy tune about how everybody wanted to be a fish, the audience erupted in riotous applause that was drowned out only by the water. I knew something magical had happened that night, but I was too preoccupied by other events to join the band afterward.

I lingered by the stage, considering my options. Diatomic Jones didn't venture far, so keeping an eye on him like Fen had warned lacked the difficulty implied. I pretended my sheet music was out of order, but I hadn't touched it all night, so my actions seemed invented. I was almost relieved when Diatomic reached out for my arm and knocked the sheet music to the floor.

"Kyra. We need to talk." Pages marked with notes and lyrics floated through the water.

"What? I got through the set okay, didn't I?" I asked.

Diatomic pulled me from the stage into a back room that was filled with kelp. Ava had recently spearheaded a project to oversee the weaving of plant life into large textiles. The resulting sheets could be used to produce garments that Mad Midge could sell at the emporium. Other merfolk had been surprised that Ava had suggested something so generous and far-reaching, but I wasn't. My older sister had a reputation for being bossy because she was Mother's attaché. It was her birthright, and someday she'd inherit the throne. But with all the time she spent shadowing Mother to the council meetings, seeing but not being seen, I completely understood why she wanted something that was hers alone.

I was afraid to tell her what I thought, but between us, I thought Ava was just about the greatest mermaid in all of Sirenia.

Right about now, I kinda wished she'd come into the room and demand we join the others. I wasn't all that happy to be pulled out of public view by Diatomic!

"You barely got through the set, and that's because it was jazz and people weren't listening for structure or precision. You've been distracted lately. Two days from now the Siren sculpture is coming out of the Nautilus Vault and we're expected to perform for the royal court. I don't think you're ready, Kyra. When your house clears up tonight, I'm going straight to your mother and requesting permission to relieve you from the gig."

"That's not fair!" I cried. "I practice all the time. And I've been to your pad twice in two days and you wouldn't practice with me. Now you want to punish me by taking away the one thing I do well, but it has nothing to do with my behavior. It has to do with you. You know I was at the Nautilus Vault earlier today. You know I found the dead guard. I think you're the one who has something to hide, Diatomic, and I think you're scared that I know your secret."

I didn't know where the outburst came from. It wasn't like me to stand up for myself or to talk back to Diatomic. Everybody who knew my sisters and me knew I did what was expected of me and I never talked back.

Except now.

If Diatomic was put off by my outburst, he kept his reaction in check. "Listen to me, Kyra. I know you were shaken up by what you saw at the Nautilus Vault, and I know it's making it hard for you to concentrate. But you have to try. Not because it's expected of you, but because this is your first test. You're young, and up to now, you've been able to exist in the protective bubble of Sirenia. Lessons and mermen and your sisters. You've been too young to have to worry about the threats of the ocean. You grew up after the council drew up the documents to protect the unchartered waters. But the world out there—the one you saw yesterday—it's dangerous."

It wasn't so much that I didn't believe Diatomic, but his immediate assumption that I was ill-prepared for such a world bothered me. I had never shown an interest in the kinds of things Zoe did or in leadership like Ava. I practiced my lessons, made friends with the fish, and did what I was told. Diatomic was right, and I'd gone most of my life not caring that I'd chosen to lean into innocence and ignore the curiosity that seemed to run in my family.

But another thing struck me. Something that seemed to run counter to everything Diatomic said. If he was really encouraging me to focus on my musical lessons, then he'd want me to practice, yet for two days he'd been the one to postpone our lessons, not me. Almost as if he had something to hide.

"You're right," I said. "I need to rehearse. If you think it's not important to me, then I'll prove to you that it is. I'll be at your place early tomorrow and we can do a marathon session. Okay?"

I bit my lip and waited for an evasive response that would confirm my suspicions. If he were being truthful, he'd have absolutely no reason to do anything other than agree.

His eyebrows dropped down over his eyes and for a moment he seemed angered by my suggestion. He crossed his arms over his tanned chest and nodded once. "You're on. Tomorrow morning, first light. We'll get started early and go as long as you're able. Show me what you're made of Kyra."

"Tomorrow morning. Right. I'll come to your place right after breakfast—"

"No," he said. "There's no reason for you to make the trip

past the Nautilus Vault. It's too dangerous. Tomorrow morning, I'll come to you."

Which was exactly what he'd say if he had something to hide.

I agreed, because there really wasn't anything I could say. But as soon as Diatomic swam off, I resolved to get some answers on my own. And if Diatomic thought he was going to keep me preoccupied all day tomorrow with a marathon lesson to test my commitment and endurance, then he left me no choice. I was going back to the Nautilus Vault tonight.

It was close to impossible to keep my nerves under control. As merfolk said goodbye and left our house, I made my way around the living room to collect abandoned cups, dishes, and utensils and swam them to the kitchen where Zoe washed them. Twice I thought about asking her advice but didn't. A teensy, tiny part of me believed if Zoe heard about something interesting, she'd tell me to stay home and investigate it for herself. And while that had always been fine with me in the past, I didn't want to let this go. It was like a secret within me, a magic bean that I'd swallowed that made my heartbeat race and my fingertips feel on fire. It was better than any flirtation I'd ever had with a merman. The only thing that surpassed it was the feeling I got when I was on stage.

Let's just say tonight had been a big night, and it wasn't over yet.

After the house was cleaned up, I pretended to get ready for bed. My face was already clean of makeup thanks to the exfoliating scrub I'd done while hiding at the Nautilus Vault earlier (I hadn't had time to reapply when I got home and, to throw everybody off, stuck with the natural look). Once I was comfortably tucked into my bed, under a blanket made from braided seaweed, it was all I could do to stay still and wait for Zoe and Ava to fall asleep first. Both of my sisters were silent and unlike most nights, I didn't make conversation.

* * *

Shortly after the electric eels that had worked our party left and the room fell into darkness, my sisters' breathing grew even. I counted to two hundred thirty seven and then got up and grabbed a small, net bag that I'd assembled earlier. I squeezed myself out of the window (Zoe and Ava had long since given up trying since their bodies had matured, but I had a boyish frame and fit through easily. I'd never given Mother a reason to believe I would try to get out after hours, so once the escape path became invalid for my sisters, it seemed as though the problem were solved.)

Once in the open water outside of our house, I swam to the Ebb Tide Emporium and let myself in. After I'd befriended Mad Midge, she showed me how to get past the security measures and help myself to her sample collection of cosmetics and self-adornment items. She knew how much I liked things like that, and I sometimes thought I was the only mermaid who talked to her about such frivolities. It was as if everybody else was afraid to talk about beauty with her because she'd been maimed. I was sure the reason Mad Midge and I became unlikely friends was because we saw each other's beauty on the inside.

I swam to the makeup counter and painted myself in exotic, vibrant tones. There would be no camouflaging myself, but my goal was one of hiding my identity, not my physical presence. The strong, sophisticated palette was far removed from the childish pastel shades I usually tended toward, and twice I sat back and considered how the change in my appearance reflected the growing change within me.

My light source was the glow of the electric eels swimming in circles in their tank—not preferable, but enough. After lining my eyes and coating my lips, I secured my hair with a black net that masked my natural white coloration. I even pulled a lace mask over my eyes because it was unique. Besides, where else are you going to wear an underwater black lace mask if not while on a covert mission? It seemed perfectly normal to me.

Once I was suitably tarted up, I secured the eel tank and put the samples back where they belonged. I left Mad Midge a note of thanks and offered to help her stock the new shipment that was due for the weekend market. It might seem as though I was dilly dallying before heading out to the vault, but I was just being polite.

Okay, I was dilly dallying a little bit.

I'm not going to lie to you. I was a little nervous to go swimming around the place where a merman had been left for dead.

I worked up my courage and swam into the dark water, seeing centimeters in front of me. Mermaids, in addition to most of the fish in the sea, were genetically disposed to seeing through the water whether it was light or dark (the exception being lingering clouds of ink), but, like the other times I'd been out this way, the cloudiness hampered my vision. As I got closer to the vault, my apprehension grew. What if the squid were bound again? What if I discovered nefarious business? What if this was too dangerous of a situation for me to handle on my own?

Before I could convince myself to turn back, I saw the outer edges of the vault. A glow on the far side of it cast light in hazy patterns. I swam closer. Was someone else here? As I rounded the corner, I saw the very end of a tail disappear into the vault. It was barely a glimpse, but it was enough to let me know that I wasn't alone.

In the dark water, what I saw wasn't enough for me to recognize much more than scales, but I was now more curious than scared. I wished I'd paid more attention in basic defensive maneuvers at Sea U. If confronted by a hostile merperson, I'd have to defend myself. Zoe would be able to handle most altercations, but for me, the threat was real.

Or maybe a fish had discovered the vault doors open and entered to scour for sand crabs? There had been plenty in the sand when I'd buried my jewelry earlier today.

I neared the vault and considered how best to find out who was in there. As I hung to the side of the door, a squad of squid approached. I remained very still as they swam past me and doubled back. Based on what I'd found, the local squid would be wary of strangers. It would take them a moment to realize I meant them no harm, but if I moved quickly, they'd squirt first and ask questions second. (Although, a coating of blue ink might be just the thing I needed to complete my new undercover look!) I waited, very still, to see how this was going to go.

What I didn't anticipate was the approach of another mermaid, one who had built up exactly zero good will with the shell-shocked squid. It was this mermaid who startled them at the exact same time when she startled me.

"What the heck do you think you're doing out here?" Zoe demanded.

I jumped, scaring the squid into squirting us both.

The water around us turned so dark it might as well have been filled with that sweet brown liquid the humans sometimes drank out of red and white cans. Zoe waved her hand back and forth in front of her face, a mistake that simply spread the ink further. Right now, Zoe's glowing tail was the only thing that cut through the thick, dark water.

Except it wasn't. Around her, glowing figures moved through the water. I spun in a circle and put my hands out, unsure what was there or whether it was dangerous.

Zoe grabbed my arm and swam me away from the vault. "Relax. Those are electric eel. They came with me."

"How did you get eel? They were in the tank at the Ebb Tide Emporium."

"I followed you when you snuck out."

"Why?" I got more suspicious. "How did you know I don't have a secret liaison?"

"You may be boy-crazy, but you've never snuck out a day in your life. You're too much of a rule follower, and if Mother discovered you were out after curfew, you'd be grounded."

"That's not why you followed me," I said. "You wouldn't care if I broke the rules because it would make you look better."

Zoe stared back at me, not saying a word. She didn't look angry and she didn't look annoyed. Whatever emotion it was that threatened to take over her features, she didn't want to show it.

Mermaids are naturally empathic and can read emotions more easily than any other living being. It's how we're able to inspire sea legends and fill tired sailors with the necessary passion to continue their journeys. It's the most genuine, sincere, pure gift that could have been bestowed upon us, and it made us the most emotionally available creatures alive. With that gift came the inability to manipulate others. It was probably how the mermaids who'd been caught and killed in the great shrimper/mermaid tragedy had been lulled into believing they were safe until the moment came they were not.

I'd never used my abilities to read one of my sisters. I'd never had a reason to. We were sisters. Related. Closer than any other bond that existed in the world. I knew Ava and Zoe were different than I was, but I never doubted for a moment we loved each other with a depth that transcended friendships and romance.

That's when it hit me. "You didn't follow me to get me into trouble," I said. "And you didn't follow me to find out where I went so you could take credit. You followed me to make sure I was safe."

"You're in trouble, Kyra. I don't know how you got mixed up in it, but you are. And you've never gotten into trouble in your life." Before I could deny it or try to pass off a lie (which she'd see right through), she pulled a handful of my jewelry out of the sack she had draped across her torso. It was the same jewelry I'd taken off inside the vault and buried in the floor.

I snatched it from her. "Where'd you get this?"

"You know exactly where I got it. Inside the vault. Couple that with you coming home with a face scrubbed so clean from makeup you might as well have been a salmon being prepared for dinner."

"Stop it," I said. "You know I'm a vegetarian."

Zoe rolled her eyes, and this time the water was clear enough from me to see the overly exaggerated expression clearly. "And now I catch you out here, all dolled up like some kind of mermaid of the evening. What is this?" she gestured around my face.

"I'm undercover," I said. "Like a spy. I know mermaids are supposed to inspire great adventures, but I thought maybe I was the kind of mermaid who could halt wars and end violence. Whoever came out here and robbed the vault tied up a squad of squid and left them bound to the building. That's not nice. I want to catch them and make them pay for being so mean."

I hadn't expected to confess, and I braced myself for Zoe's lecture or dressing down. She surprised me. She threw her arms around me and held me in a hug so tight I temporarily lost my breath. But the acceptance of my tough, adventurous sister filled me with pride, and I hugged back. Maybe I wasn't equipped to do this alone, but with her, I felt unstoppable.

"What do you know so far?" she asked.

"There's someone in the vault. I saw the tip of a merfolk tail right before you startled me. Maybe it's a new guard. I really don't know."

"We have to find out," she said. She turned toward the entrance and hesitated for a moment.

"Let me," I said. "I've been here twice in the past two days. I found the guard. I know the layout and what's there. I can pretend I came back for the jewelry I left buried in the sand."

Zoe held up the jewels. "This jewelry?"

"Yes. Bury it out here. I'll say I don't know where I lost it and that'll give me an excuse. When I find it, it'll just endorse my story. Okay?"

Zoe nodded. Together we swam toward the front of the vault.

I was filled with nerves, but I felt more alive than ever. A few feet away, Zoe squeezed my hand. "Kyra, you're a lot braver than I gave you credit for being." She smiled at me and let go of my hand and swam into the murky waters. I turned around and swam toward the entrance with her words of praise ringing in my ears. Which was great, because when I saw who was inside the vault, the confidence drained from my whole body and I started to shake.

It was Triton. His forked, golden trident lay along the top of the case that held the artifacts from the human world, and he held the siren statue that had been missing from its pedestal earlier that day.

A school of fish chose that minute to rush past me from behind. The sudden action startled me (I *was* already nervous!) and I let out a yelp. Triton turned and grabbed his spear with his left hand. He kept the statue in his right. His hair had come loose from its binding and fluttered around his head, creating an inverse halo. His coloring was pale and dark circles were visible under his eyes.

"Kyra," he said. He didn't react immediately, but his features softened. "It's after curfew. What are you doing out here?"

"The same thing as you, probably," I said. There were two ways for me to play this and I chose the one that kept me in control. "After we found the guard today, I wanted to come back and see if there was something I missed."

Triton relaxed. "After I left you at Diatomic's pad, I came back to do the same thing. I found this hidden behind a cluster of anemones." He held up the siren sculpture. "Someone ditched it and planned to come back. I took it so that couldn't happen."

"Is that why you're here?"

He nodded. "This was the first chance I had to return."

I found myself tuning into his frequency to determine if he was telling me the truth. His story was possible, but did possible mean true? Or had he simply rested upon facts that he could pass off to explain his actions and his presence tonight?

I wished Zoe had entered the vault with me. She'd know. She had experience with this sort of thing.

A ripple of sound entered the vault. It was so quiet, so soft, so gentle that it was barely detectible. For all the sounds in the ocean, there is one that plays selectively for its target audience. It comes from the throat of a mermaid and can transfix, mesmerize, and intoxicate at will. But when the sound is intended as communication from mermaid to mermaid, it provides a shorthand that remains invisible to any other living creatures. Zoe's song broke through the water and spoke to me in a series of vibrations that calmed my nerves and fed my courage. She was with me. Not physically, but in the way only sisters can be. And I instantly forgave every sibling rivalry, every time I'd felt bullied or not enough. Every instance where it seemed like Zoe thought herself better than me. It was a zero-sum game. She gave me what I needed—what I didn't know I lacked—and filled me with confidence I'd never known, not even on stage.

And I knew Triton was telling the truth.

"Does your father know you're out here?" I asked. Poseidon was notorious with his punishments, and the reason I'd never seen Triton before was because he was often in trouble.

"My father does not expect the most from me."

"But this," I gestured toward the statue, "finding this, solving this, might make him view you differently."

Pieces of Triton's black hair fluttered around his head. His lips pursed slightly, making his cheekbones more pronounced. I resisted the pull of him even though it was the most powerful sensation I'd felt (not counting Zoe's presence, which, combined, made the moment a little heady!).

"You have a way of seeing things," he said. "You caught me with the statue the day after we found a body. You have every reason to be scared of me. I know I don't have the best reputation. Most of the merfolk community avoids me. But I can tell you're not like them. I'm glad you're not like them, but I'm curious."

I swam forward to give him a quick peck on the cheek, something I'd done with lots of the other mermen, but Triton's energy was dark and intimidating and I backed away before I reached him. "You're no different than I am," I said boldly. "People think they know us. They call me the baby. They call you the bad boy. We're both more than that."

Triton seemed as surprised at hearing my assessment as I was to have said it. The water was charged with electricity, just like when I first encountered Triton at the vault yesterday. For the first time in my life, I was aware of only one merman in the whole ocean. This had to be the power of Poseidon's lineage. There was no other explanation.

Zoe's melodious melody was interrupted. The sudden absence of song jarred me. "Something's wrong," I said. I turned toward the exit.

Triton let his spear drift to the ground and grabbed my arm with his newly empty hand. His grip wasn't tight, but strong enough to keep me from swimming away. "It's dangerous out there."

"Zoe's in trouble." I snapped my tail and the powerful kick propelled me toward the exit. Triton's hand fell off me. I didn't care about anything but finding Zoe and making sure she was okay. I left the vault and searched the waters for a sign of her. She was nowhere to be found.

Zoe's calming siren song had kept me in check while inside the vault, but now, there was nothing to give me balance. I spun in a circle, twice, and searched the waters for her. When that lacked results, I glided still and used my gift to sing to her.

She didn't respond.

The waters that had been dark and mysterious were now glowing from the agitated electric eel that had accompanied Zoe. I swam toward them, and they scattered. They were frightened and acting unpredictably. There were few things worse than agitated electric eels, but for now, their light source was the only thing that cut through the water. I swam around the perimeter of the vault. When I reached the front, Triton floated in place. He held an eel in each hand and his spear rested on the ocean floor. The eel twisted but did not seem to be struggling for freedom.

"They're scared," he said.

"Something violent happened," I said.

"They're scared of you."

"Me?"

"You're glowing."

"I don't glow. That's Zoe's trouble."

"Zoe?"

"My sister. She came here with me. She was waiting outside the vault while I went in to find out who was there. She and I were communicating, and then she stopped. Now she's gone."

"I felt it," he said. "The vibrations in the water. I sensed the power of the two of you."

I barely registered Triton's comment about having felt Zoe and my communication. He shouldn't have felt anything, but this wasn't the time to think about that. "I have to find her. Someone committed a murder here at the vault, and they may have come back while we were inside. If Zoe thought she was in trouble, she would have let me know. She must have been surprised, and when she gets excited or startled, she glows."

"Like you."

"I told you; I don't glow."

Triton released the eel and swam toward me. He put his hands on my shoulders and turned me toward the reflective exterior of the vault. "Look."

He was right. My coloring, so pale I was almost translucent, radiated a glow that created a soft-focus quality. Beads of light peeked through the black lace I wore over my eyes, and the exotic makeup I'd applied at Mad Midge's now looked garish against my ethereal skin. Tiny beams surrounded my loose white hair and outlined my shoulders, arms, torso, and tail. I was like the mermaid version of a ghost fish.

Growing up, Zoe, Ava, and I all had unique physical markers from the other mermaids. It came from Mother's royal lineage and set us apart from the other merfolk who lived in our colony.

Zoe's coloring was blue. Her hair, eyes, and tail all blended seamlessly with the ocean and made her look like an extension of the water. Her movements were graceful and fluid and she was more comfortable in her own skin than any other mermaid in the ocean. But when she was passionate about something—danger, intrigue, curiosity—a coral glow lit from her central nervous system and betrayed her emotions.

Ava had a full head of vibrant pink hair and gray eyes that could induce a hypnotic trance. Her body was the most feminine and if she hadn't been the oldest, destined to accompany Mother into a life of politics, she would have been the most highly sought after mermaid in the ocean.

My gift had been my voice. It wasn't a physical trait, but a talent. I knew, from watching people listen to me sing, that my voice was special, but I'd secretly been jealous of my sisters. Flirting with mermen had become my default, a way to prove that just because I didn't have a coral-glowing tail or a curvaceous female body, I could inspire too. I'd always wondered why Zoe and Ava had been blessed with physical gifts while mine was a skill.

Tonight, I realized my gift had been dormant all along. The only thing I'd needed was to grow up.

The light surrounding me cast onto Triton. He backed up and stared at me as if seeing me for the first time. I was suddenly shy. I'd been stared at a million times before, but this time I felt vulnerable.

"This has never happened before," I said.

"Listen to me, Kyra. You are absolutely beautiful right now, but you're not safe. You have to go home until you return to your normal state. Otherwise, you're a beacon for danger."

"No," I said stubbornly. "I won't go home. Not until I find Zoe."

"I can't let you do that. It's my job to protect you."

Triton was speaking of the role of the mermen to protect the mermaids. By human world standards, it was an antiquated thought. But in the ocean, the mermaids were the ones with the power, the beauty, and the talents. Mermen were necessary but not as exalted as mermaids. They protected and served but understood that we were in charge.

It didn't much matter to me whether Triton believed in the codes of the merfolk or if these were empty words spoken out of an understanding for what I'd been taught. My sister was more important than codes of conduct. Wordlessly, I turned and swam away. Squid formed in front of me and released their ink into the water. I swam through it and realized they'd provided me the cloak of anonymity that I needed.

I darted around the perimeter of the Nautilus Vault. If Zoe were here, I was going to find her. I had to. I knew if the tables were turned, she'd find me. As I widened my circle, I spotted something laying against a tangle of branches. I swam closer and my heartbeat picked up. It was Zoe's body, limp and blue. The coral glow that should have illustrated her state of excitement was nowhere to be seen.

What was to be seen, however, was the crown from the siren sculpture, resting in the sand next to her. Zoe had been knocked out, and the sculpture had been the weapon.

I didn't want to believe Triton had hurt Zoe, but there seemed to be no other explanation. The last time I saw the statue, it had been in his hand. But when we came outside, it was not. Had he given it to someone who used it as a weapon?

Furthermore, Zoe had ceased her siren song quite abruptly, which may have been when she was knocked out. Triton had been close. He'd been the one to keep me from finding her right away by forcing me to see my glow. But Triton never could have anticipated my glow. No one could have. Did his presence have to do with Zoe's attack, or was it mere coincidence?

I was confused by the events that had unfolded since the very first day I discovered the squid bound to the corner of the building. Whatever was going on, it was worth killing for. I couldn't risk letting Zoe stay exposed a second longer. I had to get her to safety.

The ocean water provided a natural, weightless environment, and once Zoe was untangled, I could move her with ease. But the branches had shifted with the underwater currents, and her arms were bound by the mess of their branches. I pulled at one. It scraped me in protest. There wasn't time to be gentle. If the scrape had released blood into the water, sharks would be quick to venture into this territory to look for prey.

Ever since the merfolk and humans reached an agreement about the unchartered waters to protect merfolk life, the biggest threat to our existence—to any underwater existence—were the sharks. There was no negotiating with the powerful thugs. They cruised the dark depths, searching for their next meal, and occasionally took jobs as enforcers for more mercenary power-hungry organizations, but Poseidon had made it clear that an aggressive act from a shark would be met with extreme force. Despite the peaceful and loving merfolk way of life, meeting shark violence head on was necessary. When a shark detected blood in the water, they were driven by primal motivations that had nothing to do with their brains.

I hadn't sensed shark presence by the Nautilus Vault, but I knew if Zoe remained exposed, it was just a matter of time. I broke off branches hastily to free her. When she was loose, I draped her limp arms over my shoulders and held them in front of my sternum. I kicked my tail and swam her home faster than I'd ever swum before in my life.

* * *

Zoe's physical condition put a halt to both the ceremony planning and thoughts of mysteries. It was a testament to the deep respect toward Mother that the entire mermaid colony pressed pause on the event calendar while her middle daughter recovered. Zoe was alive, but a head injury left her disoriented. Mother forbid Ava and me from leaving Sirenia while Zoe rested, and it was just as well that my lessons were off because I had no reason to sing.

A team of octopi worked round the clock attending to Zoe's needs, and I flitted around the house filled with nervous energy that had no outlet. No one seemed to question what had happened, and that bothered me more than it should have. Healing Zoe was paramount, but until someone caught whoever had hurt her, restoring her health wouldn't solve the problem. Someone or something was out there, lurking in the murky waters, with an agenda.

Days passed, and I remained under house arrest. Even Ava was instructed not to leave. To her, it was a break from responsibility. To me, it was torture. I finally caved.

"Ava, I need to tell you something," I said.

"Can it wait? I was about to head in to read to Zoe."

"It's about Zoe," I said. "I was with her the night she was attacked. I'm the one who brought her back here."

"You?" The surprise in her tone was all I needed to hear. Nobody viewed me as capable of handling an emergency. I would have expected that reaction from almost anybody else. But Ava? That stung.

"Yes, me. Is that so hard to believe?"

"No," she said softly. She set her book down and rested on her clam shell bed. There was no judgment in her expression or body language. "What happened?"

I told her what the past few days had been like for me. The squid, the vault break-in. The dead guard, the floor plans on Diatomic's music stand. The run-in with Triton, the warning from Fen, the lecture from Diatomic, and the stealthy trip back to the Nautilus Vault under cloak of night and a healthy amount of face paint.

"I didn't know Zoe followed me," I said. "She freed some electric eels and swam out to make sure I was okay. She broke curfew because of me, and she got hurt and almost died." I confessed my deepest fear to date. "I don't care who stole the statue. I don't care if Poseidon cast out Triton. I don't even care if

Diatomic thinks I don't have the focus to perform at the tribunal. I just want Zoe to be well again."

I felt myself shaking with emotions. Ava studied me. "What should I do?" I finally asked.

"You can't do anything," she said. "We are not to get involved in what happens in the ocean. It's not our role."

"But she's our sister. This goes beyond someone stealing an artifact from the vault. It's personal. That mermaid code—the one that says we have to leave this to the mermen. Everybody knows Zoe was granted permission to patrol, which means even Poseidon knows the code is stupid and antiquated."

Ava leaned forward. "Zoe learned about law enforcement in her spare time. She didn't go into that situation blind. And after her involvement with the human by the perimeter of the unchartered waters, she was given responsibility. Her getting hurt may have happened anyway. Have you noticed no one has questioned her accident?"

"Yes," I said. "I've been nervous for days waiting to be questioned."

"You won't be. When Zoe accepted her responsibilities, it was with the understanding that if anything happened, the official story would be that she was acting on her own impulses. It could not be known throughout the ocean that a mermaid was granted permission to investigate questionable matters. That was Poseidon's one condition. He said—" Ava stopped talking abruptly. She bit her lip and averted her dark violet eyes so I couldn't see the emotion that filled them.

"He said what?"

"It doesn't matter."

"Ava, it matters."

She turned back and put her hand on mine. "He said Mother had to understand that granting that kind of leniency to one of her children may be what takes them away from her for good."

I considered this, turning the thought over and over in my mind. "He wasn't talking about Zoe," I finally said. "He was talking about Triton."

Ava nodded. "I've heard things about Triton, but I've never met him. What's he like?"

"He's different." I thought back to my encounters with him. "He's the most beautiful merman I've ever seen, but he doesn't try to use that. I went into the vault to use my mermaid sense to read whoever was in there, and I was sure he didn't do anything wrong. He said he came back, just like I did, and I believed him 100 percent."

"Then he wasn't lying."

"But what if a merman lies to a mermaid? Wouldn't he know how to send mixed signals?"

"Is that the impression you got?"

"No," I said. I hadn't gotten mixed signals from Triton, and I'd been getting—and giving—mixed signals from mermen my whole life. They either treated me like a child (Diatomic) or like they wanted to catch me (River, Laker, Fen, and just about all the boys who came around Sirenia). Being with Triton had been easy. Like I was presented with questions on a test I hadn't studied for but instinctively knew the answers. There was nothing, not a single thing about our encounters, that made me feel like we were playing mermaid games. But there was an intensity that scared me.

"I think Triton wants to prove something to Poseidon," I said. "He knows his reputation isn't good. I don't know why he left, but he's back and he'll need something big to win the acceptance of his father."

"Like what?"

That's what troubled me. I didn't know what Triton might have to do to prove to his father that he wasn't the bad boy he'd been painted to be. But staging the retrieval of a coveted sculpture was just the sort of thing that might do it. Rescuing the daughter of the matriarch of Sirenia was another. And between inheriting command of the ocean in the wake of Poseidon or the health of a mermaid who stuck her nose where it didn't belong, there was no real question. It was entirely possible that Triton planned it all so he could swoop in and be the hero, in which case the trouble wasn't isolated to Zoe. Because I was the one mermaid who knew he'd been there the night of the attack too.

36

"What do you want to do now?" Ava asked.

The question filled me with love. Ava had as much to lose—maybe more—than I did, but she felt just like I did. We'd do anything for Zoe.

"There are three mermen connected to this: Diatomic Jones, Fen, and Triton. You know everything I know about Triton. But Diatomic and Fen are still question marks. Why did Diatomic have floor plans to the vault hidden in with his sheet music? How much does he know about the musicians who come to his house?"

"What other musicians have you met?"

"Scat Catfish and Sea Bass Stan have both been around lately. Except when they were supposed to be there, they weren't. Does that mean something?"

"I don't know."

"And why did Fen warn me against spending time with Diatomic? I've been taking music lessons with him for ages. Why warn me now?"

"Mother trusts Diatomic with your education, but there are a lot of rumors about him. He's older than us. He's seen things we only learned about at Sea U."

"What about Fen? He said his dad is the visiting dignitary we're expecting. He's an expert in merfolk culture and would know about the statue. Fen works at the vault, so he could arrange for the guards to leave it unattended if he told them he was there to relieve them. He was at the vault, and at our house, and has been trying to warn me against Diatomic."

"He could be like every other merman," Ava said. "Trying to woo you."

I looked past Ava and considered this. "Maybe," I said. "Or maybe not. He could have something completely different on his mind."

Ava studied me. "You know, Kyra, Zoe gets credit for being the inquisitive one, but you're not bad at it either."

I felt a warmth inside me, a tiny prick of heat that swelled and flooded every scale on my tail and climbed through my body. I couldn't hide my smile. If being on stage had given me the biggest rush to date, then that was nothing compared to Ava's praise. "I want to go to Diatomic's house. He's hiding something, and I need to know what."

"Let me go," Ava said. "You've already put yourself in danger."

"We'll go together. It makes the most sense. I can use my lessons as an excuse. You'll be my chaperone. He can't turn you away, and with two of us there, we can find out more. The only problem is that Mother will never give us permission."

Ava's response surprised me. "Then we won't tell her," she said.

* * *

It took a day to agree on the details of our trip to see Diatomic. In order to secure our safety, Mother had asked a fleet of men to secure the window in our bedroom (which created some unexpected eddies inside the house!), thus removing any chance I had of sneaking out a second time. It was just as well because Ava's hips wouldn't allow her through and we'd still need a second exit. After much discussion, we agreed to make a habit of sitting with Zoe as she recovered, knowing we could exit and return from there. If Zoe had been aware of our plan, her only complaint would have been that she wasn't going with us.

On the night we planned our mission, Mad Midge arrived at Sirenia with a package wrapped in a giant leaf from a Victoria Plant. "Kyra-girl," she said. "Ya might be needin' somethin' for your evenin' out."

I took the package. "I didn't order anything, did I?"

"Nah. Dis is a gift. Anythin' can happen to a mermaid late at night and ya hafta be prepared."

I stood very still and tried not to react. "I don't know what you mean. I'm sure I'm safe here at Sirenia."

"Ya, you be safe here, girl. But when you and your sister venture out ta spy on Diatomic Jones, ya might be needin' a little somethin' extra." She blinked, which may have been a wink but with Mad Midge only having one eye, it was hard to tell. "I've been waitin' for ya ta step into your own, Kyra-girl. You're a lot like me, ya know."

I leaned forward and lowered my voice. "Do you think we're making a mistake?"

Mad Midge gave me a knowing smile. "Da only mistake you could be makin' is not ta try. Now, are ya goin' ta invite me in? I'd like ta have a word with your mother."

Mad Midge wanted to visit with Mother Mermaid? That had

never happened before in my life. I floated by the entrance, questioning everything I'd interpreted thus far. Mother swam to us and rested by my side.

"Lady Midge," Mother said. (Mad Midge wasn't royalty, but Mother made a point to treat her with the utmost respect.) "It's a pleasure to have you at Sirenia. Come in."

Mad Midge swam past me and hauled a bulging cargo net. "Thank you. I brought ya some samples I thought ya might like ta see. Fresh pastas from the human world and some delicacies you've never heard of. And a brand new collection of records for Zoe-girl ta listen to while she recovers. It could take us awhile ta get through everything."

"How considerate. Come this way." Mother swam off. Mad Midge trailed behind her, pausing just long enough to wink/blink at me again.

The most feared mermaid in the ocean had closed her shopping center early so she could keep Mother busy while Ava and I snuck out. Mad Midge was the best!

I carried my package to my room and unpacked it on my clam shell bed. Inside were two self-defense kits, a small electric eel, and a collection of pretty green jewelry that I'd been eyeing. A custom fiddle was carefully wrapped with a note that said, "special order for Diatomic Jones." She'd even had the foresight to give me an excuse to visit.

I coated the electric eel in eel muck, which hid its illumination until Ava and I needed it to make our trip. Ava braided her long pink hair and tied a self-defense kit around her tiny waist. I left my hair loose (wearing it any other way would have been curious to anyone who knew me) and accessorized with the new green jewelry. I stuffed the rest of my items into a small cargo net (along with the eel, who seemed to have been coached on what to expect from the evening), and we left.

I released the electric eel once we were a safe distance from

Sirenia and wiped off enough eel muck to reveal his glow. Ava circled me in the water. She kept looking behind us, and I sensed she was having second thoughts.

"You can go back home," I said with more bravado than I felt.

"No," she said. "I'm coming with you. It just seems like we're not alone."

I whirled around in a circle and my hair flew out in all directions. "Nobody knows we left."

"It's a feeling," she said. "There's something out here. Someone. I feel it."

I glided to a halt and tuned in to the rhythms of the water. I didn't want to tell Ava she was wrong, but I felt nothing unusual. If there was someone there, they weren't going to hurt us. "Let's go," I said. "The sooner we arrive, the better."

The eel swam slightly ahead of us, lighting our way. We'd planned to give the vault as wide of a berth as possible, but still, we had to pass it. As we approached, a menacing figure swam out in front of us.

It was Fen.

"Kyra, Ava, what are you doing out so late?" he asked.

"We could ask you—" I started. Ava put her hand on my arm to silence me.

"We're on official business for Mother Mermaid to deliver a package to Diatomic Jones," she said. "We were told the waters would be cleared. State your business, merman."

I didn't remember ever hearing Ava use her official voice, and I darn sure had never heard her lie! I watched Fen's face as he processed what she said.

"I've been accepted into guard duty. I've been assigned to the vault. Nobody told me you'd be in the waters. I saw movement and had to check it out."

"Or you came here to rob the place," I said boldly. "You've been here more than once, Fen, and both times you claimed to be on the job. Ava works with the council. Don't you think she'd know if you really did work here?"

Fen looked back and forth between our faces. His deceit fell in waves from his body. "You shouldn't be out here," he said. "That music teacher of yours is trouble. Go back home. Let the mermen handle this."

"That's the second time you insinuated Diatomic is behind the trouble at the vault. What has he done to make you suspect him?"

"I've been watching him," Fen said. "There's a reason he lives at the edge of Sirenia. He's been banished for crimes committed. He was given a choice of exile or time served and he chose exile. But you gave him an excuse to come back to the fold, Kyra, and look what's happened. A murder. A robbery. An attack on your sister. Diatomic's a criminal who's been waiting for an opportunity to get back into the game. You did this, Kyra, not me." And before I could ask him what that meant, he turned and darted into the darkness.

Ava put her hand on my arm. "Leave him," she said. "I don't know if I believe him, but he's a distraction. If Diatomic is behind this, then we need to stop him. We can't afford to get distracted."

Our electric eel chaperone had vanished when Fen appeared, and we were left in darkness. It wasn't preferable, but I'd made the swim to Diatomic's place enough times to find it without light. Ava and I held hands and undulated side by side until we reached the small pad. The front door was open and the interior glowed eerily.

I took the net and nodded once to Ava. We went separate directions, her to the left and me to the door. I knew she'd be there for me if I needed her, but we'd decided the element of surprise may be our biggest weapon. I peered inside the door, still not believing the man who taught me the gentle art of singing jazz, who played the music that I felt through my limbs, who coached my gift and backed up my performances and encouraged me to work hard and flourish could be the criminal Fen believed him to be. I'd heard the rumors, all the rumors, and yet Diatomic seemed like a merman who needed a break, not one who was looking for a payday.

And then I saw it. The siren sculpture, sitting on top of his dining room table. It was missing the crown. And as it sat there, I flashed back to the crown in the sand next to Zoe where she lay after having been attacked. Whoever had struck her had left behind that one crucial piece of evidence. The presence of the statue here confirmed everything I didn't want to believe.

I turned to the door to sing out a warning song to Ava and discovered something else. The last thing I expected to see after spotting the sculpture on Diatomic's table.

It was Diatomic himself. Face down on the floor.

I swam closer and saw a series of fresh wounds on his back to match the scars I'd seen before. Three short gouges that seem to have been made with a trident. Just like Triton's weapon.

Diatomic wasn't the perpetrator, but it seemed Triton was. And the wounds he'd inflicted on Diatomic were fresh enough to indicate he hadn't had time to go far. Which meant he was close —close enough to possibly hurt my other sister too.

My priority was Ava's safety. I sang out a warning to her and then checked Diatomic. He wasn't dead but he appeared so. I was afraid to move him but he needed his wounds to be dressed, otherwise feeder fish would soon arrive and finish him off. And there were few fates worse than being eaten alive by feeder fish—one of the earliest lessons I'd learned at Sea U.

And if not feeder fish, then sharks. I couldn't think about that.

I swam down the hall into Diatomic's bathroom and found a jar of glitter-infused silicone gel. I'd left it here so I'd be ready for any impromptu performances. I grabbed a bundle of bandages— the sheer quantity of them that were in Diatomic's cabinet gave me pause. These weren't his first injuries, that I knew firsthand. How long had he been dressing his wounds, keeping these attacks to himself? What kind of a merman was Triton to terrorize an aging music teacher who'd been outcast to the edges of the mermaid colony?

It didn't fit. I'd used my mermaid skills to read Triton more than once, and I'd gotten nothing from him that spoke of his ability to commit a crime like this. There was something familiar about him, something that told me I could trust him. It wasn't attraction either, not the kind I knew. Whatever it was about Triton, it was unlike any qualities I'd seen before. And if I had to guess, I'd say it was confidence. Triton had wanted nothing from me and that was brand new.

But what did he want from Diatomic?

I left the bathroom and swam back to my music teacher's body. On my way, I passed the rehearsal space. The instruments were set up as if he'd intended to practice. On the music stand were the arrangements I'd been hoping to learn. His guiro sat on top of his drum, and his bow fiddle rested against the wall. Sea Bass Stan, who I'd often seen resting against the mantel, was missing.

Stan, the sea bass. The living, breathing fish who'd been everywhere Diatomic went. He'd been here. He came to Sirenia. He could have followed me anywhere and I wouldn't have paid attention.

No.

The sea bass?

Was it possible?

I turned away just in time to see Stan dart toward me. In his mouth was the siren statue. A hundred things I might never have noticed came into focus, not the least of which were the three sharp, protruding teeth that lined Stan's lower jaw. He was missing several of them, but the ones remaining were separated by small gaps that left their placement approximately the same distance apart as the marks on Diatomic's back.

"You're the one who hurt Diatomic," I said. "And this wasn't the first time."

Stan circled around the room and came back at me. He opened his mouth and the statue floated through the water and landed on the silt. "I'm not in the mood to practice, girlie," he growled.

His voice was as low as the grinch song the humans sang around the holidays and when he spoke, the sand below us shook. I watched tiny airholes disturb the surface as sand crabs who'd been hiding burrowed even lower. Diatomic's pad—the place where I practiced, where traveling musicians gathered, where impromptu jam sessions sprung up and parties happened until dawn—was filled with fear. I'd believed the stories Diatomic had told me about all of that, but what I saw right now, what I felt, was that nobody had been here, not in days.

"Diatomic's hurt," I said. "You need to let me tend to him before the bottom feeders arrive."

"You're right," Stan said. "Can't have part of my group out of commission."

"Your group? What reason could you possibly have to hurt another musician?"

Stan laughed and the walls of Diatomic's pad shook. The mermaid painting that hung on his mantle vibrated off and floated down to the ground. Behind it, a series of sketches and timetables peeled away and floated to the ocean floor.

Stan's eyes lit up. "There they are," he said. He swam forward and clamped his teeth onto the drawings. I didn't need to read the labels to recognize them as the layout of Sirenia.

"What are you doing with them?"

"What do you think? The Nautilus Vault seemed like a good idea at the time, but how am I going to fence a statue? Once I saw Sirenia, I knew that's where the real riches of the sea are."

"You're going to rob Sirenia?"

"The mermaid colony doesn't deserve the riches housed there. By the time I've emptied the place, there won't even *be* a Sirenia. Coral branches and clam shells, that's what will be left," he growled.

On the ground, Diatomic stirred. He reached his hand out toward the bow he used to play the bass. Stan quickly dove toward a tossed-aside knot of rope. Faster than I could have imagined, he shook it out and swam behind Diatomic, binding his hands in the same manner he must have bound the squid. It was evident that Diatomic was in pain.

Without thinking, I swam forward, straight at Stan. I put my hands out and pushed his scaly body away from Diatomic and into the wall. The music stand tipped. It fell through the water and rested next to Diatomic's body.

By the door, a small school of bottom feeder fish hovered. Their eyes were wide and eager, and their mouths were already open, like small suction cups. There were too many of them for me to fight off. Once they attached to Diatomic, there would be no saving him. The sharks would be next.

I couldn't let them get to him. I dove down toward his body and pressed the bandages onto his back. He flinched with the contact but didn't push me away. I scooped out a blob of glitter gel and smeared it over the fresh puncture wounds. The coating instantly bonded with his skin. It was the least masculine ointment I could have used but the scent-blocking properties confused the bottom feeders. They floated inside and swam around the perimeter, trying to pick up the now-vanished trace of what they thought they'd be eating for dinner.

Stan smiled. "This ocean used to be filled with treasures ripe for the picking. I could take what I needed and get by. More than get by. I've got a network to fence stolen art and it's made my life very comfortable. Diatomic here knows it, don't you, friend?"

Diatomic grunted. I closed my eyes and read Diatomic and in an instant I understood what had happened. Diatomic had been cast out of Sirenia for crimes committed. Those crimes must have included working with Sea Bass Stan. When Diatomic had gotten out of custody and tried to live an honest life teaching and playing music, his old crime partner returned. Stan had heard about the Siren statue and saw an opportunity. He tried to coerce Diatomic into working together and when Diatomic said no, Stan set him up.

With the tied-up squid.

The stolen statue.

The attack on Zoe.

The crown left behind at the scene of the crime.

The statue on Diatomic's table.

"How did you get the statue away from Triton at the vault?" I asked.

"You don't know? You and your sister helped me with that. Triton had no idea with whom he dealt. Once he felt your vibrations, he forgot about everything else. He didn't even notice me taking it out of his hand."

I didn't understand what Stan meant about me and Zoe or our vibrations, and there was no time to process the information now. If I didn't do something soon, there would be more casualties.

Diatomic would die.

No merman deserved to be punished indefinitely for past crimes, least of all Diatomic Jones. His trouble here wasn't because he'd said no to Stan. It was because he'd risked his freedom to protect me and my sisters. I owed it to him to make sure he got out of this alive, but the only way to do that was to catch Stan. And Stan appeared to be a slippery fellow.

I swam toward him again, but this time he was prepared for me. Stan was as large as I was but double in density. I was no match for him. He opened his mouth and clamped down on my tail. The searing pain of his three sharp teeth made me scream. I bent sideways to favor the damaged section of scales and drifted to the ground. I'd never felt that kind of attack in my life and without even looking, I knew there would be permanent damage.

If Stan came back for another attack, I didn't know if my limited knowledge of self-defense would protect me.

But he didn't. Instead, he saw his window for escape. He turned to the door and made a quick dart. In seconds, he was gone. I feared for the worst—that he would head straight for Sirenia, for Mother and Zoe and all the other merfolk.

Diatomic reached out for me and squeezed my hand. "Can you stop him?" he asked.

"I don't know," I said honestly. I opened my mouth to sing, not a pretty melody to create good will or an upbeat tune to lift a crowd. The notes I sought were off-key. They mixed keys and chords, clashed with flats and sharps, and tumbled out of me messy and piercing and the least musical sounds I could muster. I sang in a way that would have gotten me banned from the musical academy if anybody had heard.

A rush of water pushed into Diatomic's pad and Ava entered. "Kyra," she said. She immediately swam toward my tail. "We have to leave."

"It's Sea Bass Stan. We can't let him go free."

"I'll take care of Stan," said a male voice from the doorway. I looked up and saw Triton.

A frisson of current so strong it was visible connected between Ava and Triton. I'd heard of such chemistry but had never seen it before. It was more powerful than anything I'd ever felt around a merman. It was a hundred times stronger than what I'd felt around Triton, and suddenly those feelings made sense.

The vibrations.

What Triton was seeking was the other half of his power, and he'd detected it when Zoe and I were at the vault. Together, our vibrations made him aware of our power—though even combined, it wasn't enough.

Ava's power was.

There wasn't time to consider what Triton and Ava's powerful connection meant. The only concern was catching Sea Bass Stan. Triton left us at Diatomic's pad and caught up with Stan. We later learned he delivered him to Poseidon. What became of the corrupt sea bass wasn't known, but I doubted we'd see him again. Between you and me, I suspected Mad Midge had traded his body for human wares. Some people on land were enjoying a meal at Sea Bass Stan's expense, quite literally.

Ava called for the octopi to come for Diatomic Jones, and when they arrived, they treated my tail too. A squad of squid joined Ava and me on our journey home, masking our presence with pulsing bursts of blue ink until we reached Sirenia.

There was no way to keep our antics secret after that. I awaited punishment, but what I got instead was a ceremony to celebrate Zoe, Ava, and me. The attention compared to the limelight of performing, but I'd take being on a stage over life and death encounters with bad guys any day.

The medical crew told Mother I'd recover but that only in

time would we know the possibly permanent damage to my tail. They left instructions for me to rest, to let my tail self-heal, to take some time off from musical lessons and errands around Sirenia. Days ago, I would have mourned the loss of my physical appearance, but today, lying in my bed with my scales torn and colorless, I couldn't help believing they were more beautiful than before because they represented something I hadn't known I had. Courage.

I didn't talk to the other merfolk about the changes within me. They had cast me into the role of the baby, and thanks to my birthright, that role was part of my mermaid DNA. But I was different now. More like Ava and Zoe than I'd ever believed. I understood that I was a part of something magical with my sisters, that we could be different but still be the same. I respected Zoe's curiosity and Ava's strength and I was eager to get well enough to develop my own skills to strengthen our trio.

Something shifted in our world that day, and not just the capture of a threat to Sirenia. I'd grown into my adulthood. I'd protected and saved merfolk who I cared about. I stepped up when Zoe, the bravest mermaid I'd ever known, wasn't able to. And I'd watched Ava, my oldest sister, get shaken to her core when she realized her destiny was floating in the room a few feet away.

Now that I was laid up, recovering from a damaged tail, with all the time in the world, I was looking forward to watching how Ava's story developed. Zoe and I had each had an unexpected adventure. It was time for Ava to experience whatever the universe held in store for her. Who knew? Maybe it would inspire a song.

Part 3: Ava

It was a day, just like any other day, when everything changed. The sun was shining, the bubbles were sparkling, the mermaids were frolicking amongst the kelp blades and coral, and I was just about to wrap up the last of the administrative tasks that I was laden with and join them when two mermen burst into Sirenia. One was Weid, an affable guard I'd known my whole life, and the other was Laker, a merman who'd recently taken up residency at Sirenia and made enough questionable choices to keep him from making friends with the other merfolk.

"Ava," Laker said. "You've been summoned to appear before Poseidon."

"When?" I asked.

"Now."

"But it's the middle of the day," I protested. I looked from Laker to Weid for signs that I'd missed something. Weid watched Laker. "You didn't say you had a message from Poseidon when we embarked on our patrol."

"It wasn't public knowledge," Laker said to Weid. To me, he said, "Are you coming?"

"Why does Poseidon want me? Mother's already there. Today was my day to stay here and oversee daily operations of the mermaid colony."

Laker seemed conflicted by my response. He didn't reply at first, and the waves moved his white hair around like a halo, occasionally hiding his eyes from view. With one hand, he reached up and pushed the choppy strands away from his forehead, letting me see his exasperation.

"You have to come with me," he said. This time his voice was lower and his tone was pleading. Weid swam to the edge of the building and disappeared around the corner. When Laker realized he was alone, his tone changed. "The other guards don't trust me. Not since the situation with Zoe and the diver. I wasn't even supposed to get this task, but mermen patrol in teams and there was no other merman to accompany Weid. I was the only one available."

Aside from his statement that I was needed at Poseidon's council, nothing Laker said was a surprise. There'd been recent reports of shark sightings in the waters that defined the edge of Sirenia, and some of those reports claimed the sharks had crossed the line. If they were growing bolder and testing whether their encroaching presence would be detected, we had to have a plan. The rest of the creatures who lived in the ocean existed by a code of respect for one another, but not the sharks. They were opportunistic bullies who ran the underwater crime syndicate. They took advantage of the weaker residents by luring them into their casinos and owning them for life based on the accumulated debts.

Sharks had already wreaked havoc on the neighboring mermaid colonies Oceania and Abalonia. Sirenia (mother's governance and the one I'd one day inherit) had managed to go unaffected, but it felt like a matter of time.

The threat of the sharks was part of the reason I was here (at Sirenia) and Mother was there (at the mermaid council meeting). For the first time since I'd been old enough to accompany her in my role as attaché, learning the ins and outs of Mermaid Council and experiencing what my life would be like when she stepped down from her seat of power and turned it over to me, we'd been tasked with different responsibilities. It was because of that threat that I'd woken up with a radiating excitement coursing through me.

It also left me feeling a little bit sick.

Back to today—to Laker—and to the request that I leave Sirenia to see Poseidon. "Even if I wanted to leave, I can't," I said. "I'm in charge, and it's too close to the end of the day to leave the colony unattended." I considered the request. Was this a test? Was Laker here, sent from Poseidon, to see how I'd respond to such unorthodox direction?

Laker scowled. "I'm already on probation. If you don't come with me, they'll question my motivations and I'll be removed from patrol duty, and there aren't any other entry level positions for me. This is my third colony in a year, Ava. If I can't make it work here, I don't know where else to go."

I didn't know the details of Laker's arrival to Sirena other than his involvement with my sister Zoe when she got mixed up with a human diver and a dead body by the old shipwreck, but I knew enough to recognize his attempt to manipulate me. Whether it was a conscious effort on his part or something he did without thinking, I didn't know, but that didn't change anything. Mermaids are inherently peaceful and have a natural dispensation toward actions designed to please others, but we were trained early on to detect language and behavior designed to bend our will. Laker was a fool if he thought I didn't notice.

"My responsibilities require me to remain here," I said. "If Poseidon needs to communicate with me, he'll make the necessary arrangements. You may think I'm being difficult to impede your hopes to prove your loyalty, but I *am* doing what is required of me. You'd be smart to follow my lead." I heard the bossy tone creep into my voice, and I cringed. This wasn't the first time I played the unpopular role of telling a merperson close to my age what to do, and that position had left me with few friends and fewer supporters. But there were reasons I held this post, and they weren't limited to birth order like everyone thought. I let the others believe what they wanted because it was easy, but deep down, I held onto a secret that informed everything I did.

Laker scowled. "You and your sisters think you're special because your mother is royalty. You have no idea what it's like for someone like me to move here without knowing anybody. You could do this one thing, Ava. For me. Your sister and her desire to get mixed up in something that didn't concern her is the reason I'm an outcast."

Behind Laker, a blue haired mermaid swam up to us. It was my sister Zoe, and from the increasing glow of her tail, rapidly turning from blue to a flaming shade of coral, she was fired up. "Leave her alone, Laker," she said. "Ava has a job just like you and I. Nobody thinks they're more special than anybody else. And if Poseidon needs to see a mermaid from Sirenia, then I'll go. I've been approved to leave the colony after curfew, and I'm the closest you're going to get to Ava."

If Laker was annoyed by me not going, then he was downright angry about Zoe's sudden appearance. The only one of my sisters yet to show was Kyra, the youngest, and the one who'd first caught Laker's eye. Kyra was beautiful and held the attention of most of the mermen. But ever since Kyra's tail had been damaged —possibly permanently—in her recent life-or-death fight, she had been laying low and practicing her music lessons. I knew she'd be fine, but I was overly protective of both of my sisters, and I didn't particularly want Laker to have a chance to treat either of them poorly.

"Just forget it," Laker said. He spun and swam out the entrance, into the deep blue ocean water, without putting up any more of a fight. Weid came back around the corner and glanced at us for a moment. I shrugged and he turned toward Laker and caught up with him with a quick pump of his tail.

Zoe watched the mermen disappear from view, and then she turned back to me. "What was that about?" she asked.

I stared at the door even though there was nothing to see. "Laker said Poseidon requested my presence at the council."

I felt Zoe's reaction without turning my head to look at her. "Are you sure it wasn't a real request? What did Weid say?"

"Weid didn't say anything. But Mother spent the day with the council. There's no reason for Poseidon to request my presence too. When Mother and I are together, she makes the decisions. Leaving here now would leave you and Kyra and the rest of the mermaids unattended."

"I can watch Sirenia for the short amount of time it would take for you to do what you need to do. I'm not incompetent," Zoe said with more than a trace of annoyance.

This wasn't the first time Zoe volunteered to help and oversee things, and I knew she was capable. But still, I couldn't. If anything happened to her while I was gone, I couldn't live with myself.

That thought followed me around night and day. If I could one day believe—truly believe—that the shark threat to Sirenia had been abolished, I could move on. But after Zoe had gotten involved in a murder investigation and Kyra had gotten maimed while recovering stolen art from the Nautilus Vault, I was surer than ever that evil was lurking around the waters close to us. Today was not the day to do things differently.

"Nobody said you were incompetent," I countered. "I just—I don't know. Something about the request felt off. If Poseidon really does want to see me, he'll send someone else. Someone I'd be more inclined to believe than Laker."

Lately I couldn't shake the feeling that everybody wanted something from me. The more responsibility I'd been given, the more I felt pulled in too many directions. Council responsibilities. Family loyalty. Favors for the colony. And the growing desire to get back in touch with Triton, Poseidon's son, who'd been the only merman to shake up my world. Until that point, I hadn't considered that there would one day be time for a romance, though as future leader of Sirenia, it was expected of me to marry and start a brood of my own.

One more pressure point to add to the rest of them.

I turned away from the door and swam into the spare room where I worked at a makeshift desk. Mother encouraged me to sit in her office to conduct business, but even though I'd been trained for such things, sitting there made me feel too self-important. The other merfolk talked behind my back as is; they required no encouragement from me.

But as good as my intentions were, I didn't get far. The temperature of the ocean water surrounding me turned warm and the scales on my tail stood out, making my nerve endings alert. The water felt electric. I floated a few inches above my chair but otherwise remained as still as I could. I recognized the sensation even though I'd only felt it once before.

The night Kyra had been injured.

At the time I hadn't stopped to consider whether it was the threat to my sister that put me on high alert or something—someone—different. That night, my only concern was getting help. But when I heard Zoe's voice behind me, I knew it hadn't been danger that made me feel this way. It had been the presence of Triton.

And the reason I knew it now was that he was staring directly at me through a window while floating outside my house.

Triton's appearance was unusual compared to other mermen. He had long black hair that he bound behind his head. Pieces of it came loose and floated by his forehead and cheekbones. His face was narrow and angular, and his lips were a shade of blue-red rarely seen in the ocean. Dark eyes under thick, strong eyebrows gave him an intensity that intimidated those who didn't know him. Between the intensity and his lineage, he was feared. His reputation supported the belief that he didn't mind the distance given to him.

"Ava," he said.

"Triton."

I didn't know if Zoe felt what I felt and I didn't care. An invisible connection held me in place. I'd been told about this, about how it would feel when I met the merman who was supposedly my destiny. Until that first time I'd met him face to face, I'd considered the whole story to be hooey.

Tonight, not so much.

The water was charged with frequencies that I had only formerly felt when swimming past a cluster of abalone. (The shells released bubbles, and when swimming past a wall of them, I could feel the vibrations.) An unfamiliar warmth radiated from my chest, through my shoulders and down my arms, and my tail fluffed up on its own. I quickly ran my hands over my scales to hide the physical reaction, but it was no use. Whatever it was that attracted me to Triton was on display. The confidence that had been instilled in me since birth dissipated and I didn't know what to do with my hands.

"I've been sent to find you," Triton said. "It's bad news."

I felt both Zoe and Kyra swim up behind me, Kyra maintaining her distance from the doorway and hiding her injured tail behind the door. The presence of my sisters provided the strength I needed to act in control. "Yes? What is it? Has Laker filed a complaint against me?"

"Laker is not your concern. Your mother is. She was kidnapped on her way to the council meeting. For the foreseeable future, the leadership of Sirenia will fall to you."

It was the last thing I was prepared to hear. In that moment, the bright, vibrant colors of the ocean faded to gray. Ever since the incident that put me in the role of Mother's assistant, I'd been told this moment might come. And I'd done what was requested of me, not questioning the decision to remove a young mermaid from the regular lesson plan and groom her for a role she was too immature to understand. I'd been ten at the time. Zoe was just entering Coelacanth University—Sea U—and Kyra was a baby, her scales still forming on her tail. At the age when other mermaids were learning to frolic and sing the very first notes of the siren songs that had been sung generations before us, I was being inducted into the Cabinet of Calamari.

And in that same moment, I stepped into the responsibility that was my birthright: taking control of Sirenia when Mother was no longer able to do so.

"Are there any leads?" I asked Triton.

"No," he said. "But Poseidon will find her."

"How?" I asked again. It was one word, one syllable, but it held a combination of desperation and hope. I'd been schooled and trained for this moment my whole life, for the day when Mother wouldn't be able to sit as the head of Sirenia, but the news that she'd been kidnapped was like a sucker punch to my abdomen. My breakfast of shrimp patties flipped over inside my stomach, and a fleeting thought about never eating again came into and out of my brain.

Triton floated in front of me. "He'll find a way. There are protocols for events such as these. Poseidon's team has made her protection their top priority. Your job is to act as leader of Sirenia in her place."

I felt Zoe next to me. My sister had a naturally inquisitive nature, and even if she hadn't made herself known, I would have figured her to be hiding behind the wall of coral branches. "Take me to Poseidon's lair. I can help." she said to Triton.

A protest sprang to my lips before he could respond, but she sent me a non-verbal communication before I could speak it. *It's Mother. We have to try to save her. He won't take me, but he'll take you.*

Zoe was right.

I put my arm out and held her in place as if keeping her from leaving. "Zoe will stay here. I'll go."

Triton looked back and forth between us. He knew what I knew—that he couldn't deny my request. It wasn't due to any display of power on my part or any of the hierarchical rules of the ocean. It was because of the current of attraction that ran between us.

Triton and I were predestined to meet. I'd been coached my whole life to recognize these feelings yet when we'd first occupied the same space, I felt like I'd been slammed into a reef by a Beluga whale.

In a good way.

"Who will oversee Sirenia?" he asked.

"Zoe," I said. "She has spent the past several months working with the human police and dive teams to patrol the unchartered waters, and she's capable of standing in for me now. I need to know Mother is safe. Take me to Poseidon."

I glanced at my sister. She straightened herself up, and her blue tail took on a coral hue that radiated out from the nerve endings within. The lustrous scales that covered her bottom half glowed. She looked more regal than she ever had in her life, and if anybody needed to decide based on how she presented herself right now, they'd trust her.

I trusted her.

"No," Triton said. (Apparently he couldn't be fooled by glowing mermaid scales and body language.)

"No?" I asked.

"No. It's too dangerous."

"You can't deny me," I said. The thought came out of my mouth before I stopped to think about it, and as soon as it did, I regretted the childish outburst.

Triton looked surprised. "This isn't going to be that easy, Ava. You thought you could control me because of this?" He gestured back and forth between us, and the water glowed with a trail of light that connected us like he was waving around an electric eel.

"I thought—you're a merman—your role—" I stammered.

"Maybe another merman would do whatever you told him to do, but not me. You handle your responsibilities and I'll handle mine." He turned and swam away.

"Leave him be," Zoe said.

"But Mother—"

"Mother is being held at Poseidon's underwater caves two miles past the barrier reef. She is safe. If you go now, they'll move her, and we may never know where she's at."

Realization dawned on me. "You read Triton," I said.

Much had been said about the unusual abilities of mermaids. We were referred to as sirens, and human gossip had trickled into our world via sailors and patrons of the Ebb Tide Emporium to know that much of what they thought was simply a product of their imaginations. No, we couldn't see straight through to their souls. No, we couldn't cast spells to lead them to their death. No, we couldn't spin magic with the moonlight that could fill their nets with fish and their traps with lobsters.

But we could read their minds.

When circumstances were right, we could read the minds of other merfolk too.

Zoe smiled, though her smile lacked her usual warmth. "Triton challenges you," she said. "It's fun to watch."

"That's why you read him? Because he challenges me?"

"You wanted to know what he knew about Mother and he wasn't going to tell you. I didn't know if I could read him or not, but I tried. You told him you trusted me with Sirenia, and that was the least I could do."

I smiled. During a tragedy, families either come together or are torn apart. Zoe had caused me countless headaches while growing up, but I couldn't be happier that she was my sister.

Word of Mother's attack spread through the ocean and soon our house was filled with concerned dugong, manatees, and tuna. Staying at Sirenia was the right thing. Not knowing who had been behind the attack made me suspicious of everyone and acting in any manner other than the one expected of me would have been a red flag.

"Ava," said a manatee named Caleb who I recognized from the Ebb Tide Emporium. "Mad Midge sent me to check on you."

Manatees weren't among the smarter mammals in the ocean, but they were reliable and loyal. That plus their physical nature were the reasons they often found work in more demanding jobs like stock, repair, and delivery. I wished I were more like my other sister, Kyra, who had managed to befriend most living creatures in the ocean and relate to them one on one, but that wasn't me. More often than not, the other fish considered me aloof and expected nothing more than condescension and orders. I found myself playing into that perception and became a self-fulfilling prophecy.

"Caleb!" Kyra cried out. She swam toward us and hugged the chubby manatee. "Is Mad Midge coming? Is she here?" Kyra looked left and right and her white hair billowed out around her head and hid her face.

I followed Kyra's glance around the interior. Mad Midge was the older mermaid who ran the Ebb Tide Emporium. She was a friend of the family and was always welcome in our house. She was a shrewd businessmermaid and the only resident in Sirenia who had a license to negotiate with the humans. Because she was singlehandedly in charge of procuring unique items for her customers, she created a safe space in which to exist—an unexpected reality for someone who almost died at the hands of some greedy sailors during the great shrimper/mermaid tragedy.

It was because of this that my pulse sped up at the thought that she was here. Ever since the news of Mother's abduction, I was on edge. What others treated as a random crime or a precautionary measure to keep Mother out of harm's way felt more personal to me. The last time I could have done something to save Sirenia, I was too young to react. That night ended in tragedy, and I'd never spoken of my role. Mad Midge was the only other mermaid who lived to tell what happened that night. I'd always wondered if she knew the truth.

I turned my attention back to Caleb. "Mad Midge couldn't get away," Caleb said. "There have been a series of break-ins at the emporium and she didn't want to leave her shops unattended."

"Does she need help? She should have asked," Kyra said.

"You have more important things to worry about." Caleb and Kyra looked at me and I forced a smile.

I watched the two of them converse. For a long time, everyone in the village had treated Kyra like she was fragile and could be broken. She'd been praised repeatedly for her appearance and her beautiful singing voice, and those gifts became her calling card. When her tail had gotten damaged, I'd feared she would lose that place of joy within her.

I should have known Kyra was more resourceful than I gave her credit for being. She'd been instructed to rest to facilitate healing of her tail, but her disposition remained sunny. She showed the population of the ocean that beauty is more than scale-deep, and I admired how she managed to not become bitter. She inspired far more sea life now than she ever had before.

"Mad Midge has been a loyal friend of our family for as long as I can remember. If there's anything we can do for her, tell her to not hesitate to ask."

Caleb nodded and swam away. Kyra put her hand on my arm and smiled gently. "I know this is hard for you. And I know you've been taught to handle everything. But if there's anything I can do, please let me know. I'm not as helpless as you once thought I was."

I covered Kyra's hand with my own and nodded but didn't say a word. Too much was riding on my performance to risk letting everybody see I was teetering on the edge of a meltdown.

I left Kyra with the other fish and swam to the back room that I used to weave kelp blades into textiles to distribute around Sirenia. The room had remained unoccupied for the evening, mostly because it was the least luxurious. When visitors came to visit, whether to party or show respects, they anticipated a display of wealth. It wasn't that we were rich, but Mother was the Matriarch, and that came with expectations. It was one of the reasons we were such good customers of Mad Midge and the Ebb Tide Emporium. Keeping up appearances was part of our life.

But tonight, I was thankful for the solitude of my room. I swam into it and shifted a panel of woven seagrass in front of the door and relaxed for the first time all night. It was then that I overheard the voices.

"She thinks she's in charge. She has no idea," said a female voice. I strained to place who it was, but with all the merfolk coming and going, it was close to impossible.

"That's what we were counting on," said a male voice. There was no question that this speaker was Laker. "This whole family thinks they're better than the rest of us," he added. "Since I first arrived, they've broken the rules and done whatever they want and they're not held accountable to the mermaid code. But I'm on the outside. Nobody trusts me and it's all because of them. I'm glad this happened. They don't deserve the support of the community."

"Laker, you have to calm down," the female said again. "We have a plan. We're going to get you your due. Just remember what we decided on. Tonight. Fourteen meters past the barrier reef. Nobody will expect us."

The conversation was too incriminating for me to ignore, but if I let them know of my presence, I'd miss critical details. Worse, I couldn't send out a mental cast to read their thoughts and identities because the whole house was filled with merfolk, and either someone would sense what I'd done or I'd come back with a jumble of thoughts from various sources.

Reading other merfolk was an invasion of privacy, a fact I'd often tried to instill upon both Kyra and Zoe (but Zoe's earlier demonstration of reading Triton told me she hadn't paid the fact much mind). In private, I'd meditated on ways to build up mental fortresses against their attempts to read me, and after a few tries, they tired of the unsuccessful efforts. Instead, they chose to read each other, which led to far too many sisterly secrets being spilled.

I closed my eyes and floated off a sea pod. The movement was subtle enough that it created minimal currents that would (hopefully) not be detected. I strained to notice the conversation which had fallen silent.

"Did you feel that?" Laker said. "I don't think we should talk about this anymore. Someone could be listening."

"Shhhhh," the female said. "It's all been planned. Meet me tonight. The sharks are expecting us. Zoe, Ava, and Kyra will be preoccupied with Sirenia. It's the perfect window of time."

"You're sure?"

"Trust me. Now let's get out of this place while we still can."

I gave them a brief lead and then pulled back the corner of the woven panel and watched as Laker and Ophelia, a mermaid I'd had a long-standing rivalry with at Sea U, swam the opposite direction.

It could be little more than a late night tryst.

It could be an attempt to undermine my new position of power.

But she'd mentioned the sharks, and that meant it could be something worse. And tonight, when everybody else was fast asleep and the colony was secure, I intended to find out.

I've never been one to ask for help. It's my biggest flaw. The curriculum at Sea U was intended for the merfolk children from the three neighboring colonies, but my education had varied from my sisters because of my predetermined path. It had only sparked question amongst the first born daughters of Abalonia and Oceania, because they should have been held to the same standard that I was. If there had been questions about starting me early onto the path of sovereignty, I'd been sheltered from them.

Nobody knew what roles Zoe and Kyra would play in the colony until they grew up and stepped into their talents and skill sets (if being nosy was a talent, in Zoe's case), but I had no choice. No matter what my natural inclinations were, I would be groomed to one day take over as leader.

I learned what the others learned: history of mermaids, history of humans. I learned about aquatic life and threats to us all. I memorized the mermaid code by the time I was in third grade and proposed an amendment lift the protective order that stated mermaids weren't allowed to travel unchaperoned after dusk. (It lacked support from others who could have been convinced if I'd approached them ahead of time, and it didn't pass.)

I got a reputation for acting on my own. It was my first experience with politics and the importance of gaining supporters before trying to change the way things were done, and I wasn't sure I liked what the political way entailed.

Ophelia proposed the same amendment repeal the following year. She changed the wording enough to make it her own, and it passed unanimously. She was hailed as an influencer, and rumblings about her future began. Ophelia wasn't born into a matriarchal family, and she lived like many other mermaids of my generation. She would never have the kind of power that would be handed off to me.

Even though we'd both wanted the same change to government, any friendship we might have had turned sour. What she didn't know, what nobody knew, was that I was bitter too. At being handed something I didn't want. At being expected to act like I was better than everybody else. At not knowing who I could trust or having an entire class of potential friends be turned against me. I spent the rest of my school years learning to trust my instincts and problem solve and be the one person I needed to depend on for entertainment, for solace, and for emergencies. I was so good at deep reflection that my emotional intelligence quotient was off the charts.

Not that anybody knew.

It was this reliance on myself and nobody else that led me to the plan that I hatched as I watched Laker and Ophelia swim away. (It was a little bit me needing to prove to everybody else that I was more than capable of taking care of things and not just from the throne). Whatever it was Laker and Ophelia knew about Mother, whatever it was they were planning, it needed to stop now. Mermaids didn't sacrifice each other, not in any circumstances. We were a peaceful genus whose life mission was to inspire creativity and great thought. There was no room for petty or vindictive behavior in the sea.

The last of the visitors left the village. I instructed the sea cows who'd been hired to oversee the gathering and clean-up aspects of the evening to hold off on their efforts until the morning and retire for the night. I was on edge, buzzing with the thoughts of what I was about to do. Both Kyra and Zoe were busy saying goodbye to our guests, and I took advantage of their (appropriate) behavior to finalize my plan.

When Zoe waved at the last of the visitors to leave, she joined me in the common area. "They're all gone," she said. "Is it just me or did that feel like a giant waste of time? We should be out there canvassing for Mother, not handing out anchovies to moochers who were here for gossip."

"They're not moochers," Kyra said. She shook her head side to side and her pearly white dangling earrings moved in the water. "They're our friends and neighbors. They're as concerned as we are. It's standard practice for the colony to convene at the matriarch's house when something like this happens. Isn't it, Ava?"

Both of my sisters turned to me. "We did what was expected of us," I said. "Now, I'm tired. If you two want to rehash the whole night, have at it. I'm going to sleep in Mother's room. The sea cows will clean in the morning."

"Why are you sleeping in there?" Zoe asked with more than a trace of suspicion.

"I want to be alone."

"Sure. You'll probably test out her crown and scepter while you're in there." Zoe said under her breath as she swam away.

I cringed at the tone of her voice. Did she think I wanted this? That I wanted something to happen to Mother?

As I watched Zoe, I felt Kyra watching me. Her eyes were

wide, and her innocence was on display. More than ever before I wanted to tell her that Zoe was wrong, that the only thing I could think about was how to find out what had really happened to our mother and to fix this. I wanted to come clean and tell her my worst fears, that this wasn't a random abduction or a security drill or even a one-off crime from some opportunistic criminal element, but that it was payback. For something that had happened a long time ago that had gotten out of hand because of me.

But that would require me to let her know my secret. It would mean I'd let out the one thing I didn't want anybody to know.

No, I had to do this by myself. I couldn't risk her safety with the same abandon that I was risking my own.

***

I waited until both Zoe and Kyra had gone to our shared bedroom and the sea cows had left for the night. Sirenia was dead silent and the only motion inside were the eddies created by the recently secured windows.

Our house had always been open, more with the suggestion of walls based on coral placement, but after recent danger that involved Kyra (of all the mermaids, nobody expected Kyra to get involved in something dangerous!), Mother had hired a team of construction manatee to create boundaries. Our lives didn't change, but when the windows and doors were closed, the water flowed differently. These days it wasn't unusual to fall asleep in one spot and wake up in another. At least in Mother's room, I couldn't float too far from where I started.

There was another reason I chose to sleep in Mother's room. It had a separate entrance.

When I could wait no longer, I bound my long pink hair in a braid that hung past my shoulders, and I rubbed my skin down with eel muck, a favorite product of Zoe (it masked the coral glow of her tail that appeared when she was excited). I slipped out. It would have been nice to have an electric eel or two to light the way, but that would defeat the purpose of swimming alone in the dead of night. Merfolk were genetically dispositioned to see underwater and even though it was dark, I found my way to the barrier reef.

The closer I swam to the reef, the more heightened my senses became. My aloneness was tangible, and with it came an awareness of my vulnerability, just like that night so many years before. I should have asked someone to come with me, but I doubted they would have said yes if I did.

It wasn't like I didn't know I had a reputation for being stuffy. I did. Even though the other merfolk kept their whispers to behind my back, I knew what they said.

I could give you a list of every moment where I choose to be aloof instead of free like the other merfolk in our village. It was easy to hide behind being the first born, being named as Mother's attaché, and being groomed to take over the throne, but the reality was, all of that had been set into motion far earlier than it should have been. The night I was almost captured.

It's not a story I often tell. Truth? My sisters don't even know. They were both too young to understand what had happened at the time. Since then, stories of the great shrimper/mermaid tragedy have been told and retold so often they play as cautionary tales, but what no one talks about, what no one knows, is that the event that singlehandedly changed the relationship between the humans and the merfolk didn't happen the night nine out of ten parties involved met with their death.

And it didn't happen the day before when the shrimpers first spotted the mermaids.

It happened the day *before* the day before. The day when *I* got tangled up in the shrimpers' net.

I'd been swimming by myself, playing out past the edges of Sirenia, practicing mermaid maneuvers, when a net dropped down into the water. It could have been argued to be either late afternoon or early evening, and either party would have been right. The sun hung over the edge of the ocean, a half circle above and below the water line. It was why I hadn't seen the shrimper boat veer off its chartered course and into Sirenia waters, hadn't seen the men on board coordinate the casting of their net, hadn't felt the danger until too late.

I'd been an easy target.

The more I'd struggled, the worse things got. That was before I learned extraction maneuvers at Sea U, before I was named under protection of Poseidon, before people viewed me as part of the leadership regime. It was before I understood there were people who wanted to capture us.

My memories of that night were fleeting. I was injured. I blacked out. Someone, or something, cut through the ropes that bound me and I floated to the ocean floor where I might have died.

Clearly, I did not.

Barely conscious, I got myself into the caves where I lost consciousness. When I woke, I was terrified. I stayed in the caves for two days filled with shame for having ventured away from Sirenia, for ignoring the warnings. I was terrified to tell mother where I'd been and I considered swimming out into the unknown, facing the deepest depths of the ocean, and never returning to my community.

What I didn't know, what I couldn't have known, was in the time I remained hidden, five mermaids had been dispatched to find me. They'd been caught by the very shrimpers who'd left me for dead.

That was the incident that led to the new rules of the ocean, where mermen were tasked with protecting the waters after hours and mermaids were held to curfew. It wasn't born out of a human sense of chivalry or merfolk being more qualified than mermaids, but because, in all the centuries that merfolk had existed, no one had ever tried to catch a merman. Sailors had heard rumors about mermaids. They knew we existed through legends, and like most legends, the descriptions, value, and use of us had gotten enhanced over time. Capturing a mermaid held a novelty that I hadn't understood until it was too late.

Four mermaids and five sailors were killed by sharks the night that I remained huddled in a cave, consumed by shame. Had I swum home and told Mother what had happened, Sirenia would be different. The mermaids would still be alive.

And that one mermaid who had survived, Mad Midge, might have had a whole other life.

Questions remained about my missing memories. How had I gotten into the cave? Why had I been spared? How had the sharks known to find the mermaids and shrimpers where we were?

The biggest question that remained unanswered was this: could I remain quiet about the truth my whole life in order to protect everyone?

I'd long since accepted the fact that there were no confidants for me. No one to listen to my spotty recollections of that night, no one to unburden myself to, because speaking of that night was admitting my role in the tragedy. That was the night I grew up.

The next day, Mother brought me with her to the underwater council. She introduced me to Poseidon's cabinet and I waited alone in a locked room while she met with him to discuss my fate. When she returned, it was to tell me that I would be accompanying her to council meetings regularly.

That was the beginning of my training to succeed her throne.

I was far too young to understand what was happening, but I knew one thing: I now had a secret.

I tired of the questions and the teasing and the accusation

from other mermaids that I thought I was better than them. Eventually I settled into being what they expected of me. It was easier that way.

Bossy? Yes. Not because I wanted to control the outcome of who did what, but because I knew what could happen if the others didn't follow the rules. It was why I hated that Zoe had been approved to work with the human dive team and Kyra had found trouble while going to her music lessons. It was why I rarely flirted with the mermen who hung around Sirenia. It was why I sometimes got frustrated with my sisters and resentful of Mother.

But I did it anyway, because of the guilt. I couldn't shake the feeling that if I'd been more self-aware that night, everything would be different.

* * *

Few spots in the ocean inspire a sense of overwhelm. When you're raised in a place with no walls, no boundaries, and no borders, you learn that everything is meant for you. The freedom associated with mermaids comes from that inherent belief that the ocean belongs to us, that we can go anywhere without restriction. Charters have been drawn up between humans and merfolk to keep the peace, and agreements have been reached between whales and dolphins who occasionally frolic in our territory too. The one group that has resisted any kind of written law are the sharks.

That's not to say Poseidon hasn't tried.

But sharks know their power. They know the fear they instill. A shark sighting for humans is scary enough to clear the waters immediately. But for those of us who live underwater with a sense of freedom, trust, and innocence, an unexpected shark sighting means certain danger.

Which is why, when my eyes adjusted to the waters in front of the barrier reef and I saw the outlines of three sharks tearing apart their dinner, I forgot everything I'd planned for the night.

In broad daylight, with a clear knowledge of where it was I wanted to go, I could outswim a shark. But three? In open waters? That I wasn't familiar with? Tonight? When I was already gripped by fear and anxiety and memories of the worst night of my life?

A hand grabbed my arm and I spun. Ophelia faced me. She held her finger in front of her face and gestured for me to follow her.

It was as fine a time as any to learn to accept some help.

I followed Ophelia toward the reef and into a cave-like opening. The closer I got to the opening, the higher my anxiety rose. It was as if the memories, long buried, came flooding back to the surface and the fear had never left. Ophelia turned and looked behind us, and then slowed. "You're safe now," she said. "The sharks are preoccupied. They didn't notice you."

"But they will," I said. "They have the most refined sense of smell in the ocean. It's just a matter of time before they come after us, and I hardly think two mermaids against three sharks are good odds."

"One against three," she said. "I have no intention of engaging in a losing battle."

I crossed my arms and gently waved the fin on the bottom of my tail back and forth to keep me upright and afloat. "Why did you pull me in here? Why not just let me out there with the sharks? If you want me out of the picture, that's an easy way to make it happen."

"You shouldn't be here. You're supposed to be at Sirenia acting as boss in your mother's absence—" she cut herself off for a moment, and then spoke. "You overheard me and Laker talking, didn't you? I monitored where your sisters were but not you. I just assumed you were hobnobbing with someone now that you're in charge."

"Ophelia, I'm not in charge. Mother is in charge. Until I hear official word that she—" I couldn't finish that sentence— "that she isn't returning, then she is in charge and I'm her mermaid-in-waiting."

"Then why are you out here? The waters are dangerous. You know that." She pointed over her shoulder toward the shark. "It isn't safe for you *or* for me."

I looked past her to the cave opening and considered what she'd said to Laker earlier. It pointed to one thing. "You're right. It isn't safe for me or for you. So why are you here?"

"You're lucky I am."

"Maybe yes, maybe no. You're planning something, aren't you?"

She didn't answer.

"Ophelia, I want in. Whatever it is you have going on the side, I want to be a part of it."

Her eyes narrowed and she cocked her head to the side. "You expect me to believe that?"

"Why shouldn't you? I've spent my life in this very position. You don't know what it's like where I am. I'm close to the throne, yes, but at what price? I never had the chance to make friends, but I can make things happen. I can be of more use to you if you let me help you than if you shut me out."

Ophelia considered my words. Unlike me, she'd left her hair untethered and it cascaded around her head like a cloud, dull yellow strands that made her head look disproportionately oversized to her body. In the darkness, the only features of hers that I could make out were dark holes where her eyes were surrounded by a thick fringe of black lashes.

The lashes weren't real, I remembered. Kyra once told me she'd seen Ophelia getting lash extensions at the Ebb Tide Emporium. Dark circles were visible below her eyes, possibly enhanced by the darkness of either our surroundings or several consecutive late night hours.

"What is it you think I'm planning?" she asked.

Back at Sea U, I'd had to accept that Ophelia knew how to manipulate those around her to get what she wanted. It was the first lesson in politics I'd ever received, and I learned it by living it. But a lot of time had passed between then and now, and I counted on Ophelia not knowing I now understood the point of having an ally. "You're right, I overheard you. I want to know what you and Laker are planning."

Ophelia looked over her shoulder and then back at me. "Wait here," she said.

"No. I go where you go."

"No deal," she said. "It's dangerous out there. You're not exactly unrecognizable, you know? And if someone is out to destroy Sirenia, then you're next. I'd be a fool to hitch my wagon to yours until I know what's what. Go deep into the caves. Wait until I come back. I'll explain everything."

She had a point, though I didn't like trusting her. I nodded and turned away, swimming deeper inside the cave. It was as I remembered it from that night in my youth. Teeth, broken off and laying on the floor, were scattered by bones. I recognized them too. Bleached white and smooth from having been dragged across the sandy ocean floor and massaged by the changing currents. At a glance they appeared to be bones that could have come from humans or merfolk.

But these discarded bones could only have come from a mermaid. It was the distinct skeletal composition that was underneath the scales that made up our tails. Their presence here in the cave indicated the sharks had no compunctions about who —or what—they ate.

The sharks had been responsible for the deaths of both sailors and mermaids the night of the tragedy. Ophelia had said she was sending me to safety, but she may have been sending me to my death.

"Who are you?" said a deep voice behind me. I looked over my shoulder and saw a large, muscular shark had entered the cave. Behind him, the outline of two additional sharks hovered. I haven't spent a ton of time around sharks, but to my untrained eye, they looked hungry.

There wasn't time to think about Ophelia's motivations now. I kicked my tail several times and swam deep within the cavernous structure. With my arms and hands out in front of me, I felt the walls for an opening, something small enough to fit through that would keep the sharks from following me. The first opening I found was a fake out, a crevice between rocks that led nowhere. The second was a narrow squeeze, but I fit. I kept my arms in front of me and moved forward until my hips were wedged into the space. I couldn't move. An impact shook the walls and the narrow opening widened. The impact had forced a fissure between the walls of the cave, and if I didn't move quickly, the sharks would soon make their way in.

A hand reached into the opening and encircled my wrist. I clamped my hand down on a wrist and snapped my tail. Soon I was out of the opening and deeper into the cave. From the current of electricity and the glowing trail of sparkly water that surrounded me, I knew the arm of the merman who freed me belonged to Triton.

We reached a cavern and glided to a halt. I tried to let go of Triton's hand, but he held tight. "You're shirking your duty to Sirenia," he said.

"I can't just sit by and pretend to rule from a chair that doesn't belong to me. Mother needs my help."

"Your mother can take care of herself."

"And so can I."

For the first time since delivering the news of Mother's abduction, Triton smiled. "Are you sure about that? Because a coating of eel muck is only going to go so far. And even if you aced defensive maneuvers at Sea U, which I'll give you the benefit of the doubt and say you did, you didn't stand a chance against those sharks."

"They already ate," I said. The reality occurred to me while I was speaking. "When I arrived, they were eating. I was lucky. Someone—or something—wasn't."

Triton relaxed against the wall. "How much do you know about the sharks?"

I studied him. For the first time in my life, I felt an overpowering sense of wanting to share the secret that I contained. I took a breath to speak, and then fear made my throat constrict and no sound came out.

Triton appeared to take that as indication that I had nothing to say. "That's the way of the ocean," he said. "We live a peaceful existence with one exception. The sharks. They live to terrorize. Over time, they've organized. They run the crime syndicate and profit from illegal gambling at the Clams Casino."

"Why won't Poseidon banish them?"

"That's not the way of the world. They're the yang to your yin. The evil to your good. The stronger the mermaid culture becomes, the more beauty and peace and creativity you inspire, the more darkness exists on the opposite end of the spectrum."

"That's not fair," I said. "You're blaming the mermaids for creating a world where the sharks are a necessary evil to keep balance."

Triton rested on a rock and lifted my tail. He draped it over his knee joint, an intimate gesture that felt perfectly natural and organic. Our eyes connected and I felt warmth blossom from my heart and radiate into my arms and torso. He picked up my hand and held it against his chest. "I feel it too," he said gently.

"It's not our time yet," I said.

"You don't know that."

"It's not." I pulled my hand away from him and twisted my torso so my tail fell away from his lap. I couldn't think about that now. I knew—he and I both knew—the signs that it was our time, and those signs aligned with the death of Mother or Poseidon. If either one of us contributed to those deaths in any way, we'd corrupt the synergy between us and would never fully realize our destiny.

"How did you know I was here?" I asked.

"I didn't. I met with Poseidon earlier this evening and was on my way out. When I entered the cavern and didn't feel water passing through the passageway, I knew someone was in there. I didn't know it was you."

He slowly floated up from a sitting position and bent down to pick up his trident. It was a three-pronged weapon with sharp, pointed tips on each prong. It was known to be his weapon of choice, given to him by Poseidon when he redeemed himself from past bad behavior and accepted his place in the dominion.

Triton held the trident out to me. "Take this," he said. "I can't come with you but I can't leave you unarmed. The sharks will recognize it. They'll know it came from Poseidon and they'll leave you alone. They won't make it easy on you, but they'll let you pass."

It wasn't the first time I'd seen Triton's weapon, but this time I stared at it and felt an eerie sense of familiarity. It was as if I had a buried memory of it, locked in a vault inside me where I chose not to look. The longer I stared at it, the more anxious I became. I forced myself to turn away and address him directly.

"What about you? Where are you going?" I asked.

"If you're right and it's not our time, then there is one task I need to complete. I need to find your mother."

Triton thrust the trident into my hand. At the moment when I grabbed it, the weapon grew hot and a shock spiked through my hand. Triton let go and swam away without the one thing that could have insured his safety. It was a risk I didn't know if I would have been able to take.

I followed him through the water. There was no way I could let him sacrifice himself for me, not now, not ever. I'd been spared once, and the familiarity of the circumstances determined one thing: I wouldn't let history repeat itself. I would not allow Triton to risk his life in order to save mine.

I turned and swam back toward the passageway. The opening was unblocked, but I didn't believe for a moment that the sharks weren't close. I swam tentatively with the trident in my hand, looking to my left and right, sending out vibrations into the water to detect the proximity of others. Not only had Ophelia been out here earlier, but she'd planned to meet with Laker. Had he shown? Was he lurking in the darkness? Or was he a part of the abduction? Had Laker turned his back on his merfolk loyalties and chosen to partner with the underwater crime syndicate? Were he and Ophelia working with the sharks?

For all the time I'd spent by Mother's side, I'd never considered these issues. I believed, foolishly, that I knew what she knew. That I was prepared for this eventuality. That Zoe and Kyra had the freedom and the adventure and I was destined to a life of boredom.

In one day, I saw how wrong I'd been.

"Well, well, well," said an eerie voice. "You look like a tasty treat."

The silhouette of a shark hovered outside the opening to the cave. The water around him was dark and I knew he wasn't the only one there. "Who goes there?" I asked boldly.

"The direct approach. I admire that in a mermaid."

"State your name."

"I am Xander," he said. "And this here is Spike and Garo."

"What did you do with Mother Mermaid from Sirenia?"

"We're not in the kidnap business, girlie," the one named Spike said. He was missing two teeth and an eye. The disfigurement could only mean he'd survived battle on at least one occasion. Scars by his eye socket that appeared to match the tips of the trident made me understand Triton may have used it on the sharks to some success before.

I shifted it to my left hand, glided to an upright position, and held it behind me. "You didn't take her?"

"No, but if we find her before you do, we're not in the rescue business, either." The three sharks laughed, releasing a cloud of bubbles and undigested chum into the water surrounding them.

The last time I'd been in the caves by the barrier reef, I'd been too terrified to flee. Embarrassment, shame, guilt all had rendered me unable to act, and instead, I'd given up. I had pressed myself into the deepest caverns of the cave and been close to starvation when I'd been found.

Had I left, I could have notified Sirenia about the sailors and the sharks. Even the warnings from a child would have been taken seriously enough to warrant investigation.

But I'd chosen inaction over action. And in that time, the two days after being cornered in the cave and being found, nine lives had been lost.

No matter what happened tonight, I wouldn't relive that mistake.

I kicked my tail, feeling the powerful motion from my back, into my hips, through the tip of my fin. The sudden movement gave me a split second of a head start, but compared to the large mass of the sharks, I was slight and nimble. I zipped between two of them and they bumped into each other when they turned to follow me.

It was enough to propel me out of reach and into the darkness. I clutched the trident close to my body and undulated as fast as my tail would allow until I reached Sirenia. The sharks may have considered following me, they may have even started for a bit, but the one thing I knew to be true about sharks was their motivation was tied to their needs. No shark had been known to commit murder on a whim. They showed up when they detected blood in the water. Their recent crime syndicate and control of the Clams Casino had more to do with them staking out a territory where fish who didn't feel loyalties to our genus could go for high stakes play. There were desperate fish deep in the ocean.

When someone lost more than they could pay, they were taken outside and taught a lesson. That lesson sometimes ended in bloodshed. And when that happened, the sharks were never far.

I canvassed the water around the caves but didn't find Triton. Of the two possibilities: he'd either gotten away while I confronted the sharks or he hadn't survived, I considered only one. He was still out there.

I reached Sirenia and eased the door to Mother's quarters open. I didn't think I'd been followed, but I twirled and, from the safety of our house, stared outside and double checked. When it appeared that I was alone, I slowly backed in and set the trident on an end table.

Zoe cleared her throat behind me.

I spun around and saw her waiting for me with her arms crossed. "Did you learn anything? About Mother's whereabouts or what happened to her?"

"No," I said. "I've been with Triton in the caves."

She glanced at the trident on the end table and then back at me. "Do *not* tell me you put a boy before Mother's safety, she said, the emphasis on "boy." "You're supposed to be the responsible one. Even Kyra wouldn't do that while Mother is missing."

I bristled at being accused of something so inconsequential, but I bit back the denial that sprung to my lips. If Zoe believed that's what I'd done, then that was better than having her risk her life too.

"Triton isn't like the others."

"Triton is your destiny, blah blah blah," she said.

The subject had been brought up before, but this was the first time I didn't deny it.

It wasn't uncommon for mermaids and mermen to have dalliances, some of which led to the merfolk population in the ocean. Merfolk were nomadic creatures who moved from colony to colony, exploring the vast underwater world and moving on when ready. Sirenia, Oceana, and Abalonia represented a link to Poseidon's rule not solely through law, but also through his connection to the leaders of said colonies. The matriarchs. Like Mother.

Few who lived in Sirenia spoke of Mother's relationship with Poseidon, but what was known was that their bond was emotional, not physical. The expectation was that the first-born daughter of a Matriarch would eventually take over leadership of her colony with the help of the daughter's predestined partner.

For this very reason, the union between a Matriarch and Poseidon transcended procreation.

Zoe, being more interested in adventure than romance, found mermen to be a waste of time. "Do I need to point out that you'll have plenty of time to spend with Triton if Mother never returns?"

"Zoe!"

"That's what this is, isn't it? That's why you spent your time away with him. You're prepping to take over Sirenia. You don't even care that Mother is gone. You've been waiting your whole life for this opportunity and now you're not even going to try to save her first." She turned around and swam away.

Despite my exhaustion, I swam after her and spun her to face me. "Zoe, each of us has a job to do," I said in my most steady voice. "I need you to do yours and I need Kyra to do hers, and I need you to trust that I'll do mine. This isn't the time for us to fight with each other."

She shook off my hand. "Maybe if you acted more like my sister and less like the boss of me, I wouldn't want to fight with you," she grumbled.

Half of me wanted to laugh. The other half wanted to cry.

"If you knew the sacrifices I made to protect you, you wouldn't care so much about me acting like the boss," I said, heat climbing my neck.

Zoe looked at me like I'd just verified her worst suspicions of me. "Oh yeah?" she said. "Then tell me, Ava. Talk to me about whatever it is that's so important that you can't discuss it with me." She glared at me, and seconds passed while we faced off with no words spoken between us. Finally, she broke silence with more hostility. "I can't imagine under what circumstance *you* going out during a crisis to make out with your new boyfriend could be seen as protecting *me*." She swam away.

There was so much wrong with Zoe's assumption that I

didn't know where to start—or whether I should bother starting at all. The reality was far more dangerous than her supposition, and if I gave her any indication that Mother might be a captive of the sharks who ran Clams Casino, then I'd never be able to keep her away. No, letting her believe what it was she believed was the better way to go. It might make me look bad, but it would keep her safe.

I washed what was left of the eel muck off my torso and tail and unbraided my hair. I doubted I'd manage much more than short bursts of sleep but I settled in on top of Mother's queen-sized clam and closed my eyes. When I woke, it wasn't a nightmare or an alarm or a growing sense of panic that pulled me from my dreams.

It was Zoe. "Wake up, Ava," she said. She shook me by the shoulders.

"What?" I sat up and pushed her away. "You need to let this go, Zoe."

"This isn't about last night. It's about this morning. We had a visitor and you need to deal with this."

I climbed out of the bed and followed her. "What are you talking about?" I asked. My sleep-addled brain was foggy, and I had a hard time processing Zoe's concern. "We had a whole house filled with visitors last night. Did someone show up after everybody else left? They can't be faulted for being tardy."

"That's not what I mean." Zoe swam ahead of me and swam through the doorway. "This is," she said and pointed outside.

I swam ahead of her, not sure what to expect. That's when I saw Laker. The problem was that Laker didn't see me. Laker didn't—would never—see anyone again. Because someone had killed him and left his merman body resting on our doorstep.

I moved toward Laker's body and Zoe pushed me back. "He's dead," she said. "I checked his pulse and his breathing. I felt for oxygenation by his gills. There's no life left in him."

"How—"

"He was strangled," she said. Zoe had experience working with the local human police, and that job had come with a certain amount of safety and emergency training. There was no point interrupting her. I'd get more by letting her show off her knowledge. "There are ligature marks on his neck and his hyoid bone appears to be crushed. His scales are ash gray, which indicates his breathing supply was cut off. If he had gotten to the surface, he might have been able to take a breath, but look at his tail."

I looked at his tail and noticed the scales were worn off by the lower vertebrae. "Someone stole his scales?"

"Someone tied something around his tail so he couldn't get to the surface."

"Who would do that? And why?"

"Your guess about who is as good as mine, but I'd bet the why was because someone's sending us a message."

I didn't say what I was thinking. If Laker had bled, the sharks would have devoured him. No blood said what Zoe thought. But this—delivering him on our doorstep—said more than I wanted to believe. Our troubles didn't end with Mother's abduction. Whatever was happening was about to get worse.

We moved Laker's body inside the house and shut the door. "Where's Kyra?" I asked.

"She left for the Ebb Tide Emporium early. It's just us."

"Did she go alone?"

"No, Mad Midge sent Caleb to accompany her. She said she'll be gone for most of the morning."

"Good. I don't want her to see him."

Zoe eyed me. "Kyra has a history with Laker. Don't you think it'll be better to hear about this from you than from a stranger? Especially since he was brought here?"

"Why was he brought here?" I asked again. "It doesn't make sense. Whoever killed him wanted to accomplish two things: eliminate Laker and let us know."

"Or whoever killed him wasn't the one to bring him here."

"How so?"

"Maybe one person killed him. Someone else brought him here. It might be that someone wants you to know about this but doesn't want to be involved."

I stared at Zoe. She was most likely right, but that wasn't what hit me. It was her ability to see that, to understand the possibilities of what had happened, that surprised me. Zoe was my younger sister, the one who constantly found herself in trouble for getting into fights and being where she wasn't supposed to be. She ignored the rules and had been grounded more than either Kyra or me. She had once been voted mermaid most likely to have a criminal record.

But here she was, calmly assessing the death of a merman who'd been dropped off on our doorstep and breaking down the possible meaning and motive behind doing so. She was rational. She had confidence. She knew what she was taking about. When did that happen? When did Zoe become this smart?

When did Zoe get to be more in control than I was?

"We need to call the council," I said. "Poseidon must be alerted."

"Not necessarily."

"Zoe, this isn't a time to break the rules."

"The rules state that the death of a mermaid or merman from Sirenia requires notification of the council, but Laker wasn't a merman from Sirenia. He showed up around the time when I got involved with the dive team. He isn't a permanent resident. He's been trying to get a position within Poseidon's ranks, but he hasn't been approved yet."

"How do you know all that?"

"Part of my job in investigation is to process background checks on new arrivals. His was in the stack. I remember how he paid attention to Kyra, and I thought if he wanted to get close to one of my sisters, I wanted to find out what he was all about."

"I don't think Poseidon would like to know you used your job to run a background check on a potential suitor for your little sister."

"So then don't tell him."

I shifted my attention from Zoe's face to Laker's. The color had drained and he was now a pale bluish-green shade. Soon, his body would disintegrate into the sand. His bones would be carried away by ocean currents and become part of the mystery of the sea. Mad Midge's team of manatee would find pieces of his skeleton on their weekly searches and bring them back to her shop to sell to humans as ocean collectibles. I could save everybody time if I went to her instead of Poseidon and told her what had happened. Mad Midge was not just a shrewd entrepreneur. She was a friend to the family.

And rumor had it she knew how to deal with a body.

But a part of me feared going to see Mad Midge. While Kyra had taken a job at her emporium and Zoe often frequented the shops there, I avoided her where possible.

It was the second time in days when I understood the only course of action was the one that protected Sirenia, not me. "I'm going to the Ebb Tide Emporium to talk to Mad Midge. Can you . . ." I glanced back down at Laker.

"I'll stay here with him," she said.

* * *

The Ebb Tide Emporium wasn't far from Sirenia, but it often felt like a completely different world. The market consisted of booths for home goods, groceries, exotic beauty items, and clothing. Electric eels were in tanks filled to capacity, ready to be rented out to those who desired ambient lighting or a glowing escort on a midnight swim. Whatever it was you might want to buy, you just had to tell Mad Midge and then sit back and wait while she procured it.

Kyra had a booth that was open a few days each week, where she sold hand-crafted musical instruments (Kyra was a gifted vocalist, though her recent injuries had related to the music world and she hadn't had the energy to perform since then). Mad Midge had taken Kyra under her fin and taught her the ins and outs of business, which had served to soften the perception of the older, maimed mermaid.

I found Mad Midge by the main ticket booth. We were on the cusp of the monthly market and she was gearing up for business. Admission would be one of Midge's main moneymakers. Fish and mammals would come from all around the ocean to shop. It was an exciting time to live in the area since the influx of tourists made Sirenia feel exciting.

For the first time, I wondered at the timing of it all. Did Mother's abduction and Laker's death have something to do with that? Was someone using the chaos that surrounded the market gathering to distract from a bigger plot?

Mad Midge was bent over an assortment of large, colorful baskets. Next to them were bags of sea glass that she distributed by color between the baskets.

"Midge?" I prompted.

The elderly mermaid straightened up and turned toward me. A tense moment stretched between us, where she studied me with her one good eye. Despite the inspection, I kept my body language strong and I stared back. Finally, she spoke. "Ava-girl. Ya lookin' for ya sister Kyra-girl? She be by da fountain, testin' a new set of pipes for da sale, ya."

Aside from Mother, Mad Midge was the oldest mermaid in Sirenia. She had long white hair that she kept secured behind her head, "for practical purposes," she said. Her tail had been permanently damaged, leaving her scales a dull, matte shade that lacked the typical mermaid luster and leaving her caudal adductor paralyzed on one side (which sometimes made her swim crooked).

I'd often wondered about Mad Midge's life before the accident. She'd been one of five mermaids to frolic that night, swimming close to the surface of the water under the light of a full moon, water dancing for the purposes of inspiring tired sailors who passed over our deep and sometimes dangerous waters. Inspiration was one of the universal roles given to mermaids, and until that night, it wasn't unusual for a bevy of us to trade anonymity for the attention gained from making an appearance. That Midge was one of the five spoke to her beauty and confidence.

She may have lost her outward beauty, but she'd never traded on her confidence. She'd chosen not to mate, an unusual choice in the mermaid world, but I always wondered if the mermen were secretly intimidated by her ability save herself.

She'd lost the eyesight in one eye during the tragedy—a small price to pay since she was the only mermaid who came out of the attempted capture alive. (The shrimpers died too, making Mad Midge the only survivor. Accounts of what had happened were limited to what she was willing to share, and there was a lot of conjecture as to whether she altered the truth to suit her needs.)

I couldn't speak for all the mermaids, but Mother made it clear that any negative talk about Mad Midge would not be tolerated.

"I wasn't looking for Kyra," I said. "I want to talk to you. To tell you about something that happened. It's something I'd prefer to stay between you and me and not be repeated to Kyra."

"Does dis have ta do with da merman who showed up on your doorstep?"

She already knew? How was that even possible? "Yes," I said, breathing a sigh of relief. Whatever information chain Mad Midge had access to, I was thankful that it had spared me the need to say aloud body this morning. "Someone transported Laker's dead body to Sirenia. It's been hours already. He's lost all color and is starting to disintegrate."

"Laker's dead?" asked an innocent voice behind me.

I whirled around and found Kyra staring at me with her giant blue eyes. "Kyra," I said. I hoped Mad Midge would jump in with some words of wisdom. "Midge already knew. I was hoping to hear her plans—"

"I've got no plans, Ava-girl. I didn't know nothin' about Laker. I was talkin' about Triton showin' up at your place yesterday. Dis news means someone is sendin' ya a message, naw. Yah, someone wants ta tell ya sometin,' tell ya dat ya shoulda done things differently when ya had da chance."

I felt a chill through me, like when a human dumped a bucket of ice into the ocean. "I've followed the code since we first got word of Mother's abduction," I said carefully. "I don't think there's anything I should have done that I didn't."

"I'm not talkin' about da abduction, Ava-girl, I'm talkin' about the tragedy." Midge came out from behind the booth and reached down to her tail. Slowly she peeled off a prosthetic layer that covered her damaged tail and exposed a ring of missing scales. I hadn't given much thought to Mad Midge's other injuries aside from her missing eye, but the exposed tail told a story of a much more violent capture and escape than I'd previously considered.

It looked just like the ring that had been left around Laker's tail, where scales were missing, and exposed merfolk skin was visible. On Laker, it had appeared pinkish and tender, slowly loosing color and fading to gray. On Midge, it was darker gray and calloused, as if it had healed over time but never to return to its natural state.

"Ya seen dis before, have ya?" she asked.

I nodded. Zoe's theory was that someone had tied Laker up and dragged him through the ocean, delivering him on our doorstep. The marks on Mad Midge's tail suggested she'd suffered a similar fate—though she'd survived. "Dere's a lot of merfolk and humans who want ta know how Midge got away the night of the tragedy, but I figure dat's nobody's business. I thought dat den and I think dat now."

And on the busiest day of Mad Midge's year, she pulled down the gate to the Ebb Tide Emporium and disappeared from sight.

My bright pink hair billowed out around my face and I swept it back and tied it in a knot with itself. I closed my fist and pounded on the gate. "Midge? Where did you go? I really need to talk to you."

"No, you don't," Kyra said from behind me. "You need to talk to me."

I slowly turned. Whatever emotions I expected to see on Kyra's face weren't there. She was poised and calm. I reached my hand out to hers and squeezed. "I'm sorry for your loss," I said. "I know Laker was your friend."

"Laker wasn't my friend," she said. "He was a visiting merman who didn't understand the code. He tried multiple times to get around the rules and manipulate the way we did things around here. His loyalties weren't to Poseidon and Mother, they were to himself. We're better off without him. I want to know why Mad Midge showed you her tail. Why is she acting like you know something I don't?"

When had Kyra grown up so much? I was used to her being the baby. Needing to be coddled and treated like she was going to break. But she accepted the news of Laker's death like it was expected. She was in control of her emotions, just like Zoe.

How had it happened that both of my sisters were more in control than I was?

Before I could keep talking to Kyra, the gate opened and Mad Midge faced me. "Ya need ta talk about it, Ava-girl."

"I would like to, but I can't."

"Maybe I need ta talk about it and ya need ta listen. Come. Follow me. Kyra-girl, stay here. You'll find out da truth soon enough." Mad Midge turned and swam away. Her damaged tail kicked lightly, skewing her to the side. She corrected her path with her arms and swam toward an enclosed structure to the back of the marketplace. Her private offices.

We entered the stone structure and swam to two giant clam shells alongside of the walls. They were open and lined in mother of pearl with bright red coloring on the edges that made them look like mouths wearing garish lipstick. Giant clams were popular for furniture in the residences of Sirenia, and for as capitalistic as Mad Midge was, it pleased me that she'd kept not one but two of the naturally beautiful clam shells in here for herself.

"Tell me about Laker, Ava-girl," Mad Midge said.

I studied her face. It was scarred from the tragedy and showed signs of aging, but there remained a wisdom that few mermaids ever achieved. I knew Mother had turned to Mad Midge for council in the past, and whether it was because she really needed it, or because she felt Mad Midge needed to be treated with public respect, I didn't know. But a standard had been set, and, outside of family, Mad Midge was the smartest mermaid I knew.

"Last night, I went to the barrier reef to look for Mother. I found Ophelia. She warned me about the sharks that hang out there and sent me inside the caves. That's where I ran into Triton, who gave me his weapon and told me to go home."

"Ya listened to him?"

"He shouldn't have given up his trident for me. I swam after him to give it back but he was gone."

"Where is da trident now?"

"At home," I said. I dropped my eyes from hers to the ocean floor. "Under my bed," I added. Fat lot of good it would do me there.

"Triton is your future, ya?"

"That's what people say. But that's for later. When Mother is gone. I don't have time for him now. I don't have time for any of this destiny stuff."

"Ya might need ta be makin' time soon, Ava-girl."

I sat up straighter and looked Mad Midge in the eye. "No," I said. "If Triton really is my destiny, then he'll be there. Nothing will change that. But Mother is missing and I need to find her. And now Laker's body was left on our doorstep, so that's another problem that will take up my time."

"Dis is why you came to me, ya?"

"Yes. I thought—" I stopped myself. It was one thing to think through the natural progression of what happens to a deceased mermaid or merman, but in this case, I was cutting out several steps in order to relieve my burden. My thought process and decision-making were going to show me in a mercenary light. "No. I came to you because I suspect you know about my involvement in the tragedy where you were maimed," I said. "This is related. Someone knows what happened and they want to scare me."

"What do ya remember about da tragedy, Ava-girl?"

I was silent for a moment. The fleeting memories that I tried hard not to consider were lurking at the edges of my memory. I'd spent so much energy blocking them, so much time pretending they didn't shape the mermaid I was, but the opposite was true.

That experience had shaped me more than any other event in my life.

"I was swimming out by the edges of Sirenia. It was the end of the day and the sun was halfway down. I don't know if I was wrong for being out there, or if the shrimpers were wrong for being out there, but one of us was in the wrong place at the wrong time. I didn't realize they wanted to catch me until I felt the net and when I struggled, I made it worse." My voice trailed off as the memory of being trapped in the tightening net came back to me. My body tensed and I flinched as the ropes grated against my scales again.

"Go on," Mad Midge encouraged.

"The net was lifted up through the water. I remember panic spreading through me, like a tightening in my chest that radiated out to my arms and tail until I was paralyzed. The net cleared the water and I looked into the eyes of the shrimpers who were lined up alongside of their boat. The way they looked at me—I knew I was in danger. I don't know what their plans were for me, but they weren't going to be kind." I shuddered again.

"What else da ya remember?"

"Nothing. I woke up on the ocean floor. The net was next to me. Something had cut through it. I got myself into the caves and I stayed there for two days. I considered leaving Sirenia and never coming back."

"Dere's a lot ya don't know," Mad Midge said.

"I know someone must have cut me loose from the net," I said. "I know four mermaids died that night. I know you're the only one who survived. I know Mother is eternally grateful to you, but she—and I—can never repay you for your loss."

"Ava-girl, what I gained dat night outweighs anything I might have lost."

"But your eyesight . . . and your tail . . ."

Mad Midge put her hand on my shoulder. Her voice softened.

"I see more of da world with my one good eye than da rest of da merfolk see with two. My life, dis life, managing da Ebb Tide Emporium, doing business with da humans, having control over my life, it's something I never would have had any other way. Mermaids are meant ta inspire love, but they're not expected to feel it. I felt it, a love so big it would have suffocated me had I let it. The power of destiny can shape us in ways we don't expect."

As I listened to Mad Midge, I wondered about what I'd been told about that night, about how many of my memory gaps had been filled in with rumors and gossip heard from others at Sea U.

"Midge, how much can you tell me about what happened that night?"

"Ava-girl, dat be a secret I promised I'd take to my grave," she said. "But I can tell ya dis: the mermaids that died weren't dispatched to find you. Poseidon went looking for ya himself. The mermaids who died ventured into the waters ta follow him. They didn't know ya were missing. They thought his presence in the ocean waters meant he was looking for a companion."

"But Mother—"

"Your mother is great Matriarch, and in many ways she's da perfect match for Poseidon. She understood her role and she accepted a few things about their relationship that other mermaids might not."

"Like what?"

"When Poseidon chose her as his mate, he gave her everything she could ask for save for one thing."

"What?"

"His heart."

"Poseidon didn't—doesn't—love Mother?"

"Yes, he loves her, but not in the way ya think."

It was impossible not to read the unspoken thoughts that Mad Midge sent out as she spoke of Poseidon. The water around her colored a soft shade of peachy pink, the bubbles sparkled, and a glow emanated from her scales. For a fleeting moment, even the damage to her tail appeared to heal itself and I saw the beauty of Mad Midge from before the tragedy. And I knew, regardless of the eye patch and the damaged scales, Mad Midge had always been this beautiful, but she only allowed certain merfolk to see it.

"He loved you," I said with understanding.

She nodded.

"He went out ta find ya," she said. "It was a noble gesture but it was dangerous. I couldn't let him go alone so I joined him. The reason I wasn't killed by da shrimpers was because I wasn't with da other mermaids. I was with Poseidon in one of da caves."

"You were watching over me? You were the one who cut me loose and rescued me?"

"No, that was Poseidon's son Triton."

A rush of warmth came over me. I remembered how powerful it felt when I'd first been face to face with Triton, and now I knew why. It wasn't just because he was my destiny. It was because he'd been the one to save me. For all the training we received: defensive maneuvers, independent thinking, mind-reading, and wordless communication, as I'd been lifted out of the water in the net of the shrimpers, I'd been helpless. That's why the trident felt familiar when I held it today. It contained the memory of my freedom within it and when I touched it, that power transferred to me.

"What if I have to choose between power and love?" I asked. Mad Midge didn't answer me. She floated in front of me, her expression the picture of serenity. As her thoughts mixed with mine, I felt the familiar internal tug-of-war, the feeling that I was being pulled in directions I had no say over going.

"If Mother dies and I step into her role, I have to make decisions. I'm not ready and it'll take all my energy to handle the responsibility. There won't be time for love. If someone undermines my confidence now, I'll always second guess myself.

It's not a foregone conclusion that I'll stay in mother's seat. There's a process where someone can challenge me. They can say I'm not qualified. If the truth about what happened comes to light, it would indicate I don't have what it takes to lead. It could be just the thing to award the matriarch to another family, maybe one that wasn't born into the line like Mother."

Mad Midge leaned forward and tapped the front scales on my tail. "Why do ya think someone wants to remove ya from da line?"

I considered my words before speaking them aloud. "If someone knows what happened the night of the tragedy, they might not want to see me in line for the throne."

"Ava-girl, ya spent your whole life pretendin' dat didn't exist. Ya closed off da world and ya shut out everybody. But dat decision to pull ya from your lessons and groom ya to inherit Sirenia wasn't made without a lot a thought. Your mother is a wise mermaid, but even she knew dere were other considerations."

"What are you saying?"

Mad Midge patted my hand. "Right now, ya got a problem ya be needin' ta solve. Don't worry about talkin' direct to me. There's a lot of words wasted when conversation dances around the issue."

I found myself wanting to ask Mad Midge what she knew about my life and about the decisions that were made for me before I could make them for myself, but her ability to shift the focus back on Laker and the immediate problem created when Zoe discovered his body on our doorstep was more important.

"Laker's body is already losing color. The scales on his tail have started falling off. It's just a matter of time before he starts to disintegrate, and when that happens, his bones will scatter. Your manatee team will likely find those bones in time, but I thought— if you tasked them to retrieve his body now and bring it here—"

"It would solve a certain problem for you."

"Yes," I said, relieved to have it out there.

"Ava-girl, things have ta happen on dere own time. Dat's the way of the ocean. Ya can't rush da process."

A wave of anger climbed my body and warmed me to the follicles of my bright pink hair. The knot I'd tied came loose and the hair billowed out and entered my periphery vision. My fists balled up without thinking and I set them together in my lap to try to hide my reaction.

"Don't get mad, naw," Midge said.

"How can I not get mad? Mother is missing." I relaxed my fist and gestured toward the entrance. "You saw Kyra out there. She wasn't even upset about Laker. And Zoe, this morning, knew all the right questions to ask. They're taking this better than I am. Everybody is. The house was filled with visitors last night, fish and mammals who wanted to pay their respects, and what did I do? I hid in the back room and eavesdropped on a conversation between Ophelia and Laker.

"I should have been mingling, meeting people, getting to know the constituents, but I was hiding. Everybody thinks I'm itching to take over, but I'm not. Mother knows how to lead. I just boss people around and try to control situations. Right now, it feels like everybody wants something from me and I don't know if I can make them all happy. I never was ready for this and might never be."

I was embarrassed by my outburst but there was no taking it back. My instincts were to apologize, but one of the earliest lessons that had been drilled into me was to stand by my actions whether they were inappropriate or not. It was a sign of confidence, of power, and of belief in ourselves. I couldn't take back what I'd said, but it felt good to have said it.

"You be puttin' too much pressure on yourself, Ava-girl. Ya, Zoe-girl, and Kyra-girl are confident. Dey both be through challenges dat shaped dem. Dey both learned about demselves. You be too worried about being in charge of Sirenia. It'll come, but you need to be in charge of yourself first. You've spent your whole life hearing you were going to be somebody someday, but nobody ever thought about how dose same words told you dat you weren't somebody yet." She nodded.

The longer Midge spoke, the less I heard her dialect. A softness came over her speech, and the wisdom that she shared with me felt deeply intimate and personal. I didn't understand how she knew exactly what I felt or what my fears were, but she did. And her words were exactly what I needed to hear.

"How do I do that?" I asked. "How do I focus on me when there's so much that needs to be taken care of? Mother, and Laker, and Sirenia, and—"

"You'll find a way, girl. Remember that. You don't need ta wait ta become da woman you're meant ta be. You're already her."

I nodded to show that I heard her, but I had nothing left to say. "I should go," I said. "There are things to tend to at home." I floated up from the giant clam shell and Mad Midge rose too.

"Ya know, with the market opening this weekend, it's not a bad idea for the manatee to go out on one last scavenger trip. Ya never know what dey might find in da waters."

We left the solitude of the stone building and swam out front. Chubby manatees were busy unloading crates from their holding zone and distributing them to booths inside the emporium. I glanced around for Kyra but didn't see her. Mad Midge swam toward the manatee and the two in front set down the boxes they were holding and joined her. I remained a few yards away but tuned into their vibrations to hear the conversation.

"I'm-a goin' ta need ya to go out to Sirenia. A merman has died and da mermaid colony has enough ta worry about."

"Shouldn't we let nature take its course?" Caleb asked.

"Dis is a distraction to keep da merfolk from finding Mother Mermaid," Mad Midge said. "We owe it ta her ta be discreet."

Caleb nodded. "Whatever you say, boss. I'll go out there with a few of the guys and handle it after we get back from Ophelia's delivery."

"Ophelia?" I said aloud. Midge and Caleb turned toward me. It was obvious that I'd been listening in on their conversation. "Is it a large delivery? I was planning to head out to see Ophelia when I left here, and I'd be happy to make a delivery for you." I turned to Midge. "Assuming Midge agrees."

Mad Midge smiled. "Dat sounds like a perfect solution. Caleb, give Ava-girl the package."

And I took it, and I swam away, and I waited until I was out of view before peeking inside and discovered the last thing I'd expected to see. Laker's personal effects.

I closed the sack and forced myself to keep on swimming. If Laker's body was still out by Sirenia, then why were his belongings here at the Ebb Tide Emporium? I couldn't believe Mad Midge had anything to do with Laker's death, not now, not after our conversation, but what about Caleb? Or one of the other manatees? Or had this been a sack dropped off and marked for delivery to Ophelia? Other than planning to meet with Laker at the caves by the barrier reef last night, what did she have to do with him?

The night of the reception at Sirenia, they'd been talking. That was the conversation I'd listened in on. Ophelia had made it clear that she had a plan for something. What?

What was she up to?

Was it possible that what I'd initially discounted as a petty grade school competition had festered under the surface and become a reason for her to come after me through my family? Because that was key. No matter what all was going on, how many things were pulling me in a thousand different directions, at the heart of it all was my family. My mother. I had to find her before it was too late.

It seemed close to impossible to believe, but in the past day I'd been faced with a lot of things I hadn't wanted to believe. Now seemed a good time to be open to suggestion. But before I cast my judgmental vote one way or another, I needed to find out more.

Ophelia lived on the outskirts of Sirenia in a cluster of mermaid housing designed to provide comfortable living in a planned community. Unlike our house, which was intended to represent an open door and a ready welcome for all merfolk near and far, Ophelia's hamlet was privately owned and gated for maximum security. It was unclear where the idea of locking out fellow merfolk came from, but it seemed a subsect of our genus preferred their privacy.

Or, it was possible, that the residents felt they had something to hide.

With the sack of Laker's belongings in one hand, I kicked my tail and made the trip to the hamlet quickly. I hesitated by the front gate, not sure what I would say to the dugong on patrol to gain access.

"Miss Ava," he said. "What brings you to the hamlet?"

"Have we met?" I asked.

"No, but I recognize you from the propaganda distributed by Poseidon's team. You're the first daughter in line to the throne, right? Not a lot of mermaids who look like you."

There was no point denying it. "Right," I said.

It wasn't the first time I cursed the way I looked. My sisters and I each had distinctive appearances that caused us difficulties at various times. Kyra had long, white hair that was thick and lustrous. Her skin was so pale it was almost translucent, and her build was slight like a water fairy. Zoe had an athletic build, and with her blue body and blue hair, also had the potential to blend in more than Kyra and me. It was her tail, which glowed bright coral from within whenever she was scared, excited, or particularly angry, that gave her away.

And then there was me. A full head of bright pink hair that was visible from the surface of the ocean and a curvaceous body that kept me from escaping through windows (and gained unwanted attention from an early age). If I hadn't been born into royalty, I would have spent my teen years fending off advances and offers that would've led to scandal. Being intended for one of Poseidon's sons had shut down that conversation.

"Are you here to ask about leads to your mother's disappearance?" the dugong asked. "We were advised that a representative would come around and make inquiries, but nobody said it would be you."

I closed my eyes for a moment and said a silent thank you to the spirits of the ocean. "Yes," I said. "Have you heard anything?"

"Me?" The dugong looked confused. "I spend my days in this booth. Why would I know anything?"

"I'm here to see Ophelia. Is she in?"

"I don't know. She's a private one. You best go back and find out for yourself. Number sixteen."

"Number sixteen," I repeated. "Thank you, Dugong."

"Name's George."

"Thank you, George."

"You're welcome, Miss Ava." He looked bashful. I swam inside the gates, and behind me I heard, "Come back and say goodbye before you leave." I spun around in the water and waved to acknowledge that I'd heard him, and then flipped onto my front and continued to her unit.

The hamlet was designed with four individual units that were connected by pathways that led to a courtyard. Each unit had windows that looked out onto the open space, and as I swam, I became aware that I was being watched. It wasn't that I saw the eyes, but I felt them. And I felt vulnerable. It wasn't every day that a direct descendant of the throne went out by herself to knock on doors. A tiny part of me thrilled with the experience and in that moment I knew when the time came to inherit the throne, I wouldn't be the sort of leader to sit in an isolated space and participate from afar.

I wanted the same freedoms as everybody else.

Unit sixteen was on the corner of the property. I swam past the back door and windows and rounded the side until I was out of view of the prying eyes. Opting for the direct approach, I swam to the front door and tapped on it. I waited. No one answered.

I tapped again. Was Ophelia here? Was she avoiding me? Or was she not home?

After the third very firm knock, I knew the door wouldn't be answered.

I swam to the side and peered through the window. There was no sign of Ophelia. There was no sign of anybody.

But there was a sign of something I didn't expect. Piles of chips stamped with the logo from the Clams Casino stacked up on her dining room table.

What was Ophelia up to?

I regretted coming on my own because this would amount to my word against hers. Zoe would have known what to do thanks to her recent lessons in investigation, but she didn't even know I was here. Kyra was slight enough to fit into a gap between the bars on the windows and either retrieve the chips as evidence or swim through the interior to see what other incriminating objects we might find.

But benefitting from Zoe and Kyra's help required me to ask them for it and I wasn't good at asking for help. It was a sign of weakness. It would indicate how ill prepared I was for what lay in my future. If only I could get in, get a chip, take it to Poseidon as evidence that Ophelia was involved with the sharks and organized crime, then I could—

"What do you think you're doing?" Ophelia asked.

Of course, Ophelia was behind me. Even if she'd been nowhere close, someone could have warned her. She was a mermaid just like me, and communication through a siren song was the easiest form of communication. I'd been so lost in my thoughts that it hadn't occurred to me that someone may have told her of my presence before I'd gotten through the gate.

"I'm investigating my mother's disappearance," I said. My hand tightened around the opening of the sack containing Laker's belongings. It was what I was supposed to deliver to her, but I couldn't bring myself to hand it over until I knew her motivations. "George let me in," I said. "He said the hamlet residents were notified that I might come by to ask questions."

"Not you," she said. "A representative. A guard. A merman. Someone not important to the grand scheme of things." She waved her hands around to illustrate "grand scheme." "Besides, don't you have better things to do?"

"Like what?" I demanded. "What could be more important than finding out who abducted my mother?"

I stared at Ophelia and she stared back. My hair billowed out, around my head, taking up space in the water and making me feel larger than life. By comparison, Ophelia's chopped yellow hair wiggled up and down and back against her head. People like Ophelia had made me feel inferior my whole life. No more.

I held the bag out to her. "I was at the Ebb Tide Emporium earlier today. Mad Midge needed the manatee to oversee some unexpected business for her and I volunteered to deliver your package. This is what you've been waiting for, isn't it?"

She hovered in her spot, her tail jiggling ever so slightly to keep her from moving. Her hands were twisted together, her arms bent at the elbows and close to her chest. Her eyes never moved from the bag. I sent out a mental cast to see what she was thinking.

She already knew what was inside.

But it wasn't fear that she radiated, or guilt, or panic. It was overwhelming sadness.

"It's Laker's belongings," I said, this time more gently.

"He's dead, isn't he?" she asked.

"Yes."

"Where did they dump his body?"

"On the stoop of Sirenia."

She nodded. Slowly, she untwisted her hands and reached out for the sack. I released it. She held it open and glanced inside, and then closed it back up. When she looked up, her eyes were bloodshot. "Laker was my brother," she said.

"Your *brother?*" I floated in front of her, considering what this meant. "But Laker arrived from a distant merfolk colony. He's a relative stranger."

"He's a relative, but he's not a stranger. He was taken from us when we were young. Before school started. My parents wanted me to believe I made him up, but I had memories of him. When he came back to Sirenia, he sought me out and told me about his life."

"Was it a good life?" I asked, though I could already guess the answer.

Merfolk were loyal and cared for each other, but there were rare occasions when families bartered with a young mermaid or merman in exchange for better living arrangements for the rest of them. It was one of the practices that had forced the creation of Sirenia, where such activity would not be tolerated. In our colony, there was a mutual level of respect and protection. If any family felt they couldn't provide for their kin, Mother would do so for them. All they had to do was ask.

But pride kept some families from asking, as did the unfounded belief that the request would put them in mother's debt. And Mother's relationship with Poseidon was no secret. Anyone who chose not to have ties to the ruler of the sea was left to seek out solutions on their own.

I'd like to say I didn't understand why anyone would ignore the generosity of Mother and community of Sirenia, but deep down, I knew that I understood it just fine. I was closer to her than any other member of the community, but I felt estranged, like accepting what was offered to me meant I wasn't capable of creating a future for myself. I'd been assigned to shadow her before I understood why, and that way of life, the treatment from others that let me know they didn't think of me like they thought of themselves, had been shocking at first but eventually became the norm. It felt like a handout of power, not food. Of respect that I hadn't earned. Of isolation I never wanted.

There were times I'd wanted to leave. To pack a bag and swim out into the deepest parts of the ocean, beyond the unchartered waters and back to the barrier reef. Into the darkness where I didn't know who I might encounter and what I might find. It wasn't the same as Zoe seeking out adventure or Kyra seeking out training. It wasn't seeking out anything—it was running away. From everything I'd been told was my due simply for being born first.

I resented it all because I didn't feel worthy. And here I was, listening to Ophelia tell me about Laker, who hadn't had that choice. He hadn't been given the chance to decide if he wanted to stay or go. He hadn't been given the opportunity to grow up as a ward of Sirenia, or to enlist in Poseidon's army from an early age. He'd been cast out and left for dead. And when he returned, beleaguered by a past of misery, instead of finding the home he'd sought, his life was cut short.

"Laker didn't want to talk about his life. I knew he got mixed up with the crime syndicate. He had gambling debts. He was tossed out of Clams Casino and a bounty was placed on his head. The sharks were eager to find him. I took him in for his safety, but I could only protect him as long as he wanted to be protected."

"The night you found me by the caves. What were you doing there?"

"I followed Laker to the casino. If he'd gone in without the money he owed them, they would have killed him. I went to intervene. I was going to bail him out, but I didn't get the money in time. And then you showed up and I had to deal with you, and now—"

And now I'd been spared while Laker had been killed. It was the second time my life had been deemed more important than someone else. She looked away and swiped at her eyes with the back of her hand. "How did they kill him?"

I held my hand up to my throat.

"And his body?"

"You already know it will be gone overnight."

Ophelia kept her eyes averted from mine for a long moment. When she looked up again, anger flashed in them. "If you hadn't shown up at the caves when you did, I might have saved his life. This is your fault, Ava. His death is on your hands. You may think you're protected by the laws of Sirenia, but this didn't happen under your mother's jurisdiction. Laker's death needs to be avenged, and if I can use you to get closure, then don't think for a second I won't take that chance."

The waves of anger that emanated from Ophelia's body hit me like a wall. I countered her rage and held my ground. I didn't blame her for her anger, but we had a history, and I wasn't about to give in.

"Where did you get those chips?" I asked.

"That's none of your business."

"Actually, it *is* my business. Any illegal activity that takes place in Sirenia is my business. Laker running up gambling debts with the sharks brings danger to our door. Your plan to pay them off with casino chips of questionable origin does too."

"Those chips were donated by the merfolk who don't believe you should be in charge. They want a different kind of system. They think there's a better way to rule Sirenia."

"Because you told them there was. You've been stirring up trouble for me and my family since we were students at Sea U. We weren't responsible for what happened to Laker. Your family was."

"Get out," Ophelia said. "Get out of our hamlet and never come back." Her eyes became bloodshot and the flesh around her eyes got red. Her fists balled up and her mouth pulled together into a tiny, squished together dot in the middle of her face.

"Thank you for your time," I said, "And my deepest condolences on your loss."

I waited another second before turning around and leaving her alone. Ophelia may have valid reasons for being upset about what had happened to Laker, but it didn't change the fact that there were more questions than ever relating to her recent behavior.

I swam back to Sirenia with one thought in mind. I needed to talk to my sisters. This wasn't a problem for me to solve, it was a problem for us. For family. My need for their help was bigger than my fear of asking for it.

By the time I got home, I was filled with questions. What did Ophelia promise the merfolk she knew in exchange for those casino chips? Did she really believe she could pay off Laker's debts to the sharks? Did her lies lead—either directly or indirectly—to someone abducting Mother from her throne? And if someone had kidnapped Mother, why wasn't anybody demanding ransom for her?

The piles of chips on Ophelia's table represented a vast fortune. Did she really think she could pay off Laker's debts and the sharks would leave him be?

Did she really believe he wouldn't return to the casino and run up the same debts?

Was Mother alive?

This last question came out of nowhere. I didn't even know why I connected it to Laker and the trouble with Ophelia. On one hand, it was more important than the other questions. Not only was she the leader of our colony, but she was my mother. She was the one who had watched out for me and protected me when I couldn't protect myself.

I was struck by the difference in parenting styles between

Mother and Ophelia's parents. After my first real bout with trouble—a doozy, since it forever changed the way the mermaids lived—had led to her to pulling me out of school and keeping me safe by keeping me by her side.

Contrast that with Laker's life. He'd been separated from his family when he was still young. Given away? Or banished? Maybe he'd been a problem child, but still. The idea that parents would barter away their son for a better living arrangement left me feeling ill.

I couldn't imagine where Laker had landed or what life had been like for him, but even he told me he'd bounced around from colony to colony looking for his place in the ocean. When he delivered news of Mother's abduction, he'd been angry with my response. He claimed it was because he wanted to establish himself in Poseidon's cabinet, but would Poseidon even consider a merman with considerable gambling debts and a bounty on his head? Wouldn't that endanger the very people he was charged with protecting?

It didn't sit right with me. I didn't know how it connected to Mother's disappearance, but I knew the two were not unrelated.

As I swam away from Ophelia's hamlet, my thoughts returned to Mother. All of this trouble started the day Laker showed up at Sirenia and told me she'd been abducted. What had Laker told me?

He said Poseidon requested a meeting with me.

And I hadn't gone. It was a direct violation of a request from Poseidon. There should have been repercussions.

There weren't. Nothing had come down from Poseidon's council to demand I take that meeting. The only contact I'd had since then was with Triton, who'd told me to stay away. But when I ended up in the caves, he'd been the one to make sure I was okay. It was as though he'd been waiting for me. In the exact same place where I'd hidden decades ago when I got caught by the greedy sailors.

It didn't feel like a coincidence.

I was halfway to Sirenia when I changed direction. The answers I sought weren't at Sirenia. That was a place of community and safety, but this wasn't the time to commune with my sisters or play safe. They'd be okay as long as they stayed with each other.

It was time for me to take a chance and talk to the one person who could shed light on things.

I swam toward Poseidon's underwater palace.

* * *

There were two ways to reach Poseidon's lair. The first was through the open water, navigating past a wall of coral, through a maze of kelp, and into the abalone forest. It was the direct approach, which was fine for expected visitors. That wasn't me. I didn't yet know if Poseidon would see me or let one of his advisors handle my arrival, but I wanted the element of surprise on my side.

I swam toward the caves.

It made sense that I could reach the palace by swimming deep into the caves. Triton had been inside and it never seemed as though he'd gone head to head with the sharks to be there. When he pulled me into safety, that's exactly what he'd done: pulled me in. He'd already been there. And I suspected I knew how.

Once, in the early days of me attending council meetings with Mother, I'd been asked to sit outside while the two of them met to discuss my future. Five minutes is a long time for a mermaid filled with nerves and misplaced energy to sit still, and I'd made it to ten. When it seemed as though I would be left unattended indefinitely, I floated up from the bench where I sat and studied the maps that hung in the hallway.

The renderings focused on the palace, but I'd been more interested in the surroundings. Mother and I had swum there together, and it fascinated me to see that on the side not facing us were the caves where I'd woken after being freed from the net that caught me. I remember tracing my finger over the paths indicated on the far side, over and over, in an S pattern, as if committing it to memory.

Which was exactly what I'd done.

There'd been no reason for me to return to the caves after that night, but the longer I stayed away, the more I disconnected from the memories. Now, having spoken to Mad Midge and opening the doors to thoughts I'd kept buried, further details came to light. One moment I'd been tangled in a net. The next, I'd woken up on the floor inside. I had no recollection of getting free.

It was starting to seem as though the help I'd received had come from the palace.

As I approached the caves, I scanned the water for signs of sharks. The water was clear today, with no hint of chum or bones or vicious toothy menaces. Still, I didn't waste time. I ducked inside, swam directly to the opening where I'd woken up, and squeezed into the opening. This time I didn't focus on the discarded bones that scattered around the floor.

The strain of the past few days had held few benefits, but the one I was thankful for was the ease with which I now slipped through the crack in the cave walls. The tenderness of having my scales scraped against the interior walls was still with me. This time I gritted my teeth and swam through, wriggling my hips when the walls felt tight, and slowly made it into the second room where Triton and I had sat.

From there, I floated and scanned the interior. A small pile of discarded fish bones and clam shells lay scattered around the base of a long, low rock. The ocean floor had been disturbed around the bottom, as if someone had spent time walking on that stretch of silt. I swam closer and found a crude harpoon resting by the rock. Triton had been here, and judging from the presence of his weapon, he hadn't gone far.

Unlike the last time I'd been near him, I didn't feel his presence. I glided to the rock wall and ran my hands over it until I found what I was looking for, a small fingerhole in the cave wall that allowed me leverage. I shifted my weight against it and flapped my fin as hard as I could. The attempt was futile.

And then, a piece of sea rock floated down from above me.

I looked up and saw a crack. The wall had shifted—so little that I barely noticed, but it had, nonetheless.

It was a minor victory, but I took it. I inserted my fingers back into the crack and flapped my tail more. My muscles ached with the exertion and I questioned whether I was strong enough to get through. Just as I was about to let go, I felt the current shift behind me. I turned. Zoe and Kyra were there, hovering in the middle of the cave. Zoe's tail was bright coral, and Kyra was so pale she was practically translucent.

"How did you know where to find me?" I asked.

"You dropped your guard and I read you. That would only happen for two reasons: you were helpless, or you chose to channel all of your available energy into a gargantuan physical task. I didn't know which."

Kyra swam closer and threw her arms around me. "Ava, I was scared that you were in danger!"

I hugged my sister back and felt hot tears spring to my eyes. I couldn't remember the last time either of my sisters had shown concern for me or had come to my rescue. The emotional surge I felt from their presence filled me with a kind of power that I hadn't ever known before.

"I'm okay. I need to see Poseidon and I think it's best that he doesn't know I'm coming. I believe if I can move this wall, I can enter his lair in secret."

Zoe kept her eyes trained on me. She was using the same analytical skills she used to help the human patrol team surveil the waters outside of Sirenia. Kyra floated close, watching Zoe. I would not ask either of them to help me. It had to be their choice.

Zoe swam closer and fed her fingers into the crevice next to mine. Kyra did a somersault and twirled, getting her closer to the base of the rock door.

"On the count of three," Zoe said.

"One—two—three!"

The three of us heaved our weight and power against the rock and it shifted out of place and revealed the doorway into Poseidon's lair. As the water rushed into the opening and the warm eddies mingled with the cool temperature behind the door, I knew it wouldn't be long until someone inside knew the seal had been broken.

There was no going back now.

51

"Stay here," I told Zoe. "You too, Kyra. You'll be safe here. The sharks can't get to you. I'll be back as soon as I can."

"Wait," Zoe said. She put her hand on my forearm. "Let me go. You don't have the same skills that I do. You might not be able to handle yourself."

"Don't you see?" I asked. "I have to go. This is my challenge. I'm the only one who can see this through."

Zoe nodded and let go of my arm. I reached both hands out and grabbed her and Kyra's hands in each of mine and we floated there in the water, in a circle joined by our fingers. I felt both of them squeeze back as hard as I squeezed them, until I relaxed my grip and let go. Before fear took over, I turned and swam into the darkness that led to Poseidon's lair. Kyra's sobs faded into the sounds of the water behind me.

The hallway was dark, and I was unsure which way to go. Yet, there was a familiarity to my surroundings. I'd spent so much time staring at those maps and running my finger over the pathways that I practically knew them with my eyes closed.

So, I closed my eyes.

I put my hands out in front of me and undulated through the water, following my instincts on which way to go. A turn here, a twist there, a narrow passageway chosen over a wide public area. The water grew warmer and warmer and a now-familiar tingle snaked up my spine and flooded to my fingertips. This time it was a hundred times more intense than the feeling I'd felt around Triton.

I turned a corner and discovered why. I was in Poseidon's chambers.

The commander of the oceans sat in a throne in front of me. He was more intimidating than the fiercest renderings of him that were housed in the Nautilus Vault. Where some might have expected him to be surrounded by precious metals and valuable stones, a display of all the wealth of the ocean, they'd be wrong. Poseidon's throne was crudely carved out of a massive rock, probably the only surface dense and heavy enough to support him.

Poseidon was bigger, broader, and bolder than any other creature of the sea. His iron fist was legendary, and the wrath of Poseidon had enough of a disruptive impact on the ocean that a system of law and order had been implemented that kept him here while his team patrolled and enforced the ways of the ocean. In addition to Sirenia, Abalonia, and Oceania, he ruled over numerous other mermaid colonies, along with unchartered territories that surrounded us. It was this last part that made him more important than any other being in the water. His power transcended the merfolk world.

I hadn't expected to slip into his lair undetected but was surprised to find him staring directly at me as I approached. Protocol dictated that I allow him to address me first, but too much was at stake to stand on formality.

"Poseidon," I said. "It is I, Ava, daughter of Mother Mermaid of Sirenia. Trouble has come to our colony. Mother is missing, a merman has been murdered, and the sharks have violated their territorial agreement."

"Is it not true that you are to function as leader in your mother's absence?" Poseidon asked.

"It is. And I've tried. But I don't think I'm ready."

"You would not be here if you were not."

"But I should know what to do. I should be overseeing everything out there, and instead it's all getting worse!" My despair took over and my calm, rational voice sounded hysterical. If there'd been any doubt about my abilities (or lack thereof), I would have proven them right there.

"My child, you are here because you seek help. That's the sign of a true leader. You inspired your sisters to come to your aid. You dropped your guard and called for help. You sought truth, answers, and understanding about your role in our world, and you came here because you recognized the power of the group over the indulgence of the individual."

"I came here because I don't know what's happening amongst the merfolk and Mother isn't there to intervene."

"Your Mother is safe." His voice boomed out from where he sat, not loud, but with underwater vibrations that caused the walls to quiver and the fish who swam around the interior of this room to scatter. Poseidon needn't raise his voice. He projected his thoughts in accordance with his voice, and the effect filled the cavernous room with power that blossomed like a fist unfurled.

"You can't know that," I said quietly. "You might be able to sense Mother's presence like Triton and I can sense each other, but unless she's here with you, then you can't know she's safe. And I need to know. I need to understand what's at risk and why things are falling apart like they are."

It wasn't common for a mermaid—for anyone—to challenge Poseidon, to question anything he said, but I did it, nonetheless. The fear I'd felt since being in charge had exhausted me, and in place of the exhaustion came a steely calm. I felt supported by my sisters, who lingered in the cavern behind me, and by Mad Midge, who'd told me the truth about the great shrimper/mermaid tragedy. I felt supported by the love of Triton, who wasn't even in the room.

Poseidon leaned forward. "You sense the presence of Triton?" he asked.

"Not now," I said. "When he's close. When we're in the same space. The water feels different."

"He did not tell me he had found you."

"I don't think he was looking for me."

A wall shifted behind Poseidon and a statuesque mermaid slowly glided out. She was draped in jewels befitting a queen, and her torso was covered with diaphanous sea kelp that had been pulverized then braided together to form the most beautiful textile I'd ever seen. And while any other mermaid would have wanted to study the technique, or to admire her jewels, there was only one word I wanted to utter when I saw her.

"Mother!"

oseidon put his arm out, keeping her next to him. "Luna," he whispered gently.

It was the first time I'd heard anyone use her name, and to hear it come from the lips of Poseidon, the most feared leader in the ocean, made my heart race. The water surrounding Mother turned a soft, luminous shade of pale gold. Mother placed her hand on Poseidon's and smiled. Her face glowed more brightly than a perigee-syzygy of the Earth-Moon-Sun system.

Poseidon nodded once and their hands drifted apart. Mother turned to me and held her arms open and I swam into her embrace. This time it was I who clung to her the way Kyra had clung to me. She stroked my hair until I released her and leaned back to make sure I hadn't dreamt her.

"Mother," I said again. "You're here."

"I've been here all along," she said. "It was the only way to protect Sirenia."

"But Sirenia isn't protected. Laker was murdered, and Ophelia is planning to enter a business transaction with the sharks, and Mad Midge told me what happened all those years ago—"

"Ava."

Just hearing my name, transferred wordlessly from Mother's mind to mine, interrupted my stream of consciousness. She held my hands in hers and her eyes were steady on mine. Poseidon remained in his chair, but regardless of his powers, he couldn't hear what she said to me if she communicated through telepathy, and all three of us knew that.

Mother continued. "My child, you could not know what was happening to our colony. To tell you would have been to violate the highest code of the sea. There are risks involved in being the Matriarch, and I took one to try to save one of our own. That was my choice. What you did after I left was yours."

"But this all started when Laker showed up and told us you had been kidnapped."

"I was not kidnapped," she said. "I entered into negotiations with the sharks in exchange for Laker's life. The debts he accrued were severe and he had no way to pay. They would not have let him live."

"But then why did he tell me you were in danger?"

Mother turned to face Poseidon. "I would like to tell my daughter the truth," she said. "It is within my rights as a mother but goes against the vow of silence I promised you before she was born. We have had our moment. I'd like your blessing to allow her to have hers."

Poseidon nodded once. He held a trident in one hand and his fingers relaxed and then tightened around the thick spear. The set of his jawline was rigid and I wondered what it was Mother was going to say and why Poseidon seemed to have to control his energy in order to agree to her wish.

(A small part of me questioned Mother's power over Poseidon too, but that part would have to wait for later.)

"Relations with the sharks have been tense for centuries and living in fear has become the norm for merfolk. Enough was enough. As I said, I negotiated a deal with them. To clear Laker's debts in exchange for underwater property out beyond the edges of Sirenia. Poseidon granted permission to free up the territory. Clams Casino would have been moved and a safe zone would have been implemented between us, leaving no possibility of another tragedy."

"Why would you go that far for Laker?"

"Laker's parents sent him away as a young merman. He lived a difficult life and has had to fight for much of it. When he returned to Sirenia, I made it my mission to accept him into our community and try to make him feel welcome."

Unlike his own family. He'd returned to Sirenia, where Ophelia and her parents lived, but he'd spent much of his time at our house. At first, Laker had shown attention to Kyra, but Kyra had many suitors and her lack of attention must have made him feel insignificant. He'd gotten mixed up in the murder investigation Zoe helped solve, but she'd gotten all the credit for that. In many ways, Laker had been around more often than not and we'd treated him like we treated any other merman. Not knowing his background, it hadn't occurred to me (or any of us, I figured) that his motivations for being close were anything other than what they seemed.

"Laker didn't want to be part of our community," I said. "He wanted to benefit from our community. He hated what we stood for—he and Ophelia."

"After negotiations, the ball was in the court of the sharks. I brought Laker into protective custody until the sharks proved they would uphold their side of the agreement. Poseidon granted a withdrawal from the Cabinet of Calamari to pay off his debts. The day after we arrived, Laker escaped with the chips."

The chips I'd seen on Ophelia's table. The bounty that would have freed him, arranged by Mother in her role as Matriarch, had been stolen in an act of desperation and greed. Whether Ophelia knew the origin of the chips was unclear, but as long as she maintained possession, she was in danger too.

Poseidon spoke up. "Triton sensed Laker intended trouble for you and your sisters. We couldn't risk allowing anyone to know Mother was here, not until we knew what it was Laker was going to do, so I forbade Triton from telling anyone that she was here."

"I could have read him," I said slowly. "If he really were my destiny, I would have known what he knew from spending time with him." I looked back and forth between Poseidon and Mother's faces. "Why didn't I know what he was thinking? Was I wrong about how I interpreted our interactions?"

"Did Triton give you anything when you last saw him?" Poseidon asked.

"He gave me his trident." I looked away and remembered what Mad Midge had told me. "And I know it was him. He's the one who cut me loose from the shrimper nets when I was caught. He's the one who saved my life."

Mother put her hand over her heart and closed her eyes. The temperature of the water rose. When Mother opened her eyes, she looked past me to Poseidon and smiled tenderly. His expression softened. She swam to him and lightly touched the back of his hand that rested on the arm of his throne. A trail of sparkles appeared in the water, not unlike the way the water turned glittery when I was near Triton.

"He saved you with that trident, and then he gave it up for you," Mother said. "It was the greatest sacrifice, and the one gesture that would cloud your mind. Once he transferred his power to you in the form of his trident, you could no longer read his thoughts. The two of you became one."

"But he left," I said. "He swam out to the sharks and I haven't seen him since."

"He's not with you?" Mother asked.

"No. He gave me his trident and he swam away."

"Then there's only one thing you can do. You have to return his trident to him and balance will be restored."

"What about Laker's killer? And the sharks? What about the threat to Sirenia?"

"It's all connected," Mother said. "Find Triton and all answers you seek will be revealed."

What she didn't say, but what I felt, was that everything I had come to know in my life as a mermaid now hung in the balance of my actions.

And humans thought being a mermaid sounded like fun.

* * *

On my list of immediate actions, there were two things: retrieve Triton's trident from Sirenia and find Triton. There was the troubling fact that being in possession of his trident would cloud my ability to read his thoughts, but it seemed fitting to be faced with a somewhat impossible task. Why should things start to be easy now?

As I swam through the ocean, I thought about what Mother and Poseidon had said, about what I'd learned when I started dropping my guard and letting others help. For as long as I could remember, my life had been defined by the tragedy and the guilt over the death of so many. I'd felt unprepared to take on the role of leader, and I'd felt like every other mermaid and merman judged me and saw my lack of abilities. But when I got out of my own way, others didn't mock me for my shortcomings. They joined me and helped.

It felt good.

I relaxed my mind and conjured up a call for help for the mermaids. I opened my mouth and let out a siren song to ask my sisters to meet me at Sirenia. I felt vulnerable but empowered. It truly didn't matter if anyone answered my call. Simply by asking, I'd evolved.

I arrived home to an empty nest. I ducked into the front door and swam from room to room, hoping to find either Zoe or Kyra (or both) waiting for me, but they were not there. Nobody was there.

The cry for help hadn't done anything. I was on my own.

After circling the interior, I swam to the room I shared with my sisters and ducked under the clam shell where I slept. Wrapped in a sheet of woven blades of sea kelp was Triton's weapon. I pulled it out from under the bed and untied the textile. Slowly, I ran my open hand over the base of it. I touched the tip of my finger to the pointed spikes on the end of each of the three prongs. I ran the side of my hand side to side between the prongs and then slid my hand back down the length of the spear. I closed my eyes and thought about Triton and the moment when he first handed it to me, how familiar it had felt. He'd let go a split second after I first touched it and a shock had passed through it, almost as if it contained an electrical current. Nerves, I wrote it off as now. Nothing more.

I floated up, away from the bed, and sensed movement out front of the house. The windows were unsecured, and I quickly identified the thick, gray body of a shark as my uninvited guest. As he swam to the left, another swam to the right. I swam closer to the window to get a better sense of how many of the evil bullies were there and that's when I saw how dirty they planned to fight.

They had Triton, bound to a boulder, outside my front door.

My fist tightened around the trident and I swam forward. "Release him," I commanded. "You are in violation of the laws that determine the underwater territories. You have no place here in Sirenia."

The shark that called himself Xander swam forward. "You're out of your league, mermaid. You may have escaped us once, but you had help. Who's going to rescue you this time?"

"I am," said a voice from my left.

"I am," said another voice, this one less locatable.

"I am," said others. One by one, voices repeated the phrase. I kept my eyes on Xander but watched him look into the water around me. The other two sharks with him circled around Sirenia and then returned to his side. As a chorus of "I am," continued, I felt an overwhelming sense of community. The sharks clustered together, baring teeth, but not advancing. When I couldn't contain myself, I turned my head and looked.

They were all there.

There was Zoe and Kyra at the front. Ophelia to Kyra's left. George, the dugong who'd worked security at Ophelia's hamlet, and Caleb the manatee who collaborated with Mad Midge. Speaking of Mad Midge, she was there too, next to four young mermen, including Weid, who'd been with Laker the day Laker demanded I take a meeting with Poseidon.

There was Diatomic Jones, Kyra's music teacher, who'd almost lost his life over a Siren statue, and even a tuna named Charlie who Zoe once suspected of murder. The waters around Sirenia were populated with every mermaid and merman I'd ever met and a few I hadn't.

They had answered my song.

"Your move, girlie," Xander said. "You've got that nice, sharp trident. Why not use it to defend yourself? Even I know you can hit one of us at this range. Do it," he hissed. "You know what will happen if you do, right?"

I knew what it was Xander wanted me to do. Sure, I could hit him. But kill him? Maybe. Even if I did, there would be two sharks left and they'd control the trident. Blood in the water would attract more sharks. The waters around Sirenia would become known as a place to feed and our world would never be as idyllic as it had once been. Life as we knew it would be over.

I swam to Triton and jammed the base of the trident into the ocean floor. When I let go of it, Triton's thoughts washed over me and I understood what I had to do.

I didn't know how to use Triton's trident, but Triton did. And while that weapon gave me the power to defend myself, it was no longer about me. Becoming the leader meant nothing if it was about control.

And so, I gave up control.

I used the trident to slice through the ropes that bound Triton to the rock. I handed the weapon to him as the sharks closed in on us. His hand closed over the base while I still held it, and a shock of lightning coursed out of the weapon and joined another bolt that came down from the sky. A boom of thunder clapped so loud the sound vibrations caused a swelling of water that crashed upon us. The undertow pulled me deeper into the ocean. I lost my grip on the trident and floated away, deep into the dark recesses of the water, alone.

A figure holding a long, glowing, three-pronged weapon swam over my head. It was Triton. He was followed by one dark shape, and then another and another. The sharks. The trident, charged with lightning that we had brought down to us, protected him as he led the sharks away from Sirenia. Sharks have the greatest electrical sensitivity of any animal, and the electricity now contained in Triton's weapon was more than the sharks would have encountered in the ocean. Resistance to the energy the rod now emitted would have been futile.

Like anybody who paid attention at Sea U, Triton knew this. The power we'd brought to the trident from the sky had been the one thing that saved us.

But Triton couldn't swim forever. If his plan were to work, he had to lure the sharks out past Sirenia to the deepest, darkest spots of the ocean. He had to leverage the lightning to strike the sharks, to call on the joint power of the sky and the sea, to use that power to destroy these three sharks and send a message to any who hoped to pick up where Xander, Garo, and Spike left off.

As Triton led the sharks away from Sirenia, I knew this was what we'd been meant to do. My asking for help, relying on the other mermaids, joining forces with Triton had saved us. The fleeting glimpse I'd had at the connection between us had opened my eyes to what my future held, but that was what it was. My future. Like I'd thought once before, it wasn't Triton and my time. Not yet.

But someday, it would be. Of that I was sure.

Thank you for following me into the ocean!

I first had the idea to write a series of mysteries featuring mermaids a few years ago, but it was something else that got me into gear. Once upon a time, I was a competitive swimmer, and I did spend considerable amounts of time in the water (pools and open water alike!). It's very possible that all that time spent staring at a black line painted on the bottom of the pool (or at the three inches in front of my face which was all that I could see in the open water) was what taught me to let my mind wander and make up stories.

But an unexpected life event forced me reevaluate what was idling on my future-project list and mermaid mysteries were on there. And while I wasn't sure exactly what they would be, the motivation became crystal clear. Life is short. Don't leave projects on the table.

If you subscribe to my Weekly DiVa emails, you know this is an important idea to me. Sometimes we do things for others, and sometimes we do things for ourselves. Both have value. Both help us continue to grow and change and become the next version of ourselves.

I sincerely hope you enjoyed spending time in Sirenia. The mermaids will be back before you know it!

Love,
Diane

About the Author

Four-time award nominee and national bestselling author Diane Vallere writes smart, funny, and fashionable character-based mysteries. After a career in luxury retailing, she traded fashion accessories for accessories to murder. Diane started her own detective agency at age ten and has maintained a passion for shoes, clues, and clothes ever since.

Get girl talk, book talk, and life talk when you join the Weekly Diva Club at dianevallere.com/weekly-diva.

The Pajama Frame

Lover Come Hack

Apprehend Me No Flowers

Teacher's Threat

The Kill of It All

Love Me or Grieve Me

Please Don't Push Up the Daisies

<u>Sylvia Stryker Outer Space Mysteries</u>

Murder on a Moon Trek

Scandal on a Moon Trek

Hijacked on a Moon Trek

Framed on a Moon Trek

<u>Material Witness Mysteries</u>

Suede to Rest

Crushed Velvet

Silk Stalkings

Tulle Death Do Us Part

<u>Costume Shop Mystery Series</u>

A Disguise to Die For

Masking for Trouble

Dressed to Confess